REV

A BAYONET SCARS NOVEL

Series & Titles by JC Emery

MEN WITH BADGES
Marital Bitch
The Switch

THE BIRTHRIGHT SERIES
Anomaly

BAYONET SCARS
Ride
Thrash
Rev

Mature Content Warning: The Bayonet Scars novels are a dark romance series which features graphic sexual content, violence, and foul language that is intended for a mature audience. Each novel features a different couple, though it's not recommended that they be read out of order due to the series story arc.

REV

A BAYONET SCARS NOVEL

JC Emery

Left Break Press

Rev

a Bayonet Scars novel

by

JC Emery

© 2014 by Left Break Press

ISBN: 978-0692223390

Cover Design by Brenda Gonet at Gonet Design

http://www.facebook.com/gonetdesign

Photography by MarishaSha

http://www.shutterstock.com/gallery-378590p1.html

Editing & Design by Rae Bateman at Metamorphosis Books

http://metamorphosisbooks.com

Proofread by Amy Shearer at Books

For Mandie,
Because I can

REV

A BAYONET SCARS NOVEL

Holly

☠ PROLOGUE ☠

THERE IS NO other place I'd rather not be than here right now. The four walls that surround me are covered in various posters for everything from the upcoming Strawberry Festival to the street sweeping schedule, and a scattered collection of educational posters geared toward kids. This room doubles as the library's community room and the children's wing. I spent hours in this room as a child. I'd find one of the bean bags in the reading nook and curl up with the latest Babysitter's Club book. Back then, I had no idea they held meetings like this here.

Alcoholics Anonymous.

I move into the room slowly, trying to keep behind a couple that enters just before me. They're practically crazy-glued to each other's side. There's the faint scent of tequila that emanates from one or both of them, I can't tell. A man rushes past me and hops into one of the last empty seats that form a tight circle in the corner of the room. His short brown hair is a mess, like he's been pulling at it all day, his shirt is haphazardly buttoned, and his tie has been yanked loose in an apparent frenzy. This is supposed to be a safe place, but nobody ever really feels safe here. Exposed, vulnerable, lacking… sure. But safe? No. At least I don't.

A few chairs down from the disheveled man sits Mindy. Her strawberry blonde hair is up in a messy bun. She's rocking black yoga pants, an exercise top, and sneakers, like she's the poster child for inner peace or something. In reality, I'm pretty sure she thinks downward dog is some kind of sex position, but hey, she looks comfortable. She gives me a wave and pats the empty seat next to her.

Kindness, I remind myself. I need to work on being kind. It's number ten of the twelve steps to recovery: admitting when you're wrong. I may not have drank the Kool-Aid, but even I can see the value in taking personal inventory, and that's part of the reason I showed up tonight. I'm not an alcoholic. According to my former therapist, I'm a martyr whose poor decisions are triggered by the unrealistic expectations I put on myself. We can call it whatever we want. It doesn't change the fact that I'm being dragged to a meeting that I don't need, nor do I want. But Mindy both needs and wants it, and if me being here can help her, I'll do it. Even if I want to claw my own eyeballs out in the process.

The couple in front of me grabs chairs from a stack in the corner. The circle is basically full now as the couple wiggles in between other attendees. I squeeze through at the other end and sit down in the seat Mindy's saved for me without meeting anyone's eyes.

"Thank you for coming," she says. I nod—keeping quiet is

for the best. I wouldn't even be here if not for her insistence. She used to be fun, but that led to her being too much fun. And the downfall was anything but. That's how I've ended up here. All the therapy in the world hasn't taught me how to say "no" to her. Meetings like this actually do me more harm than good, and my real problem isn't booze, but family. Just being in this room confirms my absolute worst fear: that I'm a failure.

I couldn't save Mindy; I couldn't save myself. I couldn't make my parents proud— I couldn't even tell them the truth about why I'd failed them. It doesn't matter that every person in this room is struggling with these feelings and their own demons. That's the thing about insecurities. Nobody else's problems can lessen your own.

The meeting gets underway like they always do. Nothing special happens. The speaker identifies herself as an alcoholic right off the bat, like they encourage all alcoholics to do. There is no shame here, they say. Mindy nods beside me, and her voice is reverent as she recites the Serenity Prayer. It's all God grant me this, and God grant me that, like it was God who put the bottle to their lips.

"Do we have anyone here who is new to A.A.? Anyone who's in their first 30 days of sobriety? We don't want to embarrass anyone. We just want to get to know you, and we believe that a fundamental part of your recovery is taking that first step and admitting that you are powerless over alcohol," the speaker says.

The man I followed in raises his hand, and the woman with him gives him an encouraging pat on his knee. He introduces himself as Joe. He, too, is an alcoholic. He explains that he had been sober for several months, but then he lost his job and it went all downhill from there. It always starts with one drink, which leads to another, and then another. That's the difference between me and these people. My life falls apart, but it's not because of alcohol. I can stop drinking when I need to, and I have. I just have an uncanny talent for bonding myself to the absolutely most needy and self-destructive people I can find.

During the sharing session, Mindy raises her hand. I was hoping she would keep to herself this meeting, but no such luck. She's never gone to a meeting in town before, but if she's nervous, it doesn't show. The idea is that we're all supposed to be anonymous, but this is a small town and Mindy's dad is a cop. It's a big deal for her to be here, which is why she asked me to come with. Hiding her past from our family isn't conducive to her recovery. I don't know if Uncle Harry has any suspicions, but after tonight he might get tipped off.

"My name is Melinda, and I am an alcoholic. I'm also an addict, but I like this group better," she says with a guilty smile on her face. The group welcomes her with kind words. She clears her throat, takes a deep breath, and says, "I have been clean and sober for three years, four months, and nineteen days now. On a good day, it's easier because I have so many successful clean days behind me. On a bad day, it's no easier than it was on the day I went to jail. I'm in a good place now and I wanted to just say it out loud that I'm glad I have my best friend back home to support me." She leans over and wraps me in a side hug. "Holly has always been there for me, and she's a great friend."

I try to smile at the room, but I'm afraid it comes out as a grimace.

"Would you like to introduce yourself, Holly?" the speaker asks. I shake my head, but Mindy elbows me in my side.

"My name is Holly, and I am not an alcoholic, but I have plenty of other issues." The attendees wait for me to continue, and when I don't, the room is dead silent.

"Welcome, Holly. We're glad you could join us," the speaker says. She moves on, talking about how an alcoholic's support system is so important to their recovery. She praises me for helping Mindy in her journey and mentions step nine: making amends, because in order to be able to truly recover, one must make amends with those they have harmed.

I reach over, grab Mindy's hand, and give it a squeeze. I have amends to make with Mindy, and being here is part of that.

The meeting moves along more quickly than I expect it to, and soon we're heading for my car. Mindy walked here after her shift at Universal Grounds. I had to meet her here because I spent the entire day out job hunting. I've been back in town a week now and jobs are pretty scarce, but I've been diligent in my efforts, so hopefully it pays off soon. As it is, I'm living with my parents again and ready to shoot myself in the face. Mom hasn't been shy about wanting me to go back to school, and she's orchestrated a conveniently-scheduled after-church celebration for my return.

I unlock the doors to my old white Jeep, and we climb in. I head for Uncle Harry and Aunt Claire's house to drop Mindy off. We're a block from her house when the loud rumble of Harleys become a deafening roar. Mindy covers her ears as Fort Bragg's resident outlaw bike club rides by. There must be at least five or six of them, and a few even have women on the back of their bikes. The scene takes me back to being in high school and wondering what it'd be like to date a bad boy. That was when I thought only bad boys could be no good for you.

As the bikes fade into the darkness ahead of us, I round the corner and pull into Mindy's driveway.

"That was brave of you," I say.

"It was time. I'm tired of hiding who I am," she says with a sigh. I lean over and engulf her in a tight hug before climbing out of the Jeep. "Gimme an update when you hear back from the high school. I have a good feeling about that job."

"I will," I say. She shuts the door and waves me off as I back out onto the street and head for my parents' house.

Childhood memories of wanting to escape engulf me. A small, pathetic chuckle builds in my throat. It figures that I would end up back here. My parents' house comes into view at the end of the street. The nearer I get, the less I want to be here.

My voice is quiet and soft when I whisper, "Welcome home, Holly."

☠CHAPTER 1☠

I STRETCH MY legs out beneath my aging desk and eye the olive-colored rotary phone with great disdain. With a quick look down at the paper with the name GRADY, CHEYENNE in the top left corner, and the student's personal information below, I blow out a frustrated breath. I'll give her father one more call before I give up.

Cheyenne Grady is a senior at Fort Bragg High School, where I am a secretary. We don't have any permanent guidance counselors—rather, we rely on administrative personnel such as myself to aide the student body as best we can. When we can't, the county's traveling counselor will come in and help out. Unfortunately, after Cheyenne's last meeting with the guidance counselor went south, he refused to schedule another meeting and instructed me to, "Figure it out."

Up until last spring, Cheyenne was a solid B student. For reasons I haven't been able to ascertain, her grades plummeted, she started cutting class, and her attitude has gone from mildly sour to just plain spiteful. And of course, Mr. Beck, our principal, saw fit to assign me Cheyenne Grady— his least experienced staff member with, in his opinion, his second-biggest problem student. Thankfully, my supervisor gets the honor of taking on Jeremy Whelan, the real thorn in Mr. Beck's side.

I should have known something was up when he asked me if I knew Cheyenne's dad. I said I didn't, and Mr. Beck smiled so wide I thought his face was going to split in two. Like I said, I should have known then.

Since taking on Cheyenne's case, I've followed protocol to the best of my understanding and thus have contacted Mr. Grady seven times over the last several months. Twice his voice mail was full, so I sent letters to the residence listed. Once he hung up on me before I could even get halfway through introducing myself. The rest of the times I've left messages that he hasn't returned. To his credit, he did return one of my calls where the only words he spoke were to ask if Cheyenne was safe. When I said she was, he hung up and didn't answer when I tried to call him back.

Now, after five meetings with Cheyenne since last spring, and with zero improvement in her grades, I'm forced to contact Mr. Grady again. I've called twice and he hasn't answered. According to Mr. Beck, it's imperative that I get his signature to allow Cheyenne entry into the counseling program, which allows students to make up assignments and missed classes during Saturday school. If he doesn't sign the form and things don't change soon, she'll be forced to attend the local continuation school outside of town that has an eleven percent graduation rate. When I first met her, she talked about going to culinary school at length, but these last several months she's mentioned it maybe twice. Without a high school diploma or a GED, she won't be able to enter a vocational program – and I don't want that for her. No matter how big of a pain in the ass she is, I kind of adore the kid. She's smart and funny, and when she's in a good mood, she's really kind. I can't help but think that something's going on at home that leads her to such self-destructive behavior.

A sharp knock rattles on my desk. Lifting my head, I force a smile as I face Mr. Beck's red, aging face.

"Holly," he says by way of greeting. "How goes the Grady case?"

"Not well," I admit. "Mr. Grady is obstinate in his refusal to communicate with me. I just don't understand how a parent can be so absent from his child's education."

"Mr. Grady is a particular individual," he says with a look on his face that I don't understand. Every time we talk about Cheyenne or her mysterious father, Mr. Beck gets a wary look on his face that tells me that there's a reason he gave Cheyenne's case to me and isn't handling it himself.

"Yes, well, he's particularly an ass," I withhold the rest of my comment, but just barely. "How important is it, really, to get his signature? Can't we get her into academic counseling without his help? I can't even get the guy on the phone to tell him why I'm calling, let alone to talk about his daughter's future with him."

"Two choices, Holly. Either get Mr. Grady's signature

acknowledging that his daughter will enter academic counseling or petition for her expulsion. We've waited long enough."

"I don't want her expelled, Mr. Beck. Something's going on here. Cheyenne is a good kid. We can turn this around."

Mr. Beck sighs and shakes his head slightly. "You meet Mr. Grady and you'll understand a few things better. Cheyenne *was* a good kid once – they all were. But she's on the fast track to the trailer park off highway twenty. Do yourself a favor and stop expending so much energy on this kid." With that, Mr. Beck taps my desk again and walks away. Once I'm sure he's out of earshot, I mutter a few choice words about his particular brand of leadership and refocus my attention to the problem at hand.

Leaning forward, I grab Cheyenne's student profile and find her father's phone number under the emergency contacts section. I practically have the number burned into my brain with how many times I've had to call. Mr. Beck may be convinced that Cheyenne is a lost cause, but I'm not. I hate the idea of giving up on kids, especially ones with such obviously screwed up parents.

I grab the receiver off the base and turn the dial, calling Mr. Grady one last time. The phone rings in my ear four times before the answering machine picks up.

"This is Grady, make it good," his deep, masculine voice sounds through the receiver. The first time I heard his voice in the message, I was slightly stunned by how rough and deep it is. Admittedly, it was an immediate turn-on. But now, I just like to imagine that it's choking on his own bullshit that's made his voice so husky.

"This message is for Sterling Grady. My name is Holly Mercer and I am your daughter Cheyenne's administrative advocate at Fort Bragg High School. Please return my phone call immediately as I need to meet with you regarding Cheyenne's continuing education at Fort Bragg High," I say in my most professional voice—the one I use to pretend not to hate the man's guts. I leave him my contact information as though he's going to actually use it and then hang up. Mr. Beck's conviction that Cheyenne won't be going anywhere in life gets under my skin. Between her clearly absent father and Mr. Beck's lack of faith, I can't help but wonder if this kid has anyone in her corner. I looked through her file, and there's zero mention of a mother in any of the records. The idea that she's just floating out in the world without anyone really having her back saddens and infuriates me at the same time.

Looking at Cheyenne's contact information, I find her address—1370 Riverwood Drive. Just on the outskirts of town and off Sherwood Road, Riverwood Drive is a street I've only ever dreamed of living on. It's all old battered concrete and dirt mixed in and shaded by a wealth of redwood trees and beautiful, sprawling homes, set hundreds of yards apart. If Mr. Grady has a home on Riverwood Drive, chances are good he makes decent money. The homes on the street were all built sometime after I was born, and before that, the land belonged to the county. Even when the parcels were first sold off, they went for a pretty penny.

Curiosity gets the better of me, and I stand from my desk

before I think better of it. Taking a single deep breath, I grab Cheyenne's student profile and the parental acknowledgment form I've been trying to get Mr. Grady to sign for months and head out.

The trip to Riverwood Drive is pleasant enough despite my reasons for making the drive across town. As I angle down Sherwood Road and then toward Riverwood, I have to fight to keep my hands from griping the steering wheel too tight. My nerves are on edge, and my belly is flip-flopping. If I keep it up, my palms are going to callous over soon.

With a quick check for the house number, I park my white Jeep Grand Cherokee on the side of the road across the street from Mr. Grady's home.

The house looks like a white single-story from the front. It rests atop a sloping hill and from the right angle, I can see an expansive bottom level that boasts a wraparound porch. To the left is an attached two-car garage, and to the right is a porch that leads to the front door and is supported by beams that jut out from the pitched ground below. The home appears to be well-taken care of and Cheyenne's beat-up Volkswagen Bug sits in the drive.

Something I learned early on in my job as office admin is that sometimes it's easy to spot signs of abuse or neglect. Some parents are obvious in their disregard by providing their children with inadequate housing, poor conditions, and a total lack of love and attention. Other cases, like this one, aren't as obvious. While the house appears in good shape, there's no telling what kind of disaster awaits inside.

While I'm certain I could get in trouble for doing it, I put the car in drive and pull into the driveway and cut the engine. I've committed to confronting Mr. Grady in person about the form I'd like him to sign, and now that I'm in his driveway, there's no turning back.

Only, I don't know when I decided to confront him.

I take several deep breaths and gather my wits before I climb out of the car with paperwork in hand and walk toward the front porch, smoothing my black pencil skirt the entire way and hoping I don't look as terrified as I feel.

As I round the garage and catch sight of the open front window, I find several lights on inside the house.

Now or never, Holly.

I lift my hand to knock then wait for the door to open, but it never does. I knock again, louder this time, and again, I wait. Still, no answer. Finally, I knock as hard as I can, determined to get a face-to-face with the man who has spent months avoiding me.

The door swings open and, instead of Mr. Grady standing before me as I expect, it's Cheyenne. Her dark brown hair is up in a messy bun, and she's wearing a pair of torn jeans and a dark red tank top with no shoes. Her expression turns flat when she realizes it's me.

"You were serious?" she whines. I had warned her once I'd show up here to meet with her dad, and she hadn't believed me. Then again, at the time, I hadn't believed me either.

"Yeah, Cheyenne," I say with a raise of my eyebrows. "Is your dad home?" To this she snorts.

"Oh man," she says, "Today is *so* not the day for a house call. Seriously, Dad's going through some stuff."

"Listen, kid, I've been trying to meet with your dad for months now, and since he's had trouble with his phone, I figured I better drop by before Mr. Beck goes through with expelling your ass."

"Okay, but he's not here. So we should do it another day. I can let you know when he's free." Her eyes are wide and she blinks nervously the more she speaks. She's a gorgeous girl, really. And as long as I don't push too hard about her grades, she doesn't give me too much lip.

"And you're actually going to give him the message?" I ask.

She rolls her eyes and huffs. I'm about to explain to her my next step should she not deliver the message to her father when the deep rumble of a motorcycle engine sounds from down the road. Motorcycles aren't uncommon in Fort Bragg—we're a coastal motorcycle town known for our hometown outlaw club. Being barely over seven thousand strong, we're a big enough town to vaguely know everybody's business, but not small enough to know all the gory details. My knowledge of the Forsaken Motorcycle Club begins and ends with two things: A.) They're outlaws, totally disregarding of the law and its purpose; and B.) They party hard, loud, and don't give a damn what anyone thinks of them. Other than that, I'm basically clueless about the club.

Despite sharing the same small town as the club for my entire life, I have avoided all things club-related. Still, I've always been curious about them and have even come to some conclusions of my own over the years. But in not one of them did I ever assume that a member would have any business in this part of town. I always figured they'd live in either the trailer park or in town in the less expensive housing. The roar of the bike nears as Cheyenne fidgets. I realize too late that the bike is pulling into the driveway.

"Do you know this guy?" I ask Cheyenne, immediately worried for her safety. The large bulking man turns off the bike, removes his half helmet and glares at my Jeep. My hands clutch at the paperwork I'm holding and my breath catches. As he climbs off and stands to his full height, I'm able to fully appreciate his size. He's tall, that's for certain, but it's the bulk of him that has my attention. He's all muscles and tanned skin with a thick neck and black hair that curls slightly and tucks behind his ears. I move to stand between he and Cheyenne just in case he's someone who intends to harm her. Though it would be a shame if he were that awful of a human being. So much pure male beauty wrapped up in one package to be a psychopath, but you never know.

"Not you, too," Cheyenne mutters. I move to look at her, but can't take my eyes away from the man walking toward us. He walks up in dark blue jeans with a black tee shirt and his leather cut over top. He places his hands on his hips and fixes his glare on me.

"Who the hell are you?" he asks. His eyes travel from my face and linger on my breasts, then down to my waist and right on to my exposed legs.

"Holly Mercer from the high school," I say and nervously reach out to shake his hand. The man emits intimidation and sex appeal like they're disposable, yet charm is something he lacks. He looks down at my hand and then back up at my face.

"Cheyenne in trouble?" he clips.

"No," I stutter and instantly regret it. She is in trouble, actually. I make the attempt to correct myself, but don't get far. He barks out to Cheyenne and then to me to explain my presence.

"Are you Sterling Grady?" I ask.

"Grady," he says.

"Pardon?"

"Don't call me Sterling," he says. I fight back the urge to do it just to spite him, but think better of it.

"I've been calling to speak with you regarding the welfare of your daughter for months now, sir. I just need a moment of your time."

"The welfare of my daughter? Let's get a few things straight, lady. My daughter's welfare is perfectly fucking fine. You want to talk about her grades? Tell her to bring them up. You want to talk about her attendance? Tell her to get her ass to class. She thinks she's damn grown, so she can take responsibility like she's grown."

"She's seventeen," I respond.

"She's totally right here," Cheyenne quips from beside me. Grady's eyes don't even bat her way, but he lifts his arm and snaps his fingers and points inside the house. She waits a moment, huffs, and then stomps off and lets the door slam behind her.

"You telling me how to raise my kid?" he asks, taking a step forward.

"I'm telling you that your daughter is on the verge of being expelled," I say. "I'm doing everything I can to help her, but I need your signature on the counseling form."

"She'll figure out that's a bad idea real soon," he says. "Kid don't really listen. This shit's on her." While I hadn't expected Cheyenne's father to be a biker—much less to be Forsaken—my commitment to be someone who has her back doesn't wane.

"That's the problem. She's a kid, not an adult. She needs guidance and advice and to have consequences for poor behavior. She needs boundaries. She needs you to tune in," I snap, surprising myself with my vigor.

"Bitch, Chey's my kid, and I know what she needs. What she doesn't need is your uppity ass coming to her home and harassing her about shit. Next time you show up here, it better be to drop to your knees and to suck my dick."

My cheeks heat, and my mouth drops open. I'm stunned into silence and embarrassment to the point of being unable to respond. Suddenly, everything makes much more sense—from Mr. Beck handing me the case and telling me not to pay it too much attention to the other admins cautiously avoiding talking with me about Cheyenne and her absentee father.

"Excuse me…," I say, unable to word anything else. Grady leans forward and smirks at me as he invades my space.

"I bet you'd like that, to suck my dick," he says in that ridiculously husky voice.

"You're disgusting," I say and lean forward as well. It doesn't matter that I'm practically shaking in my pumps. I won't let him see that. Going for mildly professional, I say, "Don't speak to me like that."

"Or what?" he says.

"As a representative of the high school, I have the duty to report any conditions students are living in which may worry me. Please don't tempt me to report your behavior."

"Report me, file all the paperwork you'd like. See where it goes."

"Don't worry," I say, "I will." And with that, I storm off the porch and down the drive to my car. I start her up and peel out with such anxiety that I can barely breathe until I'm back on school property.

That was such a bad idea.

Grady

☠ CHAPTER 2 ☠

THE TANG OF cheap whiskey rests on my tongue, practically sizzling with its ferocity. It's been a long time since I've drunk as much as I have in the past few days, but it's also been a long time since I've had to bury a friend. And fuck this shit.

Leaning over the solid, wooden table that sits in the center of the room we hold our club meetings in, I wrap my fingers around the mostly empty bottle of whiskey. From across the table, our charter's vice president, Wyatt, shakes his head. His long hair flops over his shoulders with the movement, and the lines around his eyes fold as his eyes squint. I tighten my grip on the bottle, daring the bastard before me to try and stop me from finishing it off. As far as I'm concerned, he can take his judgment and suck his own dick with it.

In the background, Jim, our charter's president, goes on and mother-fucking-on about the man we're burying. *He was a good man. He made us proud. He was a brother, and today we put him to rest.* It's always the fucking same when we have to lay a brother down—Chief being the sixth one I've had the motherfucking pleasure of putting six feet under. Because with the way shit has been going lately, a cheap pine box is a goddamn gift.

With one quick glance at my empty glass, I lift the bottle to my lips, tilt it back, and suck down as much whiskey as I can before my throat contracts and I'm forced to set the bottle down. A fiery burn erupts in my mouth and throat as the liquor slides down and settles in my gut. I suck in a deep breath and shake off the shiver that runs down my spine. In the background, I hear Jim asking us each to pour ourselves a drink and to raise our glasses in celebration of Chief's life.

The man to my left makes no sound as he pours himself a glass of shitty bourbon. Ian's always been a quiet one—stoic and tortured most of the time. It's the man on his other side, Ryan, who clanks the bottle against his glass and spills a few drops on the wooden table top. I turn just slightly to my left and eye the droplets as they invade the clean surface. Ruby, Jim's Old Lady, did a lot to clean this place up for today. I sat with her, just yesterday, as she scrubbed the stains out of our chairs and wiped down the table. She wanted everything to be clean for today. And her asshole stepson just made a mess.

I hear the men around me say, 'to Chief!" loudly. Their voices echo around the edges of the room, but I can't bring myself to raise the bottle in my hand. It's Ryan's fault my best friend is lying in a goddamn box, well overdue for his final burial. The kid's been making a mess of shit since he was small. He's selfish and narcissistic and never thinks of how his actions affect anyone else. Not that he'd give a shit even if he did.

The men around me quiet down, and I find myself continuing to focus on those fucking drops. Finally, I drag my eyes up Ryan's cut and past his ROAD CAPTAIN patch, up his throat and to the scowl on his face. The scowl that never really leaves falls for a moment when he catches my eye. All emotion disappears from his face, his eyes don't leave mine, and he gives me a quick nod, like we're tight or some shit. We're not.

"Clean up your mess," I say. He doesn't budge, but he does give the drops a moment's worth of attention before his brows furrow and he stares at me like I've got two heads or something. "Your mother cleaned this table. Don't be a prick. Clean up your fucking mess."

From across the table, Duke, our secretary, says in disbelief, "Since when do we give a shit about making a mess?"

"Seriously," Trigger says. His annoyance is profound. Nothing I say is going to make him understand or give a shit. The only thing I have is the potential of pissing him off to get him to fight me. The urge to fight, to do something, runs through my bones and thuds loud and hard in my veins.

"Why don't I have that bitch of yours lick it up?" I say, knowing damn well that talking about Alex is going to piss him off. I barely have the words out of my mouth by the time he's on his feet. His glass falls to the floor beside him, and his chest heaves in agitation. Slowly, I rise to my feet and meet his stance. The men around us—our brothers—push their chairs back and stand. Nobody says a word when I deliver the first blow, nor the second. When Trigger, who's a good decade my junior, lands a blow to my gut, it knocks the wind out of me. Still, nobody interferes. Eventually he works out his aggression and stops fighting. Laying into him isn't appealing once he stops fighting back, and I give up. And, unfortunately, the room now looks ten times worse than it did before.

This is how we work through our shit. We fight it out and when we're done, we go back to dealing with whatever we were before someone had the sudden urge to lay it down. But this time, it's not going to fix a fucking thing. The pain helps slightly. Blow by blow, it numbs out all of the goddamn feelings I've been having lately. I haven't had this many mixed emotions since the day my daughter was born. But it's been a damn long time since then, and I'm too old to feel shit this strongly. Despite having spent years numbing shit out, I'm feeling this—Chief's death—in a way I hate to admit. It makes me feel like the fucking pussy I've spent my entire life making sure I'm not.

I met Chief even before I hooked up with Layla, my estranged wife, and long before the best fucking thing in the world came along—my daughter, Cheyenne.

And now he's gone.

And it's because Trigger just had to get his dick wet.

"Our brother is dead, but his spirit will live on." Wyatt reaches to the center of the table and grabs the good scotch that we only break out when shit gets this bad. Our previous president, Jim's father, Rage, used to say that when your spirits are high, cheap booze is all you need, but when everything's gone to shit, good liquor is the only thing you've got. Rounding up the ten empty glasses, Wyatt breaks open the scotch and pours each glass full, then he slides them down the table, sloshing all the way. He meets my eyes, daring me to say a word about the mess he's making.

The ten of us raise our glasses in the air and shout, "to Chief," at once, then we toss the liquor back.

The scotch burns as it slides down my throat. When I set the glass down, black fabric with red and white stitching stares up at me, taunting me, from the table before me. Chief's memory patch. The patch we wear in honor of a fallen brother. The patch I lift from the table and hold between my calloused fingers. It can't be more than a few ounces, but it feels like lead in my hands—the ever-lasting reminder of this loss.

Fish stands from his seat and strides across the room. He returns with a wooden chest that he sets in the middle of the table. My brothers and I stand and carefully dig into the chest to retrieve needles and black thread. Then we sit down and proceed to sew our patches onto the back of our cuts, above the seam, tucked into the left side.

When we're done, we each stand and return our supplies, then walk out into the main room, which is filled with family.

Across the room, I catch sight of my kid, who is seated at a small, round table, her elbow atop it while she engages in easy conversation with my mother. Cheyenne is closing in on eighteen years old, and God help her, she looks just like her mother. She's convinced that when I say I'm going to shoot the first motherfucker I catch making a move on her that I'm kidding. What she doesn't get at her age is that I was a teenage boy back when I got ahold of her mother.

Cheyenne says something that makes my mother laugh, and the two throw their heads back with short laughter before they calm themselves and let out hefty sighs. It's then that I see the tears pooling in the corner of Cheyenne's eyes. My feet carry me across the room, and I find myself lurking over their table before I think about it too much. It doesn't matter what it is, I hate it when women cry. I'd rather be stabbed than to listen to the sounds of a chick wailing.

"Daddy," she says and stands instantly. She's barely over five feet tall and a hundred pounds. Her arms normally feel light as they wrap around my waist when she pulls me into one of her hugs, but right now, every single touch feels so heavy. I lift an arm and wrap it around her shoulders as she rests her head on my torso. One quick sniffle and the tears are gone, but the sadness isn't. Chief was her godfather—the man who would have fulfilled my role in her life had he outlived me—a role he took seriously. Chief's tribe is how Cheyenne got her name, a symbol of what I hope she will grow into—strong, fierce, resilient, and proud. I've always been proud of my girl, but standing here, holding her as she keeps her chin up high and puts on a stoic face, shows me how incredibly strong she really is.

"This sucks," she whispers into my cut.

I tighten my grip around her shoulders and whisper back, "Yeah."

Because it does.

"Where is the memory patch?" my mom asks. Her curiosity is natural, but the question still makes me flinch. I turn slowly and point to it quickly before turning back around.

"Who sewed that on?" she asks, a bit perplexed.

"I did," I say. She's seen me work a needle and thread before, though not often. She always offers to help, but that's not how things are done.

"I could have done it for you," she says, predictably.

"No," I say. "He was my brother, and my patches are my responsibility." I skip telling her that it's in the club bylaws, and that there's honor in sewing on a fallen brother's patch. I don't tell her it's symbolic for the members to sew their own patches. She won't get it anyway, so I save my breath.

Jim rounds up the entire room and gives direction for where we're supposed to be. "Brothers, on your bikes, Old Ladies on the back of your Old Man's bike, and extended family in the SUVs."

Just as everybody starts to move, the front door creaks open and slams shut. All heads turn toward the door. Standing at nearly six feet tall, with broad shoulders and caramel-colored skin, is Elle Phillips, Chief's eldest daughter. Even in her grief, Elle is fine as fuck and one hell of a woman. Though her normally hard-set features are somewhat soft now, and her dark brown eyes are rimmed with bags, she still carries herself with confidence and determination. I fight the urge to go to her and show her a side of myself that few people will ever see. But I don't. As it is, my brothers wonder about us, and today is not the day to disrespect her father any further.

Cheyenne relaxes in my arms as she reverently whispers, "She came."

"And me?" Elle asks in her raspy voice. Jim places his hands on his hips and gives her an honest smile. None of us expected that she'd come today. Not after I made the ride to Sacramento to tell her the news. Upon hearing of her father's death, she stood emotionless in her front doorway and, without a single word, slammed it in my face. I banged on that door for nearly an hour before the neighbors bitched too much, so I gave up and rode east for as long as I could, until finally I'd run out of gas in some nowhere town and had to push my bike a good two miles to the nearest gas station. I'd have kept riding, but Chief had this theory that when shit went wrong it was for good reason and it gave you an opportunity to evaluate what you're doing. So I came home, and now here we are.

"SUV with Barbara," he says. She takes one step farther into the room and shakes her head. Watching this woman refuse to back down from a man most fear to even make eye contact with practically crushes my soul. She's one tough bitch, that's for sure. But sometimes I think that, underneath all that strength and bravado, that she's still a woman who needs to be handled with care every now and then. And right now, Jim needs to show her some care. If he doesn't, I will.

"No," she says in a plea. "He was my father, and I have as much right to ride as any of his brothers do." I shouldn't be surprised that Elle, who's been riding since she was seventeen, would demand to ride alongside her father's brothers. She may be somewhat estranged from the club and her father, but there's no doubting that she loved him as fiercely as I hope Cheyenne feels for me.

Jim closes the distance between them and wraps her into a tight hug. We've never allowed someone from outside of the club—family or not—to ride alongside us at a time of tribute to one of our brothers, but I can't see anybody saying shit about it.

"I'm glad you came, Little Bird," he says, using the tribal name she was gifted at birth. Chief couldn't have known that the child he declared Little Bird would turn into something of an Amazonian-type woman who knows four ways to kill a man without the use of weapons. When they pull away, Jim holds her at arm's length and looks her over.

"This club has never allowed a non-member to ride with us to bury a brother," Jim says, telling everybody what we already know. Having known the man for the last twenty years, I know where he's going with this—he's giving Elle her wish. He just has to make sure everybody knows that he knows this move goes against tradition. "But there's a first for everything."

She doesn't smile, nor does she say a word. Her face hardens, and she nods her head. It's a long moment before she pulls away and crosses the room to where her stepmother and younger half-brother and sister, Stephen and Izzy, sit. Izzy jumps up and wraps her small body around Elle's immediately. Stephen is slower to follow. After the kids have had their moment with her, Barbara uneasily reaches out and gives her step-daughter a hug. It's an awkward moment between the two, but at least they're both trying to mend fences.

My brothers move to congregate around Jim as he starts giving orders. I pat Cheyenne's back, and she lets go, and then I join my club. Jim scratches at his chin and looks at Ryan and says, "You know the order best. Put Elle in the back with the prospect. Don't care which side."

"Prospect hasn't even been riding a month now," Ryan says with obvious annoyance in his voice. "I don't think he should ride." The kid's dad is an incarcerated brother, so he was fast-tracked into prospecting—we gave him a cut and told him he was going to have to earn his top rocker. The kid had no fucking clue how to ride when we did it, but he's family and apparently we're all about making exceptions for family these days. Jim gives Ryan the order again, and, like the idiot he is, he's about to argue when Wyatt closes in on him and he backs down. He's not a total moron after all.

We break, and the room empties as we all head outside. Between the line of bikes and the line of SUVs is a glass hearse with a Harley trike attached to the front of it. It's a bit extravagant for our usual tastes, but we let Ruby do some of the planning, and this is what we ended up renting. No fucking clue where she got a hearse attached to a Harley, but fuck if it doesn't make a statement.

Fish, Bear, and the prospect help get the women and kids into the SUVs. Jeremy tries to put his sister, Nic, into an SUV, but she refuses. Nic's as much Duke's Old Lady as Ruby is Jim's. She's just not voted in yet—that's going to take a while. But I suspect Jeremy's insistence on sticking her in the SUV comes from the fact that she's carrying his nephew. I watch as Duke catches sight of the disagreement and lumbers over. We ride with our women on the back of our bikes—pregnant or not—all the time, but Duke's been a special kind of protective over Nic since the moment she let him in. It surprises me when he pulls her into his side and tells Jeremy that it's cool.

"They're cute together," a soft voice says from beside me. The words are filled with love and happiness. If it were anybody else who sounded so happy right now, I'd have their face in the pavement beneath my feet. But as I look over at Ruby, knowing all the hardships she's endured in her life, I can't help but let her have this. "You used to look at Layla like that," she says.

"Yeah."

"How she doing?" she asks. I quickly glance around and breathe a sigh of relief when I catch Cheyenne standing by an SUV with Barbara, the kids, and my mother at the other end of the parking lot. "Relax, you know I wouldn't ask if she could hear me," Ruby says, always so in-tune with everybody's feelings.

"Fuckin' jacked. Got an Old Man up in Redding who's got her sucking dick for crank." Lying to Ruby and telling her I don't keep tabs on Layla is useless. She knows me too well.

"Stupid bitch," she says and places a hand on my upper arm. "Gave up a lot for a couple of rocks and a high, didn't she?"

When I look over I see that her eyes are firmly on Cheyenne. Layla leaving her kid because she couldn't handle reality and all that it entailed never has sat well with Ruby—nor should it, considering everything she's sacrificed for her own children—and she's never hidden that fact from anyone, especially not Layla.

"That she did," I say and decide to skip my monthly trip to go check on her. It's only a few hours' drive, and it's worth the peace of mind to know whether or not my kid's mom has overdosed, but she's hospitalized right now so that's not much of a concern. She was supposed to be here today, but Chey snubbed her for dinner last night, and like always, Layla couldn't handle it. By the time I got to her motel room, she was already having chest pains and difficulty breathing. Wyatt had barely gotten there with his truck when her mood spun out of control and the paranoia set in.

"Do yourself a favor and let her go," Ruby says. "If life has taught us anything, it's that it's too fucking short to spend it alone." She casts me a small smile and walks over to Jim, where she climbs on the back of his bike and places a soft kiss to his top rocker right between his shoulder blades. Ruby thinks she's like the biker love connection or some shit. She's convinced that nobody should spend their life alone or that they should be without what she has with Jim. But she's smoked too much of that shit we grow—not everybody wants that kind of baggage. Layla being gone is a fucking blessing in a way. It means I don't have to worry about my Old Lady doing me dirty, or losing her. That shit's already happened, and now that I'm out of it, I have no desire to make it back to that place where I have one more fucking thing to worry about. Love isn't a blessing; it's a fucking burden.

"Saddle up, shithead," Wyatt yells from his bike, seated next to Jim at the front of the caravan. I snap out of my thoughts and take my place on my bike behind Jim. My nerves turn to lead as I eye Ryan to my right. Thin, pale arms wrap around his waist, and a heart-shaped face rests against his back. *Alex*. For a brief moment, her eyes meet mine, but then she thinks better of it and looks at the ground. Fucking bitch shouldn't be here. We risked too much to keep her ass safe, and now this fucker is taking her out in the open like we've got nothing to lose.

Ryan, being the road captain, has the responsibility of organizing rides and, at times like these, organizing placement of the club. Highest ranking officers always ride at the front, but the mid-level officers and non-office holding patched brothers are up to Ryan's discretion. And the bastard just can't help but fucking taunting me. His head turns my direction, and he lifts his chin. I grip the handlebars of my bike as tight as I can so I don't jump off and pummel his ass. Chief would be here if it weren't for Alex's presence in our lives, and to have her here is a fucking disgrace to his memory.

"Chief would want this," Ryan says firmly. His words cut to my soul. Would Chief want her here? He probably would, but he was a fucking pussy when it came to women. He was also a better man than I ever will be. I know he wouldn't blame her. She didn't ask for us to take her on, nor did she do anything other than exist to get him killed. But even though I can see through the anger long enough to know that, I don't feel it in my heart.

We fire up the bikes and ride slowly through town, purposefully creating as much noise as possible. As we travel down Main Street, some of the natives stop what they're doing and watch us as we ride by. Passing by the hardware store, Old Man Hill even removes his worn ball cap from his head as a show of respect. I rev my engine and keep in line with my brothers, making sure that as we pass through, we occasionally glance at those who are paying Chief respect by watching us pass. I steel myself as I see two men, each with an arm slung over a slick black Mercedes, both wearing dark sunglasses—despite the overcast sky—and impeccably tailored black suits. *Mancuso.* Signaling that we've got company to Ryan, who gives notice to Jim and the rest of the men, I don't take my eyes off the Italians until I'm forced to keep my eyes on the road. Hopefully they're just making a statement and not making their next move in what's turned into a war.

The show of disrespect is almost more than I can handle, but I refuse to let my anger get the best of me today.

☠CHAPTER 3☠

I LET MY fingers drift over the cold granite surface that rests flat in the grass. I'm careful not to touch the engraved letters that tell the story of the best man I ever met. Rather, I trace around them. It's not the letters that make up his name—Charles Phillips—nor is it the inscription that reads "beloved brother, loving father, proud Cheyenne," that pains me. Unlike some clubs, who bury their men in a uniform fashion, Forsaken's founding members didn't want their men to ever forget that they are more than just soldiers. The club is a brotherhood, but that doesn't take away from the fact that we're also fathers and sons. The same Norse warrior that adorns our cuts stares back at me from the granite, but it's just a picture stenciled into rock. No, it's the year of his birth, followed by the year of his death, at the very bottom of the flat stone that is most upsetting. There shouldn't be a year of death on there, because he shouldn't be dead. But he is. A few blades of freshly cut grass rest atop the stone. I blow them away, suddenly discontent that we didn't wait until we could get an upright headstone in here.

Not that my younger brothers have bothered to read them, but it's in the club bylaws that were put in place when the club was founded in the middle of fucking nowhere Nevada way back in 1946. It's important, I think, to know our history and to not forget it. That's something Chief taught me back when I was barely old enough to understand what it meant. He taught me a lot about what it means to be a man, and a father, but most of all what it means to be a brother.

And he's gone.

"Well, you're an asshole," I say.

A cool wind picks up and slices right through my cut. I'm worn the fuck out and fighting a nasty hangover. Everything about being here, both at my best friend's grave and in this fucked-up world, hurts like a bitch. Even the wind, though not particularly icy, is painful.

"You always pushed me to be a better man, but look where that got me—I'm talking to a fucking piece of rock like you can hear me. You could've left me alone you know, back then. You didn't have to help my retarded ass out of those charges. But fuck, you hadn't shown up, I'd either be doing 25-to-life, or selling insurance in Albuquerque. Either way, I'd rather be dead. I wouldn't have Chey had we not rode up to the bar in Arizona.

"That night, with Layla, you told me she wasn't right. I didn't listen. I remember all that shit, like it's a broken record, but I can't shut off. Everything you told me about women is ingrained into my fucking skull. Not that you've ever been some kind of relationship expert—I hope you found it entertaining that your whore wanted to ride in the SUV with your goddamn wife and kids. You always thought you were so wise, giving out advice like you were some kind of sage, when in reality you were just one high motherfucker whose dick was too social for his own good. Doesn't matter. I still take that shit with me everywhere I go, and in everything I do. So here I am, acting like a fucking brokenhearted bitch. I hope you're happy."

We laid Chief to rest not too long ago. Mancuso's guys kept their distance and didn't interfere. Still, seeing them on the side of the road on our way to the cemetery was enough to fuck everybody up for the rest of the day. It had been so long since we'd lost a brother, especially the way we lost Chief, that none of us were really in the right frame of mind to organize his burial. Thank fucking Christ for Ruby. She did right by the guy, even down to figuring out the exact details for his coffin, which she had custom made. I give Jim shit for letting her lead them around by his dick a lot, but she's a damn good woman, no doubt. She even arranged to have a medicine man from a local Native American tribe officiate the service. It was perfect—the blending of his heritage, which he had been so proud of, and the life he chose.

Barbara, Chief's widow, asked if I wanted to say a few words. I was selfish though, and didn't want to look like a pussy in front of my brothers. As a strict policy, we keep our burial services private. No press, no law enforcement, no hang-arounds, and no outsiders. All of the old ladies, even Nic, ended up in tears. As expected, it was particularly tough for Chief's kids. His youngest daughter, Izzy, clung to her mother, and his son, Stephen, held his older, half-sister's hand. I had to look away when I saw the tears roll down Elle's cheek and Stephen lean in and comfort her. Elle Phillips is one tough bitch, and seeing her fall apart almost did me in. But it was the sight of Ryan introducing Cheyenne to Alex that shredded me. It was then that I realized I have to get right with the shit and move on with my life. It's what Chief would want, at least that's what everybody tells me.

The stark ring of my cell pulls me for my thoughts. Without looking at the caller ID, I slide my thumb across the screen and bring the phone to my ear. "You got Grady."

"Mr. Grady, this is Principal Beck. I need you to come down to the school. There has been an incident between Cheyenne and her counselor, Ms. Mercer."

"What did Mercer do to my kid?" I snap. This bitch is barking up the wrong fucking tree.

"Actually, Sir. Cheyenne lashed out and, should Ms. Mercer choose to do so, she can be suspended for her behavior."

"Yeah, I'll be there in a few," I say and hang up. Just as I shove my phone back into my pocket, I blow out a frustrated breath and scrub my face with my hands.

"Have a kid, you said," I say as I stare intently at the Forsaken logo that rests above "CHIEF" in bold lettering. "It's the best feeling in the world, you said. Look, I ain't blaming you because I didn't wrap my shit, brother. Alls I'm saying is that you could have given me a head's up."

The ride to the school is short, but it gives me time to

think shit over. My mother doesn't say too much, but she's obviously worried that I'm not snapping out of this funk. Mourning, she says, is one thing, "but this place you're in is dangerous."

As I park my bike and head into the office, I take a deep breath and focus on the task at hand. Chey's been struggling the last few months, and I don't know why. She won't talk to me, and she swears nothing's wrong. If she tells me she's "fine" one more time, I'm sending her ass to Ruby. She's probably the one person on the planet who hates that word more than I do.

"I'm here for Cheyenne Grady," I say.

It's no use, but I try to keep my bad fucking mood from getting even worse. Shit is not good anywhere these days, and now I have to deal with straightening Ms. Mercer's stupid ass out. Fucking perfect. For some reason, this bitch has it out for my kid, and I've had enough of it. I got no doubt that Chey earned herself some trouble, but why now? I bet Mercer's got an ax to grind with the club—just like her cock-sucking boss—and she's taking it out on Chey. While most people in Fort Bragg are cool with the club, there are a few who turn their noses up at us, and apparently this glorified paper pusher is one of them. We're too loud, too wild, and too dangerous.

If only they knew.

"Yes, Mr. Grady," the woman behind the desk says in a faux polite tone. The name plate on her desk reads MARGOT FLORES. She hits the ancient buzzer beside her computer and announces to the principal, Mr. Beck that I have arrived. It's but a few moments before I see him striding down the hallway with a scowl on his face.

"Mr. Grady," he says, "Thank you for coming down so quickly."

He leads me down the hall to his office—a place I've never been before. Until recently, Chey's never had trouble at school. The only trouble I've heard about has been from this Mercer bitch, which leads me to believe she's full of shit. My daughter is a good kid—she just occasionally has to deal with a rough patch, almost always after she sees her mom.

"Yeah," I say and follow him into his office. It's small, and every bit of furniture appears to be an aged wood and olive mix. In one corner, near a bookcase filled with awards, is Chey. Her arms are folded over her chest, and her eyes are wet with freshly fallen tears. In the other corner is Ms. Mercer. Her light brown hair is falling in her face as her head is tilted toward her lap. Mr. Beck gestures to a chair between the two, and I sit as he rounds his desk and takes his place.

"We had an incident during a counseling session that needs your attention," he says.

"What happened?" I ask, looking at Chey. She pulls her lip in and diverts her eyes, a sure sign that she did something she knows damn well she shouldn't have. When she doesn't meet my eyes, I wrap my hands around the wooden arm rests of my chair and take a deep breath. "Cheyenne, look at me."

Still, her eyes don't lift to mine.

"During a counseling session where Ms. Mercer expressed concern for Cheyenne, your daughter made a comment which was inappropriate and requires immediate attention. She used a curse word to describe Ms. Mercer," Mr. Beck says.

"You curse at this lady?" I ask Chey, who is determined to be unresponsive. When I finally tire of staring at the top of her fucking head, I turn my attention the other direction toward the bitch who's started all this shit. I don't know what went down, and to be honest, I only kind of care. Mercer's had it out for Chey for months now, and I wouldn't put it past her to push my kid's buttons to see what happens.

"What did she say?" I ask Ms. Mercer, who is now looking me in the eye. For such a bitch, she's pretty fuckable. Her complexion is nice and smooth, and she has light brown eyes that are complemented by her light brown hair and pale skin.

"Cheyenne called me the B word," she says. I scoff before I can stop myself and earn a disapproving look from both Ms. Mercer and Mr. Beck.

"She called you a bitch," I say. Ms. Mercer's lips form a straight line, and her eyes narrow. Yeah, she's uptight all right. Uptight as all fucking hell. I wonder when the last time she got laid was. I have half a mind to bend her over the desk and show her how to let loose. It'd be a fucking public service. I bet she's so tightly wound that she's never even jaywalked before.

"Yes," she says in a clipped tone.

"Why?" I ask.

"Excuse me?" she says, like she suddenly can't speak English. I raise my eyebrows and gesture to Chey.

"Why," I repeat.

"Mr. Grady," she says then shuts her mouth quickly. From my other side, I hear a sharp intake of breath. I look to Chey, who is glaring across the room.

"*Ms. Mercer* thinks I'm being abused or neglected," Chey says with serious attitude. She started this shit a few years back, and it's only gotten worse with time.

"Cheyenne," Ms. Mercer pleads in a soft voice. "I've apologized. It's my job to make sure you're safe."

"Holly," Chey says with more venom in her tone than a fucking rattlesnake has in its entire body. "I *thought* you were cool. I thought we were friends!"

"I am cool, but I will *not* ignore a situation that concerns me," Ms. Mercer says. There's obviously more going on between these two than I'm aware of.

"That why you called her a bitch?" I ask Chey, who nods. Her mood's picking up now that she thinks she has something on Ms. Mercer. She doesn't, because the second I get her ass home, she's grounded. But I'll let the little princess think she's snowed me for now. I just don't want to give Mercer the satisfaction of knowing I don't exactly have everything under control.

"Okay then, we're gonna go," I say to Mr. Beck.

"No, you cannot," Ms. Mercer says as she stands in objection. "You daughter cannot run around speaking like that to adults, especially adults at her school, and expect no consequence. *This* is what I was concerned about."

"Ain't nobody gonna tell me how to parent my kid," I say loudly and stand from my seat. Ms. Mercer takes a step closer to me and places her hands on her hips.

"You are a very troubled man," she spits out with such anger I think she might melt the fucking floor around us. "Time and time again, you refuse to accept responsibility for your daughter's poor behavior. Further, you have done her no favors by demonstrating to her that she can ignore consequences for mistreating others and that she is without fault. Cheyenne is an awesome kid, but she needs discipline. I'm not telling you how to parent. I am telling you that I won't stand to be treated so poorly by a student or her parent."

"Is that so?" I ask, rage boiling in my veins and my heart. I know I've been fucking up and it just pisses me off that this stupid bitch has the nerve to call me on it.

"Yes," she says in a firm voice. I take a step closer to her, but she doesn't budge. If I could think clearly, I could examine the scowl on her face and see that she's more than fuckable—she's actually kind of pretty. Not the kind of pretty I'm used to at the clubhouse with the whores who hang around at a dime a dozen, but a natural kind of pretty. The kind of pretty that a person wakes up with. Too bad she's such a cunt.

"Do you know who I am?" I ask, leaning in. She closes the distance between us and glares up at me.

"Yes," she says with a slight quiver to her lip that's kind of attractive. She almost looks like a scared little deer who's just seen a hunter with a rifle. And I think she's finally going to back down and show me that she's smarter than she looks. But she doesn't. "And I don't care."

Holly

☠CHAPTER 4☠

AN ELECTRIFIED CRACK sounds and is followed by the low buzz and fizzle of the overhead light bulb burning out. Without manufactured light, the room is basked in shadows and feels somewhat cooler. Still, beads of sweat sneak down my back, curve down my spine, and then are absorbed in the thin cotton blend tee shirt that sticks to my overheated skin. It's never very hot here, along the Northern California coastline, but the exertion from a move will get even those in the Arctic working up a sweat.

I peer up at the encroaching darkness and sigh. My eyes are strained from the setting sun and the encroaching darkness. It figures that my new apartment needs repairs already. We barely got the sofa into the living room an hour ago, and now this. The light bulb, though a small issue, is another reminder of how messed up my life is. First went my job, then my roommate/boyfriend/whatever he was, then my apartment, and finally my pride. Now the light bulb.

Footsteps echo down the hallway, creating creaks and

whines from the aging hardwood floor. That's probably the next to go.

"Holly, are you in here?" an upbeat and excited voice asks from down the hall. Before I can say anything, she rounds the corner into my bedroom and says, "Why are you standing in the dark?"

It's Mindy, my cousin; on-again; off-again; but most recently on-again roommate; and best friend. I turn in time to see her flick the light switch on and off until a frown forms on her pretty face. Her skin is smooth and taut, and her lips aren't dried and cracked as they were years back. Thank God. Mindy is just a few years younger than me, but in some ways, she seems so much older. She's wise in ways I don't think I'll ever be, and she's been through the kinds of hell I hope to never have to pull her out of again. And she's just barely twenty-three.

"Bulb's busted," I say and point to the ceiling. She purses her lips and gives me a big smile. It's the kind of smile our fathers hated when we were growing up because, when Mindy smiles like this, it means we're going to get in trouble for doing something we shouldn't. Back before the world fell apart and then everything sort of...crumbled...I used to love that smile. I longed for it when we were in the church pews on Sunday mornings and trying to pass notes. I lived for that smile back when we were in high school, and I was nearing graduation, but Mindy had just begun, and she convinced me that we so totally had to crash a frat party at Humboldt State. That smile even made me laugh when her dad, my uncle Harry—the cop—had to come pick us up at the frat party at Humboldt State because my car had been broken into and Mindy didn't give a damn about daddy's lectures because she'd gotten a freshman named Heath's phone number. And that smile nearly made me split in two when, a few years later, Mindy had returned home after leaving two days after graduation and telling me she'd married Heath in Reno.

But that was the *before* Mindy, and the *before* Mindy could be silly wild. She could get into a little bit of trouble and eat too much ice cream. But I don't know which Mindy this is, and her smiles don't sit right with me anymore. I can't bring myself to smile all silly-like and to just go along with whatever little scheme she has cooked up. I just can't trust that she won't go back to that place.

So I don't smile. I just stare at her, waiting for an explanation. It's probably not the best way to get started rooming with someone, but this is Mindy—regardless of which Mindy it is—and she gets it. She was there, mostly the cause of it, and she doesn't take things all that personally. At least she didn't used to.

"Relax," she says, with the big smile on her face waning slightly. "I was just thinking that we could walk down to the hardware store, and then we could grab a pizza while we're out. Nothing crazy."

"Sorry," I say. The words come out forced, and I sound like I'm being strangled. I don't really *want* to apologize for my reaction, but it's the polite thing to do. Besides, even though I know Mindy will forgive my rudeness and selfishness, I don't think I would. I've been over this with myself a hundred times. It's about time I stop blaming Mindy for the last four years. I silently repeat the mantra my community-provided therapist taught me: I am not powerless; I have a choice.

"It's fine," she says and waves my comment away. Her smile is totally gone now, and her eyes find the floor. It's obviously not fine, and this is one of the reasons I didn't think us living together again was such a great idea. We have too much baggage and too much tormented history to peacefully cohabitate. But peace or no peace, I can't afford to live on my own right now, so my options are limited.

"No," I say and reach out for her hand. She doesn't pull away, but nor does she offer it to me. Snaking my fingers between hers and squeezing, I pull her closer to me. "Pizza sounds great, and maybe if I eat, I'll stop being a jerk." A small smile creeps onto her face, and I know I have her. We leave the shadowy room behind and head down the long hallway until we're in the narrow galley kitchen that shares its space with a small dining area. I let go of her hand to grab my purse, and then we're out the front door and down the stairs. Within a minute, we're on East Oak—just half a block off Main Street.

Uncle Harry doesn't like the location because of its proximity to the town's resident motorcycle club, and my mother doesn't like it because I'm almost ten minutes away from her. But the rent is reasonable, parking is easy, and Mindy doesn't even have to drive to work anymore. Plus, after living with my mother for the last three months, I'm more than happy to be ten minutes away from her. So, I guess the new apartment has its perks and its time I stop griping about silly little things like busted light bulbs and bad history that I can't change.

Mindy and I walk quickly toward the hardware store that's about to close. I don't even know what time it is, but I grew up in this town and everybody knows that the hardware store closes at dusk. Old Man Hill has been closing Early Bird Hardware at dusk since he was a newlywed and was too paranoid to leave his wife home alone after dark. His eccentricities would be romantic if they weren't so freaking inconvenient during winter. Thankfully, Mindy and I make it in time. Old Man Hill does take a moment to chastise us for being out *so late* and even talks us each into buying a small, pink can of pepper spray. I have no idea what I'm going to do with it, other than likely spray myself in the face with it, since we live in one of the safest towns in the state, but oh well. It's ten bucks I won't get back, but it's also ten dollars' worth of Mr. Hill's silence.

Fresh light bulbs, garbage bags, shelf liner, and cute little pepper sprays in tow, we make the three-block trek to Sea Salt Pizza—an old favorite of ours. It's been years since I've been in the place, but I've missed it dearly, so Mindy made a good call when she told me she knew the perfect place for us to grab a slice. Not that we have that many choices. For a town of less than ten thousand, and being as remote as we are, Fort Bragg does well to keep their residents' basic needs met—like movie rentals, wine, and pizza. Still, finding decent food around here can be kind of a crapshoot since local business doesn't usually depend on whether or not the product is good. It's all about liking the owners, and thankfully for me, the owners of Sea Salt Pizza seem to be very well-liked since they've been in business for nearly fifteen years.

Sea Salt Pizza is the kind of place where you walk in, grab your own table and your own menu—if you even need one, that is—and give the staff a smile and a wave to get them to serve you. If you don't know the protocol, you're largely ignored until you catch the right person's eye. It's also normally loud from the endless chatter and the joyful clanking of glasses, or even agitated shouts as the customers in the back room are watching sports on one of the TVs. But tonight, the place is low-key and quiet. I can't hear a single TV, and there doesn't seem to be any celebrating going on. At first, I think the place is empty – then I hear him.

In a corner booth sits Sterling Grady and his daughter, Cheyenne. He sits tall and almost rigid, with his back to the corner, his deep green eyes scanning the area around him. In a way, he reminds me of Uncle Harry, in that he's hyper-aware of his surroundings. But unlike Uncle Harry, Sterling Grady is a major asshole. I can only hope that he doesn't see me because it's too late to change my mind. Mindy's already heading for a table in the center of the room. *Just my luck.*

Days-old stubble dots Grady's well-constructed jaw and extends halfway down his thick neck. His tanned skin peeks out from underneath his black and gray flannel shirt. Naturally tanned skin is something of an anomaly around here. It's so overcast all the time. He must have a job that requires manual labor. It would certainly explain the broad shoulders, thick arms, and massive chest. Even under a comfortable layer of flannel, I can see that he's built. Surprisingly, he isn't wearing his leather vest that labels him as a member of the Forsaken Motorcycle Club.

It makes my skin crawl that, despite how big of an asshole he is, I still find him attractive. He's not the first hot guy I've ever seen, but he is certainly the biggest douche bag. I really shouldn't be paying any attention to him. Maybe it's because, being back in Fort Bragg, I've noticed that most of the eligible men are either ones I went to high school with or obnoxious hippie transplants. Not that a serious jerk is a better option. He's just better built.

Mindy and I sit at our table in the center of the room, and I purposefully angle myself so I can watch him from the side, but not head on. I lean back in my seat and give the young boy behind the counter a smile and wave. He nods and makes his way around the service counter. As I'm leaning back, I peek to see who Grady is sitting with. It's Cheyenne. She's hoisting up a slice of cheese pizza and staring at her cell phone in wonderment.

"Grady," Mindy says quietly. I snap back to reality and try to fake confusion. She shakes her head and smiles. She knows me too well. "His name is Grady, and the girl with him is his daughter, Cheyenne. Don't bother telling me you weren't looking, because you were. And he's hot, but he's also really bad news."

Bad news is possibly the understatement of the century.

"You've been spending too much time with Uncle Harry," I say and do my best to tease her. With how crabby I was earlier, I need to make up for it before we get off to a really bad start being roommates again.

"No, you're just super obvious," she says with a snicker. I give the pair another glance. Grady has a mouthful of pizza and is saying something to Cheyenne. For the first time since we arrived, she sets her phone down and smiles up at him. And when she does, she turns her face just slightly in my direction. I divert my attention back to Mindy.

"How do you know who he is, anyway?" I ask, leaning in and lowering my voice.

"You better keep your big mouth shut, but I work with this girl who is with one of his club members. She hasn't really said much about him, but he's come in a few times, and it always makes her nervous. Heck, it makes *me* nervous."

"He's Forsaken?" I ask, acting like I don't already know.

"Yep. He's the guy who makes sure everyone follows the club rules," Mindy says with a gleam in her eyes. She's always loved gossip, but if you didn't know her well, you'd have no clue. She's really sneaky about her eavesdropping.

"You work with one of their wives?"

"She's not the guy's wife. She used to hate him, but then one day they ended up in this argument while I was at work and there was like, this emotional rollercoaster thing going on. It was crazy. Next thing I know she's pregnant and begrudgingly admitting that she's in love with him. Now she doesn't really shut up. They're all crazy, every one of them," Mindy says in a whisper-shout.

"Says the person all up in their business," I say.

"Whatever. Look, if you're looking for a guy, I'm sure I can find you someone far more suitable than one of *those* guys."

"I'm not *looking* looking, I was just…observing. Don't worry—there's no way in hell I'd get involved with the club."

As soon as the words leave my mouth, Grady and Cheyenne stand from their seats and head for the door. They make it halfway before he stops. He places his hands on his hips and I can hear him chuckling quietly to himself. The only thing I can think is, "Crap, crap, crap!" He turns around and strides toward our table. Cheyenne follows behind, crosses her arms over her chest, and keeps her attention focused on the front door.

"Just *observing*," he says. The way he emphasizes the word *observe* leaves little room for doubt that he overheard what I just said. I'd prefer to keep what happened at the high school limited to the people who already know about it, but it doesn't look like that's going to happen.

He bends at the waist and brings his face so close to mine that I can feel his breath wafting over my skin. I raise an eyebrow in silent question. The smile spreads on his face and he says, "Come by later. I'll give you something juicy to wrap your mouth around."

My eyes widen and horror fills my heart. I'm barely processing what he's said when I hear Mindy gasp. I can only imagine the look on her face. Above and beyond being inappropriate, he's being a dick.

"You're an asshole," I snap. He's already absorbed the words by the time I realize that maybe I shouldn't have said them at all. But it's too late, and I can only take so much taunting.

"Dad," Cheyenne says quietly. She's started to fidget and is hopping from foot to foot. At the very least, she's uncomfortable as well. He puts his hand up in the air to silence her, but all it does it motivate her to dramatically huff and spin around and walk toward the front door.

"For whatever reason, you seem to be making it your personal mission to torment me, and I'm not going to put up with it," I say, my voice rising with every word.

"I'm not into torture. Bondage, maybe, but not torture," he says. A shiver slides down my back. Suddenly, I realize how warm it in in the restaurant.

"Well, I'm not into either," I say. "Now, will you please leave?"

"I just thought I'd stop by and give you the opportunity to rethink the grievance you filed at the high school," he says. Of course, now he decides to get involved. Let's ignore the fact that the last few months he'd been completely unreachable regarding his daughter and her education, but this grievance would get his attention because it will be filed against him with the school board. As a district employee, I have the right to file a complaint against anyone treating me poorly. And I did. There's not too much the school district can really do because he's a parent, but it's better than nothing.

"Mr. Grady, the only thing I'm rethinking right now is my choice of seating," I say and narrow my eyes. He stands and raps his knuckles on the table top twice and brushes against my shoulder as he walks away. My eyes fall to the table and stay there until I hear the opening and shutting of the door.

"Holy cow," Mindy breathes and slaps her hand at the edge of the table. "What the heck was that?"

"Nothing," I say.

"Liar. You acted like you'd never seen him before," she says.

"I don't want to talk about it," I say, cutting her off. She must sense how entirely frustrating that scene was for me because she lets it go and changes the topic to something less awful.

The next hour goes by quickly as we order, then eat our Hawaiian pizza and drink our diet sodas. There's not much to say. It's mostly a sleepy job in a sleepy town. Not a whole lot happens in the office I work in, save for the occasional delinquent who's called in to see the principal.

"I'd rather talk about your job. It's bound to be a lot more interesting than mine," I say then finish the last few bites of my slice.

"It's really not," she says. "I serve coffee and sometimes food. I clean counters and try to chat up customers for better tips."

"Aunt Claire's been telling my mom all about how much you like it there," I say. "She goes on and on and on. So there must be more to it than just that." It takes Mindy a few moments and me asking her a number of questions in different ways before I finally get something out of her.

"There is this one customer who keeps coming in. He's tall and handsome and he is so well dressed. I don't know what kind of job he has, but he comes into the shop at all times of day and always in a suit," she says. Just like I knew she would, once she gets started, it's hard to get her to stop. "Sometimes he orders his cappuccino and sits in the corner reading the newspaper for like an hour or so, like he's got nothing better to do. And sometimes he just gets his coffee and goes. He's either totally uninterested or shy, but either way, I hope if I just keep being friendly, he'll warm up."

"If he doesn't, it just means he's lame," I say with a smile. "You make a killer cappuccino and anybody worth your time will appreciate your mad caffeine skills."

"You have a serious problem with coffee, you know that?" she asks.

"Pretty much," I admit.

As much as unknown variables make me nervous when it comes to Mindy, I am happy for her that she's keeping her eyes open. Her life can't have begun and ended with Heath.

We end the night on a positive note and the final words we speak to one another are after we've replaced the light bulb in my bedroom and get into our pajamas. Mindy draws me into a tight hug and says, "I'm so glad you're home. I thought I lost you."

"I love you, Minds," I whisper and give her a firm squeeze.

We let go and as she's walking away, she shouts over her shoulder, "Love you, too, but we're still going to talk about Grady later!"

☠CHAPTER 5☠

IT'S AMAZING HOW you can spend so much time away from a place yet feel like you've never really left it. At least, that's how it feels being in this space. Nothing's changed here in decades. The furniture is made of aged wood whose varnish wore off well before I was born, and the walls are so dingy that the original paint color is no longer recognizable due to age and lack of upkeep. Like everything about this town, a dirty gray hue settles over the entire room.

High heels click against the linoleum floor hard and fast in their approach. I look up from my desk in front of the principal's office to see Margot, Fort Bragg High School's Senior Secretary, and my supervisor, rushing through the hallway and then flinging herself into her desk chair in front of me. Margot can't be any younger than forty, but she's got a wily spirit and bright red hair. As far as bosses go, she's pretty awesome, and on occasion she's been able to make my job close to interesting.

Margot shoves her purse in her right desk drawer and then spins around and places her hands on the edge of my desk. "Where's Mr. Beck?"

With a quick look behind me to make sure Mr. Beck's office door is still closed, I lean in toward Margot and whisper, "In his office. I think he's napping. He's been there all day."

"Whew," she says and blows out a breath of relief. In the few months that I've been here, I've noticed that Margot has a thing for long lunches. Today is no exception, and while I don't really care what she does with her time, one of us has to be here at all times in case a student needs us, so her long lunches delay mine, and today she's so late that I'm starting to get grouchy with hunger.

A swarm of giggles sound in the hallway and then burst into the office. Four girls, all seniors, I think, stride toward Margot's desk and bat their eyelashes at her. I've seen this before, but this time, I recognize one of the girls—Cheyenne Grady. She is the absolute last student I want to see right now. Her father and I have never had a good meeting, and though she hasn't given me trouble lately, I still can't believe she called me a bitch. She's of average height for her age and average weight—meaning skinny and young and perfect—and has dark brown hair that's tinged just slightly with red highlights. If she's wearing any makeup, I can't tell. She stands on the far edge of the group and taps her fingers on Margot's desk.

A short, chubby blonde girl hands Margot a note and says, "We need the golf cart to help the football team clean up on the field." Margot eyes the note for a moment and then sighs. Her shoulders slump and roll as she turns back toward me.

"Mr. Dale is always letting these girls out of class to help the football team." The look on her face is anything but surprised. Mr. Dale's a pushover, that's for sure, and this isn't the first time these girls have come in with a note proclaiming to need the golf cart to help the football team. It sounds like B.S. to me, but Margot's my supervisor and I'm not about to tell her how to do her job. "Go get lunch," she says with a wave. "Where ya going anyway?"

"No clue," I say. "Any suggestions?" I open my bottom left drawer and pull out my purse. The tapping of Cheyenne's fingernail quickens before she clears her throat.

"You should try The 101 Club," Cheyenne says. She moves around Margot's desk and zeroes in on the candy jar I keep in the corner of my desk. She pulls out a lollipop and unwraps it, then sticks it in the side of her cheek. "My dad loves the place. He eats lunch there like every day. He's probably there now. I only get to go once in a while, but they've got killer burgers. Dad only lets me go on family days because at night it's more bar than grill, but you should totally go. Oh, and get a milkshake while you're there, too."

Despite our earlier interactions, listening to Cheyenne talk, I can see why she seems to have so many friends. I've seen her around the school a few times since that night at Sea Salt Pizza, and every time she's surrounded by girls. She may not always be the center of attention, but she's clearly a key part of any group she joins. She's said "hi" to me the times she's seen me. It's like the kid got a lobotomy or something because the sullen teen that I encountered during our counseling session has vanished. These days, every word she speaks exudes a sort of friendly confidence that is undeniably attractive in anyone of any age, but most especially a popular teenage girl.

"Thanks for the rec, but I don't think your father and I should share eateries," I say as politely as I can. Margot's head bobs around as she pretends she's not listening.

"Don't let him scare you," she says. "He's all bark. Besides, you seem to handle yourself just fine. He's harmless, I promise."

"On South Main, right?" I ask, giving Cheyenne a soft smile. My stomach is practically leaping out at her and giving her a hug at the mention of a killer burger, but my nerves are convinced that this is a bad idea, which, for some reason, makes it even more attractive.

"Yep," she says and pulls a cell phone from her pocket. "And if you hurry, you'll make it to lunch hour with half-priced fries."

Ever since the night at Sea Salt Pizza, I've been thinking about what I'd say to Grady should I run into him again. I was caught off-guard and not on my game because Mindy was there. But now I have an arsenal to unload on him should I have the chance.

"I love cheap fries," I say with a bit too much excitement. My belly rumbles in agreement, and I stand, thanking Cheyenne and giving Margot a wave. "Be back in an hour." I head out at warp speed, hoping that I don't end up pulling a

Margot and taking a super long lunch. I don't have the same luck she does in that my boss—being her—would notice. Once I'm inside my Jeep, I check my lipstick and hair just to make sure I'm not a total disaster. I'd try to tell myself that I don't want to run into Cheyenne's dad or anything, but that'd be a total lie. He's honestly the first guy I've seen since I moved back to town that roused even a little bit of interest for me which is actually really sick because he is one of the meanest individuals I've ever encountered.

"I'm not this pathetic," I mumble to myself as I pull up to The 101 Club. I should reconsider and just grab a crappy salad at one of the fast food joints in town. I probably shouldn't have lunch in a bar, even though Cheyenne mentioned killer burgers, half-priced fries, and milkshakes. No matter how stalkerish I feel about showing up here when I know Grady is likely here, it's no match to greasy food that makes even a teenage girl swoon.

So I hold my head up high as I put my Jeep in park and climb out. My therapist—which is really just code for my grandpa—tells me all the time that I need to look at my return to Fort Bragg like a fresh start and not an admittance of failure. He's recommended that I try new things and not let myself fall back into only doing the things and going to the places I used to before I left here for the Bay Area. If I want a different outcome, I need to do something different. So going to a place I've never been before is right up my alley. Unfortunately, so is lusting after a major asshole.

I try to shake my nerves off as I walk inside for the first time. Despite Cheyenne's recommendation, the place is basically empty and sure doesn't seem like the kind of place that has killer burgers. Still, I give it a shot. There's something kind of awesome about the place with its mismatched furniture that somehow all goes together and its too-cool-to-give-a-crap-about-décor vibe. Everything but the lights overhead, which are a flashy metal and conical-shaped, running down a long line over the bar, seem to be as old as I am. It's like The 101 Club doesn't know what it wants to be – something I can relate to.

In the corner is a pair of elderly men, cooped up and playing chess. They're angled away from the rest of the room, creating a bit of privacy for themselves. I walk up to the bar and pull myself up on a stool. A middle-aged man rounds the corner from the back room and puts himself behind the bar. He looks me over once and then nods his head and shoves a menu at me.

"Lunch hour's almost over, so order quick unless you're here to drink," he says. My stomach is in knots to the point that I almost do want a drink, but drinking at lunch is never a good idea. Drinking at lunch leads to drinking with the girls after work, and that leads to waking up hung-over. And that's the thing about drinking. It stresses me out, making me paranoid about what Mindy would say, but the more I drink the less I care. About everything.

He doesn't smile, nor does he greet me. I'd think he was being rude, but I get the impression that this is just how he is all the time and it's nothing personal. I go to thank him, but before I can, he disappears to where he came from. The front half of the menu is filled up with French fries done up in about twenty different ways, and the back side is a variety of burger choices. I look it all over quickly and make my selection and wait for Mr. Personality to return. When he does, he places his hands on the bar, looks me in the eyes, then gives the menu a glance before returning his attention to my face. It takes me a beat too long before I realize that this is his way of taking my order.

"I'll have the Mendo Burger and Coastal Fries with a vanilla shake," I say. He jerks his chin in the air, grabs my menu, and turns around. He grabs a clean—at least I hope it's clean—glass from behind the bar and the soda machine. Pushing a button, he fills the glass and then shoves it toward me.

"No shake. Water," he grumbles.

"I was told you serve shakes here?" I say in a questioning tone.

"Shakes are for family. I don't know you."

I bite my tongue to keep from making a snarky comment. I have no idea what this guy might do to my food before I get a hold of it.

It's only a few minutes before Mr. Personality returns with a red basket with my burger and fries inside. He sets it down on the bar. No sooner than he does, I hear the telltale sounds of a group of bikes heading toward the bar and grill. I gulp down my worry about being here, in Grady's space, and pick up my burger. Before I can take a bite, the man before me puts his hand over mine and I place the burger back in the basket, looking up at him in annoyance.

"Time to go, sweetheart," he says.

"Excuse me?" My voice is flat, beyond annoyed. The rumbling of the bikes grows louder, and I tamp down that nervous worry in the back of my belly. I'm hungry, but I'll get the burger to go if I have to. I just need food before my unpleasant side takes over.

"Don't know who you are, don't care. But now's not the time to find out. Best for you to go." He takes the basket from me and tosses it in the garbage behind him. I barely catch sight of the bacon and ranch on top of my Coastal Fries as they sail into the trash.

"Time to go," he repeats. I bite down on my bottom lip so hard I worry it'll bleed. The very real possibility that one of the nearing bikes could belong to Grady makes me more agreeable to leave and find another place to eat lunch. With an empty belly and heart heavy with sorrow that I won't be getting to taste that killer burger that I didn't even get to sniff before it was brutally taken away, I stand from my stool and collect my purse. Just as I'm turning to leave, two men in black leather vests walk in. Each with patches, and each with their eyes on me. I drag my hands down the front of my pantsuit and smooth the material down. One of the men can't be any older than early twenties, and the other must be no more than thirty—though both look as though they live hard lives with their faces in the wind, their bellies full of booze, and their veins pumping full of adrenaline.

The bikers are part of the club.

His club.

There is something undeniably attractive about the lure of bad boys—men who live by their own rules and don't give a damn what you think about them—and they know it, too. Even though I grew up here, with the club always at a short distance, I've rarely found myself in the company of more than one of them at a time. Like Grady at Sea Salt Pizza—he wasn't wearing his vest.

From the corner, the elderly patrons rise and pack up their chess set. The bikers part, and the men sneak between them and disappear out the door.

"Where ya going, babe?" the one on the right says, his voice reminding me of a snake, slithering and creepy. I stop and look up at them both, my eyes bouncing between them. The one on the right has dark features—dark hair, darker skin, dark eyes—and the one on the left has light brown hair with a pleasant summer tan. So different and yet so similar—their stances, their attire, their attitudes—both equally menacing, both equally dangerous. I've had my fill of menacing though.

"Leave her alone, dude. You're gonna scare her," the one on the left says as his eyes slide up and down my frame. He smirks. I open my mouth to respond before thinking better of it. I move to slide between the two men, but the dark-haired one takes a step sideways, effectively blocking my path.

"Just sayin' hi, babe," he says, leaning forward and grinning at me. I catch movement from out of the corner of my eye—the man behind the counter. He's raising a bottle of Jack Daniels to his lips and chugging away.

"Hello," I say in a squeak. An icy cold settles over me. Call it women's intuition or a heightened awareness of my surroundings. Whatever it is, suddenly, I have a very bad feeling about standing here with these men. I've never known a member of the club to forcibly take a woman, especially in such a public venue, but there's so many other things that can happen here and now that I'd like to avoid.

"You ever ride bitch?" the man with the snake-like voice asks. I don't quite understand the question, but I get the feeling that no matter how I answer, the outcome won't be pleasant.

"Excuse me?" I snap at him. His question has caught me off guard and left me annoyed. My temper's ignited by his comment, and I find myself being more brazen than I should be. Then again, I basically threw my manners out the window when I called Grady an asshole. "Now, please move out of my way."

"Tell me your name and I'll move," he says. His eyes fall down to my breasts and then drag back up. I know he's lying. Everything from the look in his eyes to the way he smirks at the end of his sentence tells me that I can't trust this man. But what options do I really have? I could lie and give him another name, but I have to live here, and his club runs this town. It seems like a bad idea to lie to him because, should he find out I've lied, then he has the potential to have a reason to have to engage in conversation with me again. And more than him knowing my real name, that's one thing I don't want. For some reason I haven't had the same fearful reaction to Grady.

"Holl—," I start to say when heavy footfalls distract me. From behind the men, a hulking form appears. It's Grady.

His wavy hair is slicked back, held in place by a pair of sunglasses. His heavy leather vest rests on his wide shoulders, covering an aged and faded black tee shirt. His strong jaw is covered with a few days' worth of facial hair, and he has a smile on his face. Every encounter I've had with him tells me that his smiles are rare.

Just before he runs into the man in front of him, he comes to a halt. His smile widens, and he lifts his hands up and shoves the dark-haired man in front of him. I take a step back, but it's not far enough. The man slams into me. He steadies himself by grabbing me by my hips. I should be afraid, but I'm flustered by Grady's presence and not thinking clearly. Grady's broad smile becomes salacious as his eyes fix on mine. He licks his lips and winks. Feeling uncomfortable with the dark-haired man's touch, I swat him away, and when that doesn't work, I swat harder. He doesn't even react.

Grady moves around us and walks over to the bar, hitches a thumb at me, and asks Mr. Personality, "What's with the pussy?"

I blanch at the term. My mouth forms a hard line, and I narrow my eyes. From behind the bar, Mr. Personality pours both himself and Grady a glass of clear liquor. He mumbles something I can't hear, to which Grady nods his head. They each toss back their glasses and set them on the bar. The dark-haired man has yet to let me go, and the proximity to him feels like an invasion.

"My name is Holly, now let me go," I say. From the corner of my eye, Grady moves back toward us and sidles up to the dark-haired man.

"Let her go, Fish," Grady says to the man. I don't know what kind of nickname Fish is, but it doesn't sound all that scary. Still, I don't think I want to know how he got it. "She might report you."

"I'm just playing around," Fish says as his grip tightens on my hips. He pulls me forward, and I fight him off by placing my hands over his and pulling. His eyes narrow, and a snarl forms on his face. His name may sound silly, but the look on his face is anything but. "Holly knows that. Don't you, *Holly*?"

"Yeah, sure. Whatever," I say and clear my throat. My voice shakes, and my words trail off at the end. His palms grow balmy to the touch, so I lift my hands from his and fold my arms over my chest.

"Fish, now," Grady snaps. His voice brokers no argument from Fish, who removes his hands, steps back, and raises them in the air. He licks his lips and whistles. "If anybody is going to piss off the pussy, it's me."

"Dick," I mutter as my eyes slice toward him. Fish raises his eyebrows and whistles, giving Grady a proud smirk.

"Get out of here," Grady snaps without giving me another look. He moves beside me, reaches out, and taps Fish on the shoulder, then jerks his thumb over his shoulder toward Mr. Personality, who has yet to move from behind the bar.

Outside, a car horn beeps in short, perky sounds. The men around me tense, and their eyes fall on the front windows. I doubt they can see anything through the dirty gray windows that are half-covered by signs advertising the popular brands served here. The horn continues to blare, but this time in long notes that make me consider covering my ears. I take a half step toward the front door to escape, the only action I can think of that seems sane, but Grady raises a hand in front of me and shakes his head. His eyes never leave the front windows.

It all happens so fast that I can barely keep up. The men around me pull out black guns from their vests as a hail of bullets flies in through the walls and partially covered windows. Wood splinters, glass bursts open, and the men hustle around. An arm sweeps around my midsection, blocking me from the assault. A spray of blood bursts in front of me as a scream escapes my lungs. I'm pulled to the floor by the hulking man around me, and his glassy eyes glaze over and then close.

☠CHAPTER 6☠

NOW ON THE floor, I'm being crushed by a solid wall of flesh. It's like dead weight. Grady's body lays over mine with such stillness that I fear for his life. My stomach hurts, almost like I'm cramping, but worse. I can't quite figure out what's causing it, only that between the weight of Grady and the discomfort in my stomach, I can barely breathe. The very thought that he could be dead sickens me to the point where I think I'd rather pass out again than to lie here underneath his dead body. I think of Cheyenne losing her father, no matter how questionable of a father he may be, and I feel just awful that he protected me and lost his life for it. It takes longer than it should to occur to me that Grady's taken a bullet because of Grady and that *I'm* the victim here.

"Grady!" a deep voice shouts from somewhere nearby, though I can't see where from. I can't see much, really. All I can see is thick black hair that curls at the ends and has thin gray streaks in a few places, and tanned skin. He really doesn't look old enough to have a daughter Cheyenne's age, even this close up. He's too much of a bastard to be this attractive.

"Ian," an impossibly deeper voice commands, "help me lift him." Just beyond the thick head of black hair, I can see the two men working to gently pull Grady off of me. A moment passes before they've made any progress, and then he is being lifted up. First, they drag his upper torso and then pull him to the side. For a brief moment, the respite from the impact leaves me breathless, then dizzy with relief. Then it happens.

A fresh wave of pain hits me right in my gut as the two men drag Grady off my lower torso. My muscles spasm, and my lungs fight desperately for air. It's too much, the feeling, and not enough, the clarity, all at the same time. It's awful. The whole thing, from when they first started lifting him until now, has taken less than a minute, but it feels like forever.

A half of a second after the pain subsides some, Grady gasps for breath and struggles against his friends. I watch with rapt attention as his eyes shoot open and lock on mine. A beautiful green—deep and rich—zeroes in on first my face before they lower. His eyes travel down my body, but not the way a lover's do. It's not the way I've imagined he would explore my flesh after a heated argument that's left us both livid.

His eyes slide down my frame in a sterile manner as he inspects me. I follow his attention, and when I find the source of my discomfort, I gasp and let my head fall back onto the hard wooden floor. A spot of blood is seeping into my blouse from my abdomen. The deep red stain focuses my energy as I close my eyes and try to block out the awful throbbing. It's no use. Now that I know what's causing the pain—a bullet wound to my lower gut, just above my hip—there's just no ignoring the horrible dread that's set in.

Large, strong hands reach out and put pressure on my wound, providing absolutely no relief. It's not like it is in the movies, when you're injured and you can still talk and give orders, or when someone puts pressure on your wound and it feels better. No, that would be far too lovely. I arch my back and cry out for some relief, but nothing comes. The movement only makes it worse as tears stream down the sides of my face.

When I reopen my eyes, Grady is hunched over me muttering something to one of his friends. I can't understand a word of it. His head is turned and he's speaking quietly. But then he speaks louder, and I finally understand something. *I'm fine*, he says a few times to his friends before he turns his attention back to me. Blood darkens his once-black tee shirt on his upper shoulder and streams down his arm.

I force myself to keep my eyes open and to watch him as he puts pressure on my lower abdomen. Everything around me stills for a moment before a sort of white noise creeps up, low and in the back of my head, moving toward the front until it overtakes everything around me. Gone is the sound of my heavy breathing, and gone is the sound of Grady barking orders at his friends, who take off without another word. They're gone, but Grady doesn't move.

Except for his lips—they're moving. Slowly, I start to be able to hear him. He's asking about a car and then it sounds like he's asking about my wound. All the sounds start to cross and it sounds like a buzzer is going off in my ear. I squint my eyes at him to show that I'm trying to listen, but I don't understand. It does no good. His lips move faster, and, with one blood-streaked hand, he reaches out and lifts my head off the wood.

Everything about him consumes me. From his eyes to his bulking frame to the smile lines around his mouth. He doesn't look happy now, but I can tell—he was happy once. It certainly hasn't ever been in front of me. I thought I could see a bit of it the other night at the pizza shop before he spotted me. It's inconsequential to my current state, but I think I was wrong about him and Cheyenne. I'll bet he's happy around her. Probably never been happier than the day she was born. And I'll bet he smiled a lot when she was little. Maybe he has a wife who makes him smile, or a girlfriend. Maybe it's just the club. But his smile lines are deep and long, and they give him away. He's been happy, and that makes me want to be happy for him.

"Hey," he shouts in my face, loud and mean. I blink a moment before realizing that I can hear him. And I want to rejoice, but in my current condition, I know it's not a good idea. Not that I can rejoice. "Good, you can hear me."

I go to open my mouth, but it doesn't work. I move my lips until I can force a breath out, and I finally croak, "What?"

"You've been shot," he says in an annoyed voice. Yeah, still a dick. "And I need to get you out of here. Are you going to give me any trouble?"

"Why?" I say before I can finish the thought, and then try to correct myself. "No," I say.

"Good," he says. "Do you have your Jeep here?" I nod and manage to mutter that it's in the parking lot. Before he can ask, I tell him the make and model, which is saying something because I didn't think I could do much else aside from breathe heavy and let myself pass out.

"I have to remove my hand from the wound," he says. I don't think that's such a good idea—last time there was no pressure on it, it hurt even worse than it does now. But it's too late. I'm pressed hard against his chest as he strides out of The 101 Club with purposeful steps. I'm facing behind him, and the only thing I can think as I look at The 101 Club is that I never got the chance to try the lunch I ordered. For some asinine reason, that's bothering me more than anything else right now. That and those damn smile lines on his face. I just want to see him smile. But the burger—*that* almost makes the bullet wound hurt even more.

He tosses me into the passenger side of my car. I scream out in pain as the throbbing comes back with a full-on vengeance. There's little else I can do but cry and scream for it to stop. Not that my crying or screaming will do anything, but it seems a perfectly sensible option right now.

Rushing around the front to the driver's side, Grady lumbers into my Jeep and adjusts the seat as quickly as he can. The Jeep rocks as he settles in, and I force my arms to move from my side and place them on my wound. And it hurts like a bitch. It hurts like how I imagine childbirth to hurt, only in a slightly different way. No less painful, though. Because I can't imagine anything more painful than this.

I suck in a breath to tell him the key is in my purse, but I don't know where my purse is. He reaches beneath my steering wheel and yanks down a bunch of wires. I've seen enough crime shows on TV that I'm only confused for a moment before I get it. He's hot-wiring the car. And while I'd normally be panicking about him messing up my car, the blinding pain in my abdomen has me not giving a crap about the state of my old ass Jeep's wiring. So I keep my mouth shut and try to focus on putting pressure on my wound.

A few seconds later, we're pulling out of the parking lot at rapid speeds and flying down South Main Street toward the center of town. I want to caution him that Jeeps flip easily should we hit something, but I don't. That's just my dad's wisdom seeping through at a very inconvenient time. And I don't need to be telling him what to do right now. He seems to have it under control. I, on the other hand, might have a seriously embarrassing accident if I don't figure out how to control the muscle spasms in my stomach soon. I close my eyes and decide not to pay attention to where we're going. It doesn't matter anyway. For some reason, Grady has chosen to help me and make himself my nursemaid, and while I'd normally be freaking out that we're heading away from the local medical center, I don't really care right now. He could take me to a wood chipper and throw me in, and I'd have nary a complaint. Bullet wounds hurt *that* bad. I can't say it's something I ever wanted to experience, but now that I have—and I'm hoping I live through it—I think I can endure just about anything.

"Put more pressure on that," he says and looks over at me. I catch his eyes before they slide back to the road.

"I'm trying," I manage to wheeze out. "It really hurts."

"I get that, but if you're not careful, you're going to bleed out. So try harder."

With the way I'm slumped down in the seat and unable to bring myself to move, every time I put more pressure on the wound, my hand slips and my back bows towards the seat, shoving me down further. I manage to get a better hold on it and to force the blood to actually stop seeping through my fingers. A thin stream coats my slacks and arms. Looking down, I examine myself. There doesn't seem to be as much blood as it feels like is pouring out. With how painful it is, I'm sure I could fill a kiddie pool in no time.

"I can't," I gasp. He swings the car to the right at speeds that I know for sure are illegal. My body shifts toward him, his right arm shoots out and he gives a tug on my left arm. My entire body tenses as he pulls me close to him. He wraps his arm around my back and places his hand on top of both of mine above the bloody wound and he presses down so hard it gives me a whole new reason to cry. I'm fairly certain he's applying more pressure than necessary just because he's a dick.

"Quit screaming. It's just a fucking flesh wound," he grinds out. I close my eyes once again so I don't have to see the look on his face or the way he's driving. In all fairness, he does have only one hand on the wheel, but still. If I could bring myself to focus in on anything else, I might be terrified by the way the buildings fly past us so quickly that I can't even really see what any of them are. With my eyes closed, I can focus on the pressure from Grady's large hand and not the ache of my muscles.

"Stop it," he screams, and his hand puts even more pressure on my abdomen. I gasp for breath, and he lightens his grip just slightly before the car slows down for a second.

"You keep screaming, I'll be forced to knock you out," he snaps. I suck in a shallow breath of air, and then another, and another. I want nothing more than to tell him off. He has no right to threaten me, even if he is helping me. This is his fault anyway.

"Where," I mumble, feeling my lips lazily smack together, "are we going?"

"My house," he says. I should be focusing on why we're not going to a hospital, but I can't. All I can focus on is the mind-numbing pain.

☠ CHAPTER 7 ☠

THE FIRST THING I notice as I pull myself from sleep is how rank my breath is. My teeth and tongue are covered in a layer of fuzz that would offend most bums. I let out a stinky, frustrated breath. Waking up, no matter the time, always sucks. But this morning sucks even worse, because I'm cramping all over. My back aches, and so do my legs and arms. I move slightly and cringe from the stiffness that's set into my entire body. I lift my head from my pillow and open my eyes, finding that I'm shrouded in near total darkness.

Across the small room is a wide, single-pane window that's mostly covered by thick blinds, but slivers of pale light shine through. It's just barely enough to confirm the fear that's been creeping up since taking that first rank breath of alertness. I'm not at home.

I'm not the kind of girl who can assume that she tied one on the night before and let a stranger take her home. And I'm *really* not the kind of girl who wakes up, achy all over, in a room she doesn't recognize. At least not anymore.

"Mindy," I rasp out and swing my head from one side of the room to the other. Everything around me blurs, and I slow myself down so I don't pass out. I call for Mindy again, only to find that she's not answering. Surely, if I'm in a strange place, there must be an explanation for it. And Mindy and I do just about everything together now that I've moved home, so if I'm here, that must mean she is, too.

The door on the far side of the room swings open. An imposing body, too large to be a woman, stands in the doorway, blocking the light hanging overhead behind him. His shadow casts into the room, disappearing in the darkness, and a brief spark of recognition ignites somewhere in me. *A huge bulking frame leans over me with his hand on my lower abdomen, above my hip.*

Grady.

I move back toward the headboard, but dull pains emanate from just above my right hip and I let my arms fall to my sides as I sink back into the mattress. It reminds me of everything that happened, and I groan. The last person I want to rely on is Sterling Grady.

He lifts his arm and flicks the light on, temporarily blinding me. When my vision returns I see that my surroundings are sparsely decorated, with only the basics present. This space is clearly impersonal.

Grady stares at me from his position in the doorway. He looks so cold and calculating. Something feels different about him now, not that he's ever been particularly friendly in the past. He strides into the room, and it's like he's brought an arctic blast with him. He's all hulking muscle and wide strides and penetrating gaze.

"How are you feeling?" he asks. He clears his throat and eyes my belly. It's likely the first kind thing he's said to me.

"I'm sore," I say. "Shouldn't I be at the hospital?"

"What do you remember?" he asks, totally ignoring my question. Just like always, he redirects the conversation to where he wants it to go. Control freak.

"Pardon?" I say, trying to stall. My women's intuition is on high alert, telling me that something isn't right here. I've spent most of my life with the club at arms' length, and have gone to school with a few of the members of the club—and some of their wives and girlfriends. I'm not naïve enough to think that the club doesn't run this town. Uncle Harry is always complaining about how the club members can get away with murder—and he's quite convinced they have—as long as they continue to fund new playgrounds and keep the drug deals beyond the town's border.

"You're bruised up pretty good. It wasn't much more than a flesh wound, but you are one dramatic bitch. You're going to be sore for a little while, but you're fine. Now, tell me—what do you remember?"

"I," I say and then shut it down. Calling me a bitch time and time again is a cheap way to throw his weight around. I only wish it didn't bother me. His demeanor is off-putting and makes me think twice about telling him the truth. I remember everything, I think, but he doesn't need to know that. I want to yell at him that I've never been shot before and that I don't do well with the sight of blood. Even the suggestion of dripping blood freaks me out, but I suppose a man in his position is used to seeing bullet wounds and he wouldn't understand.

"I don't know."

Three long strides and two frustrated breaths later, he's in my space, looming over me. His eyes narrow and he places his hands on his hips. "You lying to me?" he asks.

Even though I lived in the Bay Area for years, there are some things I never could forget. Like the rumbling of the engines as the Forsaken Motorcycle Club makes its way through town. So loud and powerful that the bikes shake the earth beneath them. And the men—mostly young, and all built like brick houses—all have these badass "I can do what I want" attitudes. Even the memories of the sticky sweet air when you're even within a few blocks of the ocean faded in time, but the few club memories I have never did. The mugginess of the air and the Pacific, and even the people here—it's nothing compared to the club and all that it means.

My Uncle Harry would have everyone believe that the club is the epitome of evil—that they're good for nothing—and he tells everyone who stands to listen how he wishes to rid the town of the club for once and for all. So even admiring the deep roar of the engines and the chaotic presence of the club, I never ventured to even so much as smile at any of them. Sure, when they did things to help the community, like putting a new roof on the library, the town gathered 'round the ribbon cutting ceremony and thanked the club—most especially the president, Jim Stone, and his wife, Ruby—but beyond attending those events in the back and without personally thanking them for anything, I've done well to stay away from them.

And now…

Oh, Uncle Harry would be so angry right now. And my father—he would have a fit and demand that Uncle Harry swoop in with his boys and the captain of the force to get me out of here before Grady does something awful. Because Uncle Harry has Dad convinced that the club is full of a bunch of rapists and drug dealers who pride themselves on being cruel to those around them. I can't say much for Grady, but the club president never struck me as particularly awful. I've seen Jim Stone with his wife and their sons, Ryan and Ian. The way Ruby looks and talks about Jim—according to Mindy—she absolutely adores him and doesn't take crap from anybody. So I'm thinking that maybe Uncle Harry is a bit misguided and that he just doesn't like the fact that the club has more control and influence over his town than he and his fellow officers do—even if Grady is no better than road kill in my opinion.

"No," I say. I really do hate to lie, but I don't know what kind of situation I'm in here. There's no telling what he's going to do with me. I'm an injured witness to a shooting incident in town. I'm also the *bitch* who has the audacity to be concerned about his daughter's future. If he knows that I remember everything, I could be in a whole mess of trouble.

He leans over me, his large frame blocking out all light, and all I can see and sense is him. Tilting his face toward me, and catching my eyes, he shakes his head. "I don't believe you," he says.

I shouldn't lie. It's not so much a morality thing as it is a "I'm bad at it" thing. I really am absolutely horrid at lying to just about anyone regarding anything. Even to save my own skin, apparently.

"I'm not asking you to believe me," I say.

"Are you scared of me?" he asks in a dry tone. His lips twitch upward and his eyes practically dance with amusement.

"You wish," I say, and force myself not to purse my lips. It's my tell—or the one that everyone close to me says always gives me away. Grady doesn't need, nor does he deserve, to know this about me.

"You're awful mouthy for someone who's laid up in *my* house," he seethes.

"You should have taken me to a hospital," I say, and drag myself up onto the stack of pillows behind me, ignoring my discomfort.

"What do you remember?" he says, irritation evident in his voice.

"Nothing really," I say and try to think how to word what I'm going to say to him. "I was going for lunch. I wanted a burger."

"That's it?"

"That's it," I say. My lips purse against my will, but when I catch it, I stop myself.

"Listen, I can't help you if you don't let me. Bad shit went down, and you got hurt. I'm sorry for that."

"I don't remember anything else, but this has to go two

ways. I just remember really wanting a burger. Now, answer my question—why am I not in a hospital?" Even though I know the words come out of my mouth, I'm still surprised to hear them aloud. In the back of my head I can hear my conscious screaming at me to shut up. The more I keep asking questions, the more obvious it's going to be that I remember something.

"Holly Mercer, age twenty-six, cousin Mindy Mercer, Uncle Harry is a sergeant for the Fort Bragg P.D. Dad is an electrician, mom stays home, and older brother, Theo just got married. Pretty wife," he says with a slight smile on his face. It's not a kind smile—it's more like he's happy to have the upper-hand. I gulp and steel my jaw to keep my fear from showing too much. He already knew who I was, but him knowing my family as well as he does is disconcerting.

"How do you know all of that?" I ask, stumbling over my own words.

"It's my job to know," he says. "Now, I'm going to ask you a few questions, and do keep in mind that I already know some of the answers, so it's in your best interest to be honest."

"Why do you need to ask me anything if you already know the answers?" I can only explain my attitude by saying that I'm in pain. Because any other explanation involves admitting my own stupidity. Pissing him off when I'm mobile and we're in public is one thing, but alone in his house when I'm unsure how quick I can actually move is quite another.

"Do you know what this cut means?" he asks and points at

his leather vest.

"Yes," I say, barely able to hold back the comment that's on the tip of my tongue. My stomach aches, and my back is practically throbbing from the soreness of lying in bed for what I assume to be hours on end. It's unwise, but more than almost anything, I want to tell him it makes him look like a member of the village people.

"Then you know what I am," he says. It's not a question; it's confirmation. I nod.

"I figured out what you are a long time ago," I say and let the insults fly in my head. Asshole. Jerk. Idiot. Criminal. "I want to go home."

"That can be accomplished a few different ways. It's up to you."

"Okay," I mutter. "Lay it out for me."

"Now we're talking." His stoic face relaxes some. "You saw something you shouldn't have, and you're smart enough to know that I can't let you leave here and run your mouth about it. I can't keep this town clean if you won't let me."

"The club helps the town, and the town helps the club. I get it." I say the words, but I don't buy them. Towns across the globe survive just fine without this kind of extortion ring working.

"Good girl," he says with a nod. I shouldn't find the slick way the words fall off his tongue to be attractive, but I do.

"You came back to town a few months ago—broke off your ass. Lived with mom until this past week. You don't make shit, and you got some debt. Bet you could use some cash."

It's true, I do have debts that are long overdue to be paid. I hate that I can't pay them, but I don't think taking money from this man is the right answer.

"I don't want your money. I won't say anything."

He doesn't say a word. He just straightens his back and walks across the room then leans against the wall. Everything about the way he moves and talks exudes a sort of confidence I don't think I've seen in anyone else. He's definitely been here before. I wonder how many people he's been able to intimidate into doing his bidding.

"That's generous, but that's not how this works. You're giving us your silence, and we need to give you something in return—and 25k is nothing to turn your pretty little nose up at. Anything else means we owe you, and make no mistake about it, babe—Forsaken don't owe anybody any favors."

Grady crosses his arms over his chest and stares at me thoughtfully. I give it a moment to think the situation over. I don't have any options, really. I've heard enough from Uncle Harry how this works. People don't say no to the club—not drug dealers, or addicts, not the police, and certainly not the rest of us. Uncle Harry won't give details, but he's said enough. The people who do say no to the club end up paying for it in some way they don't like. I don't want to be one of those people, but maybe there's another option.

"I'd rather get your signature," I say. "On Cheyenne's counseling form."

"This again?"

"Yeah," I say. "Either she enters mandatory counseling and attends Saturday School or she's expelled. Mr. Beck would prefer the latter, but I'm trying to stop that from happening. The district will allow her to make up some of her missed classes on Saturdays. It's win-win for you. She doesn't get expelled and you don't have to spend a dime."

"Look, lady, you need to stop telling me how to parent my kid."

"I just don't understand why you don't care that your daughter is facing expulsion."

"I care. Trust me, I do. But I got a whole mess of shit to deal with right now that's beyond your comprehension. My kid is smart enough to know when Dad's distracted and she's taking advantage of it, and we're working on that. I won't trade your silence for my signature, because my kid is not part of club business, but if you can stop fucking nagging me about this counseling shit, I'll consider it."

"Stop by the office any time in the upcoming week to sign the form," I say, feeling a little victorious.

"The money?" he says.

"You're going to pay me to keep silent?"

"It's better than the alternative," he says. I nod my head, but don't ask for clarification. I'm trying really hard to think of this like a business transaction, and I can't do that if I let myself dwell on what he's saying. This situation is bad enough without going down that road.

"Okay," I say.

"Okay?" he asks. "That's it? You don't have any questions?" His eyes narrow, and he stares at me skeptically. It's like he's expecting some kind of fight or something.

"Yeah," I say and nod. "I don't even want to know what

the alternative is, so yeah, my mouth is shut." I'd rather not have this conversation with him, much less to discuss the details.

"No talking to your pig uncle, no talking to your roommate, no talking to anybody. Someone asks where you were yesterday, you tell them you took a drive out of town. Someone wants to know why you didn't show at work, you tell them you were sick. I don't give a fuck what you say, but you do not—under any circumstances—tell them you were at The 101 Club. You feel me?"

"Yes," I say and grit my teeth to fight back the look of irritation that I'm sure has crossed my face. Yesterday. That's just freaking awesome. I've only been working at the high school for a few months now, and no matter how cool Margot is, I don't think she'll be down for me skipping out without phoning in. Even if I do get to keep my job, I'm still going to have to deal with Mindy. She's got to be freaking out right now. Oh, God. Oh no, I'll bet Mindy's contacted Dad and Uncle Harry. If she's really freaking out then she's probably called grandma, and the last thing I need is for grandma to be driving around town at ten miles an hour, with her car window down, shouting my name like I'm a lost poodle. This really freaking sucks.

"You got something to say?" he barks out.

"I have a boss who has to be wondering where I am. I have family who must be scared because they can't find me. So pardon me, but I'm a little upset right now." The venom in my words is fiercer than I expect it to be. Money or no money, I have no idea how I'm going to recoup from this crap.

"You think you're the only one who's been inconvenienced here? The twenty-five grand I have to spend to keep your mouth closed pisses me off. Normally when I give a bitch money it's for her to open her mouth, not close it."

"I'm in this situation because of *your* bullshit, so don't push this off on me. Also, I don't know why you're so obsessed with getting your dick sucked, but maybe if you spent more time being a decent human being and less time calling women bitches, you'd have better luck." On the outside, I'm trying really hard to keep a straight face, but on the inside I'm totally screaming for help. Nobody in my life has ever pissed me off this badly before, and it would be just my luck that I can't seem to get rid of him.

"Bitch, please. I get my dick sucked plenty."

Somewhere in the distance, I swear I can hear sirens going off. I can hear screaming, and I can sense danger. But none of that is actually happening. It takes me a moment to realize that I'm barely holding in a scream. My face heats, my pulse races, and my entire body locks up so tense I think I might explode.

"Did you just call me a bitch again?" I shout as loud as I can. My voice is screechy and on the edge of breaking into a full-on wail. If I thought I could take him, I think I'd slap him right here and now. Thin as the grasp on reality might be, I can still see clearly enough to stop myself from trying to hobble from the bed and show him exactly how much I detest his use of that word.

Grady's jaw ticks, and, in an instant, he's pushed himself

off of the wall. Several long strides and he's got one knee on the edge of the bed and the other is thrown over my hips. His broad torso blocks the light from the hallway, and he rests his left forearm on the pillows beside me. He reaches out with his right arm and grasps me by my neck and jerks my head in close to his face. He breathes heavily on my skin, dampening my face in his scent.

"I'm being nice. Do not think that means I'm going to put up with your mouth. My brothers and I are going to count on you to keep quiet about the shit that went down. You cannot go off half-cocked like you just did. If you don't keep your mouth shut, I'm going to let one of my brothers enjoy the pleasure of your company."

"Are you threatening me?" I ask. My voice is so steady and cold that I don't even know how I'm doing it. Inside I'm freaking the hell out. Maybe it's the trauma of the situation that's driving me, or maybe I'm just stupid.

"I don't make threats. I make promises."

We continue to stare at each other with neither of us moving a single muscle. His eyes are hard and unwavering as he glares at me. His full lips and strong jaw invade my space and demand attention. I know I shouldn't be thinking these things, but I can't help it. I've always secretly loved bad boys with their "devil may care" attitudes. Even when I was younger and Uncle Harry made sure I knew damn well that the club was off limits, I still looked. And now, here I am, with one of them hovering over me. And while he's gorgeous and built, and dangerous in a thousand sexy ways, all I really want to do is to knee him in the balls. Repeatedly.

How dare he...

"Oh God," a perky young voice shouts from the other side of the room. "What the hell? Gross!"

Grady jumps back and stands awkwardly, like he's just been caught doing something he shouldn't have by his mom. Only, it's worse. He's been caught by his teenage daughter. I freeze for a moment and then pull the blankets up further over me just as my cheeks redden. I don't know why I'm embarrassed. I should be asking her to call the cops to get me out of here. I'm fully clothed but, somehow, it's my first reaction and likely one that only solidifies the image that Cheyenne thinks she's seen.

☠CHAPTER 8☠

WHAT THE FUCK are you doing home?" Grady snaps and turns to his daughter. Cheyenne takes two tentative steps inside the room and crosses her arms over her chest. Her nose is turned up, and her mouth is turned down. She looks positively grossed out, and truth be told, I can't blame her. Teenagers don't expect their parents to be human.

"Half day, Dad. God," she says in exasperation. I think for a moment and realize that she's lying. I tilt my head to the side and watch as she delivers a beautifully crafted lie that, if I didn't know our school schedule, I'd think was the honest-to-God truth. I could kick her ass for ditching, especially after how much work I've been putting into keeping her in school. Oh, we're going to talk about this.

She blows out a breath and bounces from foot to foot. "I told you this like last week. You *never* listen to me."

Cheyenne looks down at me, and her eyes bug out. She gives me a questioning glare before her wrath finds its target: her dad. "Holly, really? Oh my God. What the hell! You totally lied to me when I asked if you two were together!"

Her voice rises into a scream. Unlike the last time he was being screamed at, he doesn't lunge across the room and scare the crap out of her. His shoulders fall, and he rubs the back of his neck. He may be a big badass when he's with his club, and he may be an even bigger ass when he's around me, but he looks like a totally different person in his daughter's presence.

"What is your point?" he snaps. "What I do on my time is my business." And just like that, the big, bad, scary dude is back and in full force. Only, Cheyenne doesn't wither under his stare. She rolls her eyes and huffs. In a near mimic, he lets out a heavy breath and grunts. If this situation wasn't so ridiculous and so uncomfortable, I might even find the similarities between the two to be humorous.

"We have a deal, Dad," she grumbles. "You promised you wouldn't do...do...do *that*." She points her finger at me then finishes with, "with anybody who works at my school. I mean, is no place sacred? I gave you a pass because I like Holly, but you totally freaking lied to me about it!"

"Chill out," he grumbles. "It's not what you think. And cool it with the attitude, Cheyenne. Do not forget who you're speaking to." Cheyenne smashes her lips together and shakes her head.

"Well," she says in a slightly less heated manner, "This explains all the sexual tension."

Grady and his band of felons have put me in a pretty bad situation here. I'm not about to let my life fall completely apart all because I wanted a burger for lunch. My life is in shambles enough already. The least I can do is to, for once, be proactive, and to do something about my situation.

"We're sorry we didn't tell you," I say quickly. Grady's head spins around so fast I think the damn thing might fall off. The smile that spreads on my face is almost painful. He doesn't like this, not at all, which makes it that much more fun. Cheyenne's eyes grow large with surprise, and her mouth falls open just slightly.

"We are?" he asks with a raised brow and a look of scorn on his chiseled face. I roll my eyes at him and give Cheyenne a wink.

"It's new. I'm sorry you had to find out this way. The truth is, your dad has been chasing me for a while. Then yesterday when I went to The 101 Club on your suggestion, we ran into each other. I just… couldn't resist his charm any longer." Not even halfway through my lie, my face is heating and I'm starting to sweat. I'm such an awful liar that I shouldn't even be attempting to pull this off, but I'm not about to be the only honest one in the room.

Grady's eyes slide from me to Cheyenne before returning to me. "And what did we do at The 101 Club?" he asks. From behind him, Cheyenne gives him a confused glance.

"Nothing. I got sick," I say in a last-minute surprise of genius. Or stupidity. The jury is still out. "You brought me back here because you said you wanted to take care of me."

"*Dad* wanted to take care of you? Oh man, he must be in *love* then," Cheyenne says. Her stare becomes uncomfortable, and then she bursts into laughter. Rich, joyous guffaws emanate from her as her chest shakes and she scrunches her face up. Whatever I've said is apparently so funny that she's nearly in tears with her laughter.

Grady turns back to me and gives me a hard stare. Feeling emboldened by his daughter's presence, I stare into his eyes and smirk. "Baby, did you call my boss and Mindy to let them know I stayed over because I was sick?"

"No," he says. "That's not my shit to handle." I take too long deciding how to react. Now that I've dug myself into this ridiculous lie, I have to stick with it, and part of that is pretending to expect him to have called my boss and family to let them know I'm safe. But I'm too late, and Cheyenne reacts for me.

"Dad, you really didn't tell anyone she's here? Can't she, like, get in trouble for that or something?"

"I can," I say sadly and look up at Grady. I'm not sure what's changed with Cheyenne since the day she flipped out on me in the office, but something obviously has. First with the greeting me in passing, and then the lunch recommendation—no matter how poorly that turned out—and now concern over me losing my job. Regardless of what kind of a father she has, she seems like a good kid who's just been going through something.

Grady's jaw ticks, and he sucks in a deep breath. The more infuriated he becomes with me, the more it eggs me on to keep the lie going. I must have lost a lot of blood to be acting like such an insane person. I'm going to end up lying myself into "the alternative" if I'm not careful.

"Oh good, you're up," an older woman says as she pushes past Cheyenne. She shares Grady's and Cheyenne's dark hair and green eyes. She has lines around her eyes, and her natural-looking, sun-kissed skin is free of makeup. As she approaches the bed, I notice that she's wearing dark-washed denim and a lavender button-up blouse that has spots of dirt smeared on the lower half.

Standing beside the bed now, the woman who I think might be Grady's mother turns to Cheyenne and says, "You're supposed to be in class. Now get your butt back to school."

"Half day," I say instinctively. "Last minute decision on behalf of the staff. Seniors have a half day so the staff can plan their graduation trip." I give the woman a smile that she doesn't quite return. She looks speculatively toward Grady and then to Cheyenne.

"Then go do homework or something," she says to Cheyenne, who turns around and stomps out. The minute Cheyenne's footsteps fade into nothingness, Grady turns and glares at me.

"You fucked up," he says.

"No," I counter. "I was saving my own butt since you were so eager to leave it out to hang. At least now I have a plausible excuse for disappearing for an entire day."

"Get one thing straight—you don't call shots around here," he barks back. The woman looks between us before lifting her hands in front of her.

"Oh, Sterling, let's not fight," I say sarcastically. If it bothers him that I call him by his first name, after he's told me not to, he doesn't let on.

"Look, just pretend to be saying your goodbyes in here,

give the girl her money, and let her go. We'll tell Chey you were a jerk and she dumped you," the woman says.

"Ma," he says in a plea. "That is the stupidest shit I've ever heard."

"Well, it's no worse than that lie she made up," his mother says. "I was listening from the hall."

"You think Chey will buy that?" he asks her.

A wry smile spreads on her face, and she says, "That you were a jerk? Yes, I think it'll require that she use her imagination, but I think it'll work." I try to keep the laughter building in my chest from erupting, but it's no use. I dissolve into a fit of chuckles and finally calm down with a happy sigh.

"You're hilarious, Ma," he says. "Now go distract Chey so I can get *her* out of here."

Giving me a small smile, his mother points at her chest and says, "I'm Lisa." Before I can even formally introduce myself, Grady is shoving her into the hallway and shutting the door behind her. When he turns around he's not all easy smiles and sarcastic glances anymore. His face is hard, and a scowl has found its way to his lips.

"How hard are you going to make this on me?" he asks. I try to summon the strength I need in order to explain myself.

"I haven't made anything hard on you. All I did was create an explanation my boss might be able to live with," I say.

"Fuck your boss," he says. The hostility in his voice reminds me of how he stormed out of the office after the incident between Cheyenne and I during her last counseling session. Margot had spent a solid five minutes muttering on and on about something to do with Grady that I wasn't even paying attention to. But now I'm wondering if I should have.

"You got any kids?" he asks. I tense at the question. "Of course you don't. My kid's mom ain't around because she's one fucked up bitch. My brother, Chey's godfather, is fucking dead, I got work shit, and there's nothing I can do to make any of that shit any better. But you— she likes you. You think my kid needs to see you at school every day and think we had a relationship that went to shit? You think that's gonna be good for her?"

I didn't know. Cheyenne never mentioned her mom, nor did she mention her godfather. I'd seen the news reports about the biker who died in a head-on collision with a SUV just a week or so ago. I knew it had been a member of Forsaken who died, but... I didn't know. If there is anything he could say to make me regret my lie, that would be it. I let my shoulders slump as I ingest the weight of his comment. I don't have kids—not even close to it in fact—and I don't come from divorced parents. So I guess I really don't know what any of that's like. And if my little lie causes Cheyenne any kind of grief, then I'm sorry for that. I was just so focused on aggravating him that I didn't think about how my lie would affect Cheyenne. Still, twenty-five grand may be nothing to scoff at, but it won't keep me afloat for even a year. Money or no money, I just can't afford to lose my job.

"I need my job," I say.

"I don't really give a shit what you need," he hisses.

"That's pretty damn apparent," I say, louder than I intend.

"I was just doing my job and trying to help a kid that nobody else seemed to give a crap about!"

"How many times I got to tell you—keep your mouth shut about my kid," he shouts. His voice booms and practically reverberates off the walls of the room.

"As many times as it takes for you to listen to me," I yell back.

"Shut up!" he screams. He crosses the room, presses his balled fists into the mattress on either side of me. He's so close that when he huffs, his breath heats my skin. He's so angry that he's practically shaking.

I lean forward so fast that I accidentally ram my nose into his. The impact stings, but I only pull back an inch and force myself not to flinch. I'm so angry and feel so guilty that my heart slams in my chest. When I speak, I keep my voice low and steady.

"Look, it's done." This man has worn the sense right out of me. I can't think of another situation where I became so thoroughly fed-up that I totally lost myself. Grady is just a special sort of infuriating. I feel awful about Cheyenne, but there's nothing I can do about it now. "You can't rewrite history, so just roll with it."

"Fuck," he says, pushing off the bed. He huffs and mumbles to himself a moment before turning around and facing the wall next to the door. His right arm twitches, and he draws back his left leg, brings it forward, and slams it into the wall in front of him. "Fuck, fuck, fuck."

I sit motionless and wait, praying that he calms down soon. The angrier he gets, the longer it's going to take me to get out of here. I just want this nightmare to end, but everything I say that's meant to make things better just ends up making them worse. So I decide to just not say anything else.

He huffs and grumbles for several more minutes before finally turning to face me again. "Let's get a few things straight—I am not a patient man. I've been kind so far, but make no mistake about it, I do not like improvising. You want to tell the entire fucking world that you fucked me, go right ahead, baby. You tell everybody I put my dick inside you and pummeled you so hard you're having trouble walking today. You tell everybody how I fucked you hard and fucked you raw. In fact, you want my dick so badly, take it."

I cover my face with my hands the moment he reaches down and starts to unbuckle his belt. A moment passes before he says, "Thought so." And then he disappears. It's minutes later when Lisa comes into the room. She doesn't say much except that she's going to help me up and out of the house. With no little amount of embarrassment, Lisa tells me that my injury is little more than a nasty bruise on my hip from where Grady fell on me and his gun slammed into me, and a mild bullet graze. Even if I'd only been going on with the dramatics in my head, I'm still mortified that I thought I'd been badly shot. All in all, she's really quite kind about it.

On my way out, I don't see Grady or Cheyenne at all. I tell myself that it's for the best. Really, in all the years I've distantly fantasized about the club and the men in it, never did I think I'd be in this position. I walk gingerly to my car, aided by Lisa, and when I climb inside, I find that it's been cleaned, with no sign that I was bleeding all over the seats just yesterday.

"Someone will be by with the first payment in a few days," she says. She's got her hand on the outside handle of the open driver's side door.

"Oh, I don't really want the cash. I just want to be left alone," I say.

"Word of advice? You want to be left alone—take the money and be done with it. Arguing is only going to invite trouble," she says. I go to defend myself, but she holds her hand up and shakes her head. "I'm just the messenger."

She shuts the door and steps away from the car. I take that as my cue and pull out of the driveway then drive slowly away from the Grady residence and back to my normal life.

☠ CHAPTER 9 ☠

YOU'RE SURE—YOU don't have *any* ibuprofen?" I ask Margot as I rub my temples. Mr. Beck has been in his office with Jeremy Whelan for the last ten minutes and it's starting to get loud. It doesn't matter that the door is shut and his office is all the way down the hall. I can hear practically every single word of what's being said. Jeremy, a senior who is unlikely to graduate, is asking for a work permit. For the fourth time. He's awfully persistent and if I didn't know his story, I might think it a little weird that he wants a job so badly. Most kids are reluctant to work, but Jeremy's sister, Nic is the only family he has as far as I know. Nic works with Mindy and neither of them make much. I just wish Mr. Beck would give Jeremy a break— even if the kid is being a real pain in the butt.

My elbows are resting on my desk and I'm hunched over. Everything aches from my ache to my head to my soul. Even the no-longer-bruised spot above my hip aches. It could be cramps or I could be crazy. With how awful I feel right now, it doesn't really matter. The only thing that matters is that apparently nobody in this godforsaken building has any pain killers and Mr. Beck's voice carries. I look at the clock on the wall and see that they've been in there arguing for longer than I thought. It's been closer to fifteen minutes of straight-up bitching.

"Sorry, girl," Margot says.

"Hey Margot, what the hell is actually going on in there?" I ask and blow out a frustrated breath. I know Jeremy needs a work permit, and Mr. Beck won't give him one, but what I don't understand is why Mr. Beck hasn't kicked him out of his office yet. Margot wheels around and leans against my desk. Her eyes are wide and excited. I plaster my best friendly smile on my face and wait for the dirt.

"I thought Sterling would have told you," she says. We've been dancing around the topic of my alleged association with Sterling Grady for a while now. I just shake my head no and try not to fuel her curiosity any further. "Well, anyway. So Jeremy got a job working at Forsaken Custom Cycle. He came to me for a permit and I had to deny him because his grades are too low. He begged me to give him the permit, but I told him to talk to Mr. Beck."

"Yeah," I say. I knew all of that. "But why hasn't Mr. Beck kicked him out of his office?" I've never seen a student be so flat-out disrespectful to Mr. Beck before. It's not that Mr. Beck is a particularly tough man or that he's intimidating, but most students have some kind of respect for his position and try not to tick him off. When I went to school here, the only kids that got away with much of anything are now members of Forsaken.

"After the second time Mr. Beck denied Jeremy's permit, Jim Stone came in and personally asked Mr. Beck to approve it. He didn't and Mr. Stone got pretty mad. I think Mr. Beck is scared of getting another visit from the president of the club."

It all makes sense now. Mr. Beck is the typical administrator who thinks he knows better than everyone around him. He's always avoided confrontation with the club as best he can which is why he won't expel Cheyenne— or Jeremy for that matter— himself, but he pushes both Margot and I to do it for him. If only I had known this before I made the trip out to Grady's house, I could have saved myself a lot of grief. I didn't want trouble from the club, either, but I guess Mr. Beck is really only concerned about keeping his own ass out of the fire. That jerk let me chase after Grady for months— even during summer session— and he never once bothered to tell me who he is and what I was walking into.

"Jeremy's family could use the money. Mr. Beck can't help at all?" I ask. Sure, Nic is with one of the guys in the club now, and I'm sure he's going to take care of her and their baby, but that doesn't mean anything for Jeremy, I don't think. I don't really know anything about how the club members earn their money aside from the rumors that swirl around town. If Jeremy says he needs the job to help his family, then I trust that he does.

The door to Mr. Beck's office swings open and Jeremy stalks out. His feet stomp into the linoleum below and he moves so fast that he clips the corner of Margot's desk on the way out. With a angry push, the main door to the office flies open and he rushes out, letting the door slam behind him. Margot and I jump in place and move back into place to pretend like we've been working the entire time.

It's just a moment later when Mr. Beck is standing at the end of the hallway. His face is red and in an agitated voice he says, "Holly, can you come in my office, please?"

With a deep breath, I stand from my seat and cross the room, following behind Mr. Beck and into his office. My head is still pounding, but I try to push my own misery out of my head and just deal with whatever it is the boss man wants. He sits behind his desk and folds his arms over his chest. I'm not terribly happy with him right now and don't want to be in here any longer than I absolutely need to, so I opt for closing the door and leaning against the nearby wall.

"Everything okay, Dick?" I say. Richard Beck asks his colleagues to call him Dick, but he's never once asked me to. Margot calls him Mr. Beck so I assume he hasn't asked her to, either. The fact that he doesn't see me as equal to him has never really bothered me until this moment.

"Holly, where are we at with Cheyenne Grady's expulsion?"

Mr. Beck knows damn well that I don't intend to file paperwork to have Cheyenne expelled. He and I have had this conversation already. In fact, we have had this conversation several times, and I guess it still hasn't seeped into his thick skull. I never had any trouble with Mr. Beck when I was a student. He was always just the principal – a distant authority figure who let the fact that he was underpaid and overworked be known to just about everybody he came in contact with. But Mr. Beck has shown himself to be a real nitwit. He's far too scared to expel Cheyenne Grady on his own, and he's not compassionate enough to give her a break. No, that's why he sends his staff out to do a job we are not paid to do.

"Her expulsion is on hold. Mr. Grady signed the counseling acknowledgment form and Cheyenne knows that she's expected at Saturday school this weekend." It wasn't easy getting that stupid form signed, but it has been, so the job got done. If I spend too long to think about it, I'll come to the conclusion that Mr. Beck never expected me to get Grady to sign the form, and that is just going to piss me off. So instead, I pretend that he's not that big of a tool, even if I know in my heart that he is.

"You got Sterling Grady to sign that form? After months of trying, he finally did it? Does this mean that the rumors are true, that you're seeing Sterling Grady? " he asks. His eyes are wide, his mouth has fallen, and his face goes blank. And whatever tiny little bit of hope that I had that Dick isn't actually a dick vanishes. I should have known that with the way Margot dances around the subject that Mr. Beck would eventually hear the rumors.

"Yes, the form has been signed."

"Ms. Mercer, I can't tell you how to live your life, but I do want to warn you that Sterling's bike club are not the kind of people you want to associate with. Look at Cheyenne Grady and Jeremy Whelan – both of their dads are part of that gang – neither of them have much of a future. Those people go around having kids they don't discipline, nor do they care about. It's none of my business what you do in your off-time, and I apologize for stepping over the bounds, but I like you, Holly. I don't want to see you get hurt or mixed up in their criminal enterprise."

I'm silent for a few moments too long, and Mr. Beck starts talking again. He's never been shy about his disapproval of the club and its members, and that's fine. But it's not Jeremy Whelan's fault that he was given the short end of the stick, and it certainly isn't Cheyenne's fault, either. They're just kids, and I don't really care what *Dick* thinks of the club. He's taking it out on a couple of kids, and that's not fair.

In the weeks since my visit to the Grady residence, I've discovered that there are three other students in this school with worse attendance records, poorer grades, and more difficult temperaments than either Cheyenne or Jeremy have exhibited. Despite the fact that I've brought those students to Mr. Beck's attention, he's shown little interest in pursuing expulsion for them. I suppose Mr. Beck lets them slide because two of them are athletes and the other one is the child of a local business owner. I'm willing to bet none of their parents have a criminal record, and *that's* what this vendetta is really about. Either way, it ends here.

"Is there a reason you won't issue Jeremy Whelan a work permit, but you allow Edwin Nielson to continue playing football despite the fact that his GPA is two points below Jeremy's and he has four more unexcused absences as well?"

"It's at my discretion to determine whom I may and may

not make exceptions for. Jeremy has exhibited no desire to better himself. Edwin Nielson has been struggling with recovering from his football injury during a practice at defense camp over the summer."

"So, because Jeremy doesn't play football he doesn't deserve a chance to graduate high school?" I ask. My jaw locks at the end of my sentence and I have to force it loose. Everything I feared about having this conversation with Mr. Beck is coming to fruition. Our football team isn't even that good, and we haven't made state in the last decade, but Edwin Nielson is popular and his dad isn't an outlaw, so I suppose that's enough for Mr. Beck to show him a little grace.

"I'm glad you got Mr. Grady to sign the counseling form. Now, if you'll excuse me, I have a busy schedule," Mr. Beck says by means of dismissal. I exit the room and shut the door behind me as quickly and quietly as possible. I didn't know it could happen, but my head now feels even worse than it did before I entered Mr. Beck's office. Now that he's shown how utterly unfair of a human being he is, I can't help but rack my brain trying to figure out if there's anything I can do to help Jeremy, and by extension, help the club. Grady doesn't need to know that I still feel immense guilt over possibly causing Cheyenne anymore grief. Maybe I can ease some of that if I can help Jeremy.

I'm barely in my seat when Margot turns around and says, "Tell ya what, just take an extended lunch. I'll eat something here. Go grab something for your head at the store, take a walk. Do something. Just get out of here for a little bit."

"You're right." I should get out of here for a bit. It's past the time I normally take lunch, and I've been cooped up at my desk for weeks now. Actually, I've kept myself cooped up at home as well. After leaving the Grady residence I started noticing that someone was following me. At first I figured I was just plain paranoid, but the chances of seeing the same exact person following a few car lengths behind me every single day is probably pretty small. It wasn't until I saw him in a beige sedan parked in the school parking lot when I came out of work one day last week that I knew for sure that the club had somebody watching me. I can only hope the guy hasn't told Grady that I know he's following me because I let my temper get the better of me and I gave him a one-finger wave. It was not one of my finer moments, I'll admit.

I'm leaving the office when I spot my favorite student leaning against a row of lockers. She's got her back to me and her head tilted up as she listens to Jeremy Whelan grouching about Mr. Beck no doubt.

He lets out a heavy sigh. I pull my cell out of my purse and peek at the time— and sure enough, just as I thought— they're both supposed to be in class right now. Jeremy spots my approach before Cheyenne does, but I'm quick to side up to Cheyenne and put on my best smile. I've never seen them talk before, but I'm not surprised they know one another considering their connections to Forsaken.

"Going to see Dad?" Cheyenne asks with a wiggle of her brows as she jerks her chin at my purse on my shoulder. She's good at this— trying to distract people from the task at hand. It worked the first few times we'd met, but I'm onto her game now.

"Heh," I say and try to stop my eyes from rolling into the back of my head at the suggestion of seeing her father. "No, pharmacy. I have a killer headache, and I wonder why."

"The more difficult you are, the more he talks about you," she says wistfully.

"That's great, but really," I say in exasperation. "You two are going to be the death of me. Do either of you realize how much Mr. Beck wants you both kicked out of this school? Do you?"

Cheyenne bites her lip and her eyes shift to Jeremy's. He folds his arms over his chest and scowls down at me. I hate it when the students get taller than me, which unfortunately, happens a lot with the boys. It makes it difficult to feel like I'm really an authority figure when I have to look up to scold them.

"We're just talking. Chill," Jeremy says. His eyes cut to Cheyenne briefly and she gives him a soft smile. Oh, hell. She's got that look on her face that all teenage girls get when they have a crush on somebody. I wonder if her dad knows about this development. Speaking of her dad, I might be able to use the club to diffuse the attitude and get their asses to class before someone else realizes they're just lingering around campus.

"Hey," I say and raise my finger to Jeremy. "Close your mouth and get to class." He doesn't move, but he does smirk down at me and roll his eyes. Okay, he's more hard-headed than I gave him credit for. He knows I work here, but apparently he doesn't care. Either that or he's just trying to show off in front of Cheyenne. I'm betting it's the latter. So I go with my old standby when a student doesn't listen. I pull my cell from my purse and nod my head. "Wilcox, right? Joshua Wilcox? That's the name of your sister's boyfriend?"

Joshua Wilcox was a year behind me in school, but he and his two buddies, Ian Buckley and Ryan Stone were legendary around campus. Josh now goes by Duke— for a reason I'm not aware of— and like his felonious friends, he's a member of the club.

Jeremy's face falls and his arms drop to his sides. He clears his throat and scratches the back of his neck. Silently, I thank Mindy for gabbing about work so often. Apparently Nic used to have a hard time with Jeremy, but since she started seeing Josh, the boy has straightened up a lot. Mindy says all Josh has to do is give him a look and the kid behaves.

"That's what I thought," I say and put my phone away. Thankfully, Jeremy doesn't call my bluff. I don't have Josh's phone number, but even if I did, I'd never call it. I only know him by proxy and what I know of him tells me that I'm better off not getting to knowing him. "Class. Now."

Jeremy gives Cheyenne "the nod", pulls a cell out of his pocket, and quickly sends a text message. Just as he shoves the phone back into his pocket he disappears in the direction of his class. Now that I know mentioning Josh really does work as well as Mindy says, I'm going to use it liberally. Cheyenne tries to step away and sneak off down the hallway, but I'm not having that. I've gone to bat for her— I'm still going to bat for her— and she's ditching class.

"Oh no you don't," I say and snap my fingers. She stops in place, turns around, and walks back to me.

"He's cute, right?" she says. Her eyes are big and dreamy and her cheeks are a dark pink. Crap. She doesn't just kind of like him, she's got full-blown love-face going on.

"Adorable," I grumble. "But seriously, do you have any idea how hard I'm trying to keep your butt from getting expelled? I thought we talked about this, Cheyenne."

"We did and I *am* being good. I was on my way back to class from the bathroom and Jeremy was standing here. He was really upset and I didn't want him going to class like that! He just needed a friend to listen to him."

"Mr. Beck is not going to give a rat's patootie why you weren't in class if he catches you out here," I say. I mentally kick myself once the words are out of my mouth.

"Did you just say *rat's patootie*?" Cheyenne asks. Her eyes are wild like I'm some kind of alien or something. Mindy and her damn phrases are rubbing off on me and making me sound like an imbecile.

"Not the point, girly," I say in an attempt to redirect.

"You're not going to tell my dad, are you?" she asks. I've tried twice now—unsuccessfully—to "break up" with him, but somehow, despite my attempts, Cheyenne says he's told her that we're still together. I think she's starting to realize that something is rotten in Denmark, but she's still asking these kinds of questions. I have no clue if I'm lying to say we're still in a relationship or if it's ended, and things are just messy. When asked, I try to play aloof and act like he's in the doghouse—and really, if I could shove his ass in one, I would.

"You gonna behave?" I ask. She's not my kid so I don't want to be the one to tell her that nothing is going on between her dad and I, but eventually I'm going to have to draw a line in the sand with this stuff.

"You gonna tell him?" she asks with her eyebrows raised. She's getting a little too high and mighty for my taste so I mean mug her until she backs down and sighs in defeat. "You know, my dad's dated a *lot* of women, and I mean a *lot*, but they usually try to suck up to me so I'll like them. I'm just saying."

A slow smile spreads across my face and I point in the direction of the English class she's supposed to be in right now. "Careful, kid. You're starting to sound like an extortionist. Now go to class before you get in trouble."

"Dad's right. You *are* a ball-buster," she says. The smile on her face is blinding when she says, "You're awesome, Holly!" She throws her hands up in the air and backs away towards her class. When I'm confident that she's actually going to class now, I head for my car with my own huge smile on my face. Her father may be a Grade-A asshole, and he's certainly a very troubled human being, but I was most definitely wrong about at least one thing about him: he's loves his daughter. I might not like him very much, but I can definitely respect a guy who manages to raise such an awesome kid.

☠CHAPTER 10☠

IT'S ENTIRELY POSSIBLE that my headache has disappeared because I'm no longer hearing Mr. Beck's voice. The last I remember the dull thumping in my brain was before I walked out of the office and saw Cheyenne and Jeremy talking at the lockers. Even both of them giving me attitude didn't bug me, and by the time I was in my car on the way to the pharmacy, my shoulders had relaxed and I was able to take a deep breath without regretting it from the pressure in my skull.

Still, while I'm here, I pick up some ibuprofen, just in case. After my conversation with Mr. Beck today, I foresee many more headaches in my future. I'm not entirely sure what it is about Cheyenne Grady, but after the talk we just had, I'm more determined than ever before to help her succeed in school. I just have to figure out how to do that without taking Grady's money, and that means avoiding him and his guys as best I can. It's not been easy these past few weeks, but I've successfully ditched the two guys who, in addition to

Grady, have tried to hand me a thick manila envelope. I know Lisa Grady told me to just take the money, but it's just not something I'm comfortable with. I mean, they can't chase after me forever, right?

After I grab the extra strength 60-count bottle of ibuprofen from the shelf, I head straight for the refrigerated foods. I'm overdue for lunch, exhausted, and willing to try anything that I don't have to make myself. The pharmacy isn't very big, but it's grown in the last few years in order to keep up with the national drugstore chain that moved into town. I know for fact that the 24-hour chain pharmacy has better prices, and probably better food judging by the selection that they have here, but I like my money to go to local businesses whenever possible.

The refrigerated food section consists of a single refrigerator that's better equipped to house only soft drinks it's so small. Despite its size, there are three sandwiches, two salads, what they're calling freshly made soup, and a wrap to choose from. If I learned anything from the short time I spent in college, it's to not consume meat from questionable sources. The wrap, sandwiches, and soup all have that some form of meat in them, but neither of the salads do. Being cautious, I opt for the salad. On my way to the register, I grab a couple small bags of peanuts, a bottle of Coke, and a pack of gum. I like to keep a few snacks in my desk drawer, but since I haven't been going anywhere, I haven't had a chance to refill my stash lately.

Just as I'm leaving the register after paying, I start to get that feeling I'm being watched. Unfortunately, it's a feeling that I have become accustomed to these last few weeks. I didn't see the short guy who's been following me around lately on my way here, but that doesn't mean he's not out there lurking somewhere. The thought creeps me out, causing me to pick up my pace and rush out of the pharmacy as quickly as I can. My poor Coke is being shaken all to hell inside the plastic bag that I'm gripping with my left hand. I fish my keys out of my purse and clutch them with my right hand as I head straight toward my Jeep. Nervously, I keep looking behind me, so distracted by the possibility that I'm being followed that I don't even notice the man leaning against my driver side door until them almost on him.

"Well, look who decided to venture out," Grady says in a grumble. His presence puts me on the edge immediately. I take a step back, fold my arms over my chest, and let my face give him a full explanation of how I feel. My eyes narrow, and my mouth turns down into a pout.

"How did you know I was here?"

"Remind me, babe, to give Jeremy Whelan a break next time he does something to piss me off," he says. I have to bite back the smile that's going to rat me out. I want, more than anything, to tell Grady that Jeremy is going to end up pissing him off quite a lot in the future. I'm willing to bet that, with a daughter as pretty as Cheyenne is, Grady has had his fair share of heart attacks. As much as his displeasure at Cheyenne's interest in Jeremy would entertain me, it's none of my business. I've learned my lesson—when it comes to Cheyenne, Grady doesn't want to hear my opinion. Not that he's particularly fond of my opinion on any other topic, either.

I'll have to remind myself that Jeremy Whelan has such a big mouth. It's curious that he saw fit to tell Grady of my whereabouts. Little asshole.

"Is your ass trying to clean the door of my Jeep, or are you trying to make a point?" I ask. In an odd reaction, he smiles. He almost looks friendly, and if I didn't know better, it might relax me some. But I do know better. Grady smiling is never a good thing. I'm tempted to scan the parking lot to see if he ran someone over or maybe he sliced my tires. The paranoia is getting to me. I tell myself that I'm just being dramatic.

"What? I can't just stop and say hi to my favorite secretary?" he asks. I raise an eyebrow and check my tires real quick. They all look fine, but there's so many things he could do to damage the functionality of my Jeep. Brake wires can get cut, power steering fluid can mysteriously leak all over the pavement, and if he's feeling particularly evil, he could even rig the thing with explosives.

"What did you do?" I ask suspiciously.

His smile widens, and a chuckle rumbles in his chest. I almost think he looks happy, but then I remember who I'm talking to. He shrugs and looks around as innocently as I imagine he can. I don't want him to know how much his being here actually bothers me. I mean, this entire situation is getting out of hand. Sure, I have kind of done it to myself. But why should I have to compromise my beliefs just because he has something to prove?

I shouldn't.

Mr. Beck is not someone that I want to be agreeing with right now, but I have to wonder if this kind of intimidation is standard behavior for the club. And if this is par for the course, then what kind of town am I living in? Maybe I'm just naïve, and totally out of touch, but in all my years living here in Fort Bragg, I never really considered that the awful rumors that circle about could be true. Yeah, I never imagined that the Forsaken Motorcycle Club were a bunch of choirboys, but I never really believed the rumors that they were thugs, either. Maybe I'm completely off base about Jeremy Whelan if he's tipping Grady off to my whereabouts.

"You're kind of paranoid, aren't you?"

Duh.

"No, of course not. Our meetings have gone so well in the past, Sterling. I'm thrilled you could pay me a visit," I say. More sarcasm falls off my tongue in those few sentences than I think I doled out during my entire adolescence.

"Told you, babe. Don't call me Sterling."

Now I'm the one with the huge smile on my face. It's true, he has asked me not to call him Sterling. It's almost funny that he thinks I would care after the way he's treated me. And what the hell is up with him calling me babe all of a sudden? While it is much preferred to bitch, it still makes me uncomfortable.

"There a reason my kid likes you so much?"

"I can only imagine that Cheyenne enjoys having a conversation with somebody who doesn't refer to every woman as either bitch or babe," I say. I'm not sure where this conversation is going, especially since he's being so…human. "Well, this has been fun, but I really must be going now," I say. I must be having horrible luck with the male species today, because he doesn't move. Not only is this conversation awkward and strange, but it's actually not progressed anywhere, nor has it served a purpose. At this point, we're just standing here like a couple of idiots. We might as well be chatting about the weather and our expectations for the upcoming baseball season.

He waits another moment before he finally pushes off the car and strides right up to me. I order my brain to shut down any and all thoughts about the way he carries his large frame as he moves toward me. He's still an asshole, I remind myself. Even assholes, I suppose, are entitled to look good. I consider myself to be a woman of self-respect, and decent self-esteem, so the fact that he's able to get my mind racing about the build of his body really just pisses me off. Men with so little respect for other people shouldn't be allowed to look this good. Ever.

"Oh, and Holly," he says as he leans down. He's invading my space, and if I wasn't overwhelmed by being in such close proximity to him, I might be able to think clearly enough to be annoyed by it. "You're avoiding me. I don't fucking like it. Eventually, you're going to run out of steam, and you'll be tired out. Just do yourself a favor and take the money. Because, make no mistake about it, baby, I have stamina to go for days." Arrogant jerk.

"You're bipolar," I say. My blood pressure is rising. I have to hold my hands down firmly at my sides so I don't reach out and slap the smirk right off his face. His perfectly strong jaw is mostly covered with facial hair. It doesn't look like he's really shaved since I last saw him.

One moment, he's practically standing over me, and the next, he's walking away across the parking lot. I blink back my surprise and try to clear my head as I walk back to my Jeep. With my head in a daze, I grab at the driver's door handle. Just as I think I'm an idiot for trying to open the locked door without the use of the key, the handle gives way under my grip and the door opens.

"Great, now you're imagining things," I mutter to myself as I climb in and shut the door behind me. My purse and plastic bag from the pharmacy fall onto the seat beside me. I could have sworn I locked the doors before going inside, but I guess not. All my frustration and paranoia are clearly having a considerable effect on my ability to think clearly. I pull the Jeep out of the parking lot and get stuck at the first light on the way back to work. The loud roar of an idling motorcycle engine sounds behind me. Lifting my head, I find Grady on his Harley in my rear view mirror. The longer I sit at the red light, the more I consider the validity of "accidentally" putting the Jeep in reverse and backing over him. But murder is wrong—it's even one of those pesky Ten Commandments. I've been trying to live my life in a way that I can be proud of and not cut corners like I used to, but the man behind me it making that commitment more difficult than it needs to be.

Hunger gets the best of me, and I reach over into the plastic bag in search of one of those bags of peanuts. The rustling of the bag almost distracts me from the odd crunch that sounds every time I hit the bottom of the plastic bag. Feeling more than a little off my game, I pat the bottom of the bag a few more times. Something isn't right. I give the bag a shove and, sure enough, there is something underneath it. A large manila envelope sits on the passenger seat, half covered by my purse and shopping bag. I'd know that envelope anywhere. It's the same envelope, right now to the nasty little note I wrote on it, that Grady and his friends have tried to give me several times over the last few weeks.

That asshole.

No really, that asshole.

I knew something about that entire conversation was off, and I *knew* my car door wasn't unlocked when I went into the pharmacy. Here I thought I was losing my mind, but no. Sterling Grady hoodwinked me in order to drop an envelope with twenty-five grand into my car without my knowledge. Just as the light changes to green, I grab hold of the window crank and roll it down. The two cars in front of me take their time to get moving, and I take advantage of this by grabbing the envelope from the seat beside me. With my left hand full of twenty-five grand, I lift it out the open window and wave it at Grady behind me. My eyes are intently focused on the rear view mirror. I can't see the look on his face, but he's definitely paying attention. His mouth opens, and he's shouting something over his ridiculously loud engine. It takes me a moment to realize he's screaming, "Don't do it!"

Don't do what? Oh, he thinks I'm going to drop it out of

the window. I shake the package at him as I start to roll away. His eyes dart around nervously as he changes gears and follows me. He's still shouting and occasionally using one of his hands to point menacingly at me. He must actually think I'm going to just toss the money out the window. But I couldn't do that, could I?

My fingers loosen and, before I can stop myself, I've let it fall onto the pavement. I can barely see Grady holding up traffic in my rear view as I drive away from the scene of the stupidest thing I've ever done. I'm a block away before I can breathe again, but I haven't calmed down. By the time I get into the staff parking lot, I'm having a mild panic attack, my chest heaving and my lungs straining for air. I haphazardly park the Jeep and turn her off, but I don't move.

"I dropped," I mutter aloud in a dumbfounded whisper, "twenty-five...   twenty-five...twenty-five-fucking-thousand dollars out of my moving vehicle." Before I know it, I'm slapping at my steering wheel and cursing myself for my own stupidity. I don't regret getting rid of the cash, no, I'd made that conviction already. Lisa Grady told me weeks ago that arguing was going to invite trouble, and now I'm afraid I just invited more trouble that I can handle. But I can't just sit in my car and think about that all day. I have a low-paying job to get back to, and a life to resume living, holed-up at my desk and in my own home because I'm avoiding everything Forsaken. I just don't know how much longer this can go on for—the following, the fighting, the chasing, and the total departure from sanity.

Maybe I should just take the money and be done with it. I

can figure out a way to get right with that somehow. I've contemplated telling Grady why I'm not comfortable taking the cash, in full detail, but he wouldn't care anyway, so what good would it do? It wouldn't.

I grab my shopping bag and my purse and head inside the office. Margot immediately notices my arrival and looks up from her homemade sandwich. I must look awful—she pouts at the sight of me. I wave her off and don't even try to explain. No good comes from her thinking about Grady or my possible relationship with him. She tries, she really does, but curiosity gets the better of her. We live in a small town, and gossip is what small towns do best.

The first time Margot brought Grady up was when I'd returned to work after the whole shoot-out thing. It was a necessary conversation that I hated to have. The second time she brought him up, it was after Cheyenne and her friends made a trip into the office. Margot zeroed in on how Cheyenne had come over to my desk, asked how I was feeling, and then asked why she hadn't seen me at her house again. I told her it hadn't worked out with her dad, and that was when she informed me that he told her we were still seeing each other. Cheyenne left all confused, and Margot asked if it was serious between Grady and me. The best response I could muster was that the only thing Sterling Grady is ever serious about is his daughter and his club. That pacified her for a while, but when Cheyenne's visits to the office became more frequent and her excuses for visiting less and less plausible, Margot started doing this thing with her eyeballs that tells me she's holding back a million questions that are killing her to keep inside.

I toss the bag and my purse down on my desk and pull out my chair. A door slams with such force that I jump in place. I don't even have to look to know who it is. Had I given myself even a moment to consider the consequences for tossing the money out the window, I could have talked myself out of it. Grady may not be the heartless monster I once assumed him to be, but that doesn't mean he's not angry with me. It just means he probably won't hack me into tiny bits. Anything else, though, is a distinct possibility.

He takes his helmet off as he storms through the door then plops it on my desk. I try to straighten my back and force myself to look him in the eye. Everything about him, from his wild eyes to his heaving chest, displays an intensity I didn't know possible. I've made him mad before, and I've even pissed him off so bad that he's kicked walls and threatened me; but this is a different kind of intensity. His eyes slide over mine, back and forth, back and forth, almost as if he's trying to figure something out. Maybe some rationale behind my behavior, or the truth as to why I refuse to take the money. If he figures out what possessed to me toss such an ungodly amount of cash out of my old, beat-up Jeep's window, I'd like for him to explain it to me, because I can't manufacture any kind of explanation. The best I can say is that the man is so infuriating that he makes me lose my faculties when he's around and I end up doing the stupidest stuff.

It happens so fast that I almost miss the movement. He lifts his arm and wraps his hand around the back of my neck. Fear strikes at my heart in expectation of a pain that doesn't come. I stumble forward as he pulls me so close to his body that we're practically flush from my chest all the way down to my knees.

"We need to have a talk," he says in the quietest way possible. I try to nod, but his grip kind of immobilizes my head.

"Okay," I whisper. He turns us just slightly and slowly walks me backward. It's awkward, walking like this, with his feet practically stepping all over mine, and me being unable to see where I'm going, much less the path we're taking. A shadow falls over as we enter the small nook around the corner from the hall that leads down to Mr. Beck's office. I hit a hard surface that I recognize as the door to the janitor's closet, and Grady stops, now absolutely flush against me. I breathe slightly easier knowing that Margot can't see us from her desk, because whatever is happening here is plenty embarrassing without having to re-live it via the gossip chain He's much larger in such close proximity, with his entire body resting against mine and his hand cradling my neck. Slowly, he tilts my neck so that I'm forced to face him.

"You threw twenty-five grand out of a moving vehicle," he says.

"I'm crazy," I say immediately. He smashes his lips together, which distracts me from the whole intense eyeball thing he's got going on. His lips part and he pulls in a deep, shuttered breath. I try to form a coherent sentence, but it's difficult. He's kind of intoxicating in this small space. "You make me crazy."

"Why don't we just get this out of the way, huh?" he says quietly. "I want to taste your pussy." My face heats at the thought of him putting his tongue to a good use for once. Pressure builds in my head, and it's only then that I realize I've stopped breathing.

"You see that—that nervous excitement you're feeling? I'm under your skin. You don't have to like it, but I'm there," he says so quietly it comes out as a whisper. He reaches out with his free hand and strokes my arm with a single finger. His touch is light, but it sends chills down my spine. "Something you should know about me, babe. I don't go into shit blind. You think I don't know you, but I do. I know every asshole who's been inside of you, I know every place you've called home—even the places you don't want me to know about. I know the way you like your coffee, and I know how you think. The shit I don't know, you'll tell me. Eventually, I'm going to know every dirty little part of you, and if you think I make you crazy now, just wait until I bury my dick inside you."

I think I'm stunned into silence, because my brain isn't functioning in the least, but then my mouth starts moving and I realize, in horror, that I'm talking. "We're making each other insane. I've heard about this before—meeting someone who actually drives you to develop a mental health disorder. What else could possibly explain the fact that I'm not completely disgusted by you?"

"You want my dick," he says quietly. I clamp my mouth shut to stop myself from protesting. At some point I'm going to admit to myself that the lady doth protest too much, and that possibility scares me.

His free hand travels down my arm and then over to my belly. My muscles tighten nervously as he places his hand on my hip where the bullet grazed my flesh. His thumb rubs small circles over the small scar that doesn't look like it's going to disappear anytime soon.

"How's the nick?" he asks. The room is heating up quickly, and I think the only thing I could do about it would be to put some distance between him and me.

"Fine," I say. My lungs barely have enough oxygen in them to get the word out.

"No more avoiding me," he says. I'm an idiot—I nod in agreement. Somewhere in the back of my brain, I want to argue with him about it, but not avoiding him gets muscled, taut man parts pressed up against me, and even if it is at work, and it is embarrassing, it's been a while.

"No more being an asshole," I say. If he's going to give orders, I'm going to at least bargain for a fair deal.

"I'll try," he says. It's something, and I should take it, but I don't.

"I won't avoid you so long as you're not an asshole," I say. My eyes catch sight of his lips, and I'm distracted all over again.

"Don't avoid me and I won't be an asshole," he says. The intensity of the conversation is broken just slightly by the small smile that appears on his lips.

"I doubt you're capable of that," I murmur. He bends down and presses his forehead to mine.

"Take the money."

"You're being an asshole."

"Money."

"Asshole," I say.

"You can try to fight me, but I got you," he says and takes a step back. His hands fall from my neck and hip. As he backs away, he licks his lips and looks me up and down. I push off the door to the janitor's closet and follow him out into the open office. He grabs his helmet from my desk and turns to leave. Still in a daze, I turn at the wrong time, and his hand slams down against my backside.

My eyes are so big, and my skin from head to toe darkens to a crimson red that feels uncomfortably hot. I barely get my head turned in time to see him open the side door and disappear.

Margot's eyes are intently focused on the paper in front of her, but it's obvious that she's about to die from shock and curiosity, perhaps both.

I plop into my seat and try to ignore the subtle stinging of both my ego and flesh at the fact that I was spanked. At work. In front of my boss. By an outlaw biker.

☠CHAPTER 11☠

I LOOK DOWN at my store-bought, pre-made salad with disdain. It's one of those salads that looks yummy enough in the store, but when you start eating it, you realize why it was so cheap. I guess that's what I get for buying a pre-made drugstore food product. The lettuce has been shredded, and the cheese tastes waxy. And to boot, I made the mistake of checking out the expiration date and realizing that today's the last day for recommended freshness. Call me crazy, but ever since I saw that, I'm basically convinced that my lunch is going to kill me. After what just happened, I might be okay with that.

"This is ridiculous," Margot says from her desk. She recovered from her shock a few minutes ago when she started humming themes songs from television shows interchangeably. She swivels around and drags herself over. She places her elbows on the edge of my desk and leans in. "That thing looks awful. Just go grab something else for lunch."

"I'm fine, really. It tastes fine," I say in protest, but I'm not a good actress and she sees right through my pitiful attempts at lying. I've spent the last fifteen minutes trying very hard to pretend like that scene between Grady and I didn't just happen. Margot gives me a curious glance. She's not going to let this go. I haven't eaten lunch out of the office since that day I went to The 101 Club, and she's started to notice. Before then, I'd gone out for lunch regularly. I'd even made a comment or two about hating to pack a lunch. It makes me feel like I'm eight years old all over again, but I don't like the alternative much, so I stay in. And now that I know what happens when I go out for lunch in a post-Grady world, I really don't think I want to do that again.

"Uh oh, that's two fines nearly back to back," Margot says with a sympathetic smile. "You can talk to me, Holly. That scene was kind of intense."

"Okay," I say and lean in. I have to give her something to sate her need for gossip. The woman is a damn bloodhound when there's a story to be scooped. "I'm a little tight on money right now. I just don't need the added expense of buying lunch."

"Is that what your fight was about, that you won't let him help you with money? I mean, you can't *really* be tight on money with Grady around," she whisper shouts with a mischievous smile on her face. My stomach drops, and my face falls at the mention of his name. Margot has done so well not to mention him much in recent weeks that her teasing catches me off guard, but what do I expect after that show of caveman idiocy? I really don't want to talk about

Grady or the band of hooligans he has keeping tabs on my every move. They've already invaded every other part of my life. I don't want them to now invade work as well. I guess that went out the window the moment he stormed in here demanding to speak to me.

"Oh, I'm sorry," she says. "Is that impolite? I just meant that…I have a cousin with glaucoma. I know he buys from a guy in Willits who says he gets his stuff from the club. I just figured with those nice houses and bikes they have and all…oh, nevermind."

Margot's worked herself up into a tizzy. She leans back in her chair, rubs her hands together, and pouts. She keeps doing this. As if Grady's totally inappropriate ass slap, and Cheyenne's repeated visits to my desk aren't enough, I also have Margot who just can't let this fake relationship go. Only, both Cheyenne and Margot think it's real.

"I just have to ask—is everything okay with you two?" Margot says as her brows furrow and her lips form into a pout. I blow out a breath and push away the awful, rotted salad and decide to end this once and for all.

"I don't know what we are to each other, nor do I know what he's doing. He's insane. I can't even tell you what that little stunt was. We had a very brief encounter, and I haven't been with him since," I say. I don't count him knocking on my apartment door and me not answering us being together. Nor do I count me trying to avoid him in a parking lot us being together. And I certainly don't count his impromptu drop-in and rear-end assault as us being together. Those are the only times I've seen Grady since that day, and when I'm in a relationship, I typically require a little kindness and affection. Though, the pre-rear-end assault part wasn't so bad.

"Oh, I'm sorry, Holly." Margot reaches over and pats my hand, then slides back to her desk.

"It was hot though," she mutters. "No man has patted my ass like that in at least twenty years."

She manages to leave me alone for a few hours, but when attendance reports come in a little after four, she jumps from her chair. "Sorry," she says, "but I...uh, I have to cut out early. You okay here?" She inches toward the door.

I stare at the reports. Margot never says where she's going, but she has to "cut out early"—as soon as attendance reports show up—at least once a week. I shrug her off, deciding it's for the best. Cheyenne is still missing classes, not as many as she was before her dad approved her counseling, but enough that I've had to fudge the last two reports so she doesn't get in trouble. "No problem. I'll see you tomorrow."

She pauses at the door and turns back to me. Her mouth opens, then closes again in a very un-Margot-like display of hesitation. Finally, she says, "I'm sorry about Grady, but you'll find someone better suited for you, hun." And then she's gone.

What the hell does she mean by that? I may not be some badass biker chick or anything, but is it really so unimaginable that a man like Sterling Grady could be with someone like me? Maybe I'm just not interesting enough to date a biker. I should try an accountant or someone else with

an equally boring sounding job. But what the hell does she know? It wasn't Margot he had pressed up against a door. It was me.

I'm about to pack up for the day when the main office door swings open. Looking up from my computer, I see none other than Cheyenne rushing toward me with wide eyes and shaking hands. She looks over her shoulder at the door several times before she rounds my desk and stands beside me. I turn to face her and practically whisper, "Cheyenne, what's wrong?"

"There's a man leaning on my car. I tried to call my dad, but he didn't pick up. The guy said he had a message for Dad and he wants me to give it to him."

Jumping to my feet and maneuvering around her, I cautiously walk toward the door and keep an eye on the inset window. "Did he leave or was he still there when you came in here?"

"He was still there. I didn't wait to hear the message. Dad has *very* clear rules about talking to strangers, and that's like, the one rule I don't intend to break, ya know?" she says. I inch toward the door and stop breathing for a good few seconds before I catch myself. I can't let myself freak out right now. Cheyenne needs me to be the adult. She came to me for a reason. The only problem is that now *I* want an adult to come deal with this for me.

Leaning against the old, rusted classic Volkswagen Bug that Cheyenne drives is a man in a black suit that costs more than my monthly gross pay. He's all fine lines and perfect fit, and his body language exudes a confidence that only comes with a pay grade I'll never know. His sun-kissed skin tells me he's not from around here. Nobody from Mendocino County is particularly tan, especially not during this time of the year. We're much too late into the fall to still have a lingering summer tan. The man fills out the suit well, which tells me he is either naturally gifted with a great body or he works for it. His black hair is gelled back, and he's sporting some expansive as all hell sunglasses despite the fact that it's cloudy out.

"You don't know who he is?" I ask Cheyenne. She slides up beside me and presses herself against my side as she forces me to share the small window in the door.

"Does he *look* like anyone I know?" she asks. I bite my tongue to keep from telling her what I think of the people she knows.

"Stay here and try your dad again," I say then squeeze out the door. Once I'm on the other side, I'm mentally screaming at myself. What the hell am I doing out here? I should go back in and call the police, but I know that when Forsaken are involved, you don't call the police. I really don't need to give anyone in or associated with the club ay more reason to have to talk to me about anything. As it is, I've been ditching Grady and his buddies who keep trying to give me money for the last few weeks. He's made it perfectly clear how he feels about my avoiding him. I just can't deal with him right now, though his world keeps finding ways to impede on my own despite my attempts, and I don't like it.

"Sir," I say as loudly as I can bring my voice to get, "I'm going to have to ask you to leave the premises."

"I have a message for Forsaken," he says in a thick accent that sounds definitively East Coast. His words are all compressed in telltale spots and then dragged out in others. It's not Boston, but it might be New York.

"Then deliver it yourself," I say with a snap. I knew the moment Cheyenne said a man had a message for her dad that this was a club problem, but this man doesn't look like anybody in the club. They're all rugged beauty and blue collar, working man's attire. This guy is sleek and all business in a very expensive way.

"That's not how this is going to work," he says. His mouth turns up just slightly in the corner. "Please tell Grady that..."He doesn't get any farther—I cut him off, totally unable to listen to this crap. My blood pressure is likely through the roof right now. My hands shake, and my knees feel weaker than I'd like to admit, but I don't show this to the best of my ability. My palms sweat, and my heart thumps wildly in my chest.

"Stop, just stop!" I shout. "This has nothing to do with me or Cheyenne. So just get out of here and leave her alone."

The man against the car moves his hand in his pocket so the corner of his suit jacket is shoved back. Beneath it, a bright gold gun shines in the overcast rays of the sun. "Yelling at me is not wise." "Now," he says and clears his throat. "Please tell Mr. Grady that Mr. Mancuso's business associates are in town and they would like to schedule a meeting with him to discuss an acquisition. We'd like to avoid a hostile takeover if possible, but we understand that the club is quite fond of our assets and some aggressive tactics may be necessary."

"And why can't you tell them this yourself?" I say with my eyes glued to the gun at his hip. He makes it sound all business, but there's an underlying message that I'm missing.

"Two birds, one stone. I wanted to check on Cheyenne. She's a beautiful young girl. She should be with her family. I'd hate to see her ripped from them." Regardless of what I think of Grady and his stupid deviant club, that has nothing to do with Cheyenne. She's just a teenager, and she's obviously scared out of her wits. Forgetting the gun entirely, I stare up at this man and meet his eyes. The shake of my hands is gone, and now it's just a mild straining in my muscles, like my body is instinctively preparing to run.

"Leave her alone!" I scream. I've heard so many stories about the club and what they're capable of. I want to tell this man that he had better not let the club hear him say that or it'll be the last thing he does. But that's not my place, and the club's affairs aren't my problem. But Cheyenne *is* my responsibility right now, and I have to think of what's best for her. Surely getting her out of here and away from this man is priority one.

"I do hate to be yelled at," he says dryly and slowly moves his hand to the gold gun and grips it. "Please don't make me hurt you."

My stomach drops, and I take a single step backward. Our eyes are locked on one another. I move back another step when he takes a step forward. The immediate need to get out of there takes over, and I turn around and run back to the door as fast as I can. I don't turn to see if he's following.

I just fling the door open and, once I'm on the other side, quickly slide the locks into place. My eyes lift up and peer out the window. The man is gone.

"What did he say?" she asks. I keep my mouth shut about it and instead bolt over to my desk, where I grab my purse and fish out my keys.

"Nothing, but we have to find your dad. Right now," I stammer out.

"He isn't answering my calls," she whines. "I tried Uncle Wyatt, but he isn't answering either. Should I call my Aunt Ruby?"

"Who?" I say as my eyes dart around the room. I try to think of a game plan. I know we need to get out of here, but I'm not sure how since I don't know where the man is. Would he really hurt us, or was this all about just scaring us?

"Uncle Jim, the president of the club. His wife," she says as she chews on her bottom lip and looks around fearfully. Recognition dawns on me, and I remember who Ruby is. I don't know what good calling her would do, but I don't argue. When I nod, Cheyenne pulls out her phone, slides her finger across the screen, and brings it to her ear. We need to act. I reach out and grab her hand and lead her down the back hallway toward Principal Beck's office. It's closest to the staff parking lot, and maybe, just maybe, we can get out that way without incident.

I keep my ears open as Cheyenne gives her Aunt Ruby the lowdown at warp speed. I've experienced it, and I'm not even sure what she says, she says it so fast. All I can hear on the other side is mumbling. Cheyenne makes the call short and slides the phone back into her pocket when she's done. Looking at me with tears welling in her eyes, she says, "They're in Church. They don't have their phones. Aunt Ruby is calling the prospects now. She said to stay put."

"You want to stay here?" I ask incredulously. I can't imagine anything worse than staying here like a sitting duck. Everything in me tells me that I have to get her out of here and to her dad.

"No—yes," she says quickly, and then corrects, "I don't know."

"We're not staying," I say. My body buzzes with fear and anticipation of all the awful things that could happen here. If I can get us in the car, we'll be safe. But here in this building with who knows how many old rusted locks and broken latches? Not just no, but hell no. I am *not* staying here.

"Okay, if you're sure," she mutters. Nothing in her voice or demeanor tells me that she trusts me. I can't blame her. I shouldn't be trusting me, either. I just can't stop thinking of the ways that man could get in here and how we're isolated enough from anyone else that nobody could hear our screams. The custodian could be anywhere on campus, and we no longer have campus security—they got laid off. So it's likely just her and me and that crazy bastard outside. No and thank you. We have to go.

At the back door, I tell Cheyenne to stay put, and then I rush around to the windows, looking to see if the man is anywhere in sight. Thankfully, this part of the building has pretty good visibility and not much blockage. Taking a deep breath, I grab Cheyenne's hand again, tighten my grip, and rush out the door with her. It's a short distance to my car, parked in the third spot from the door. I don't pause to look around, for fear that I might trip to waste time.

"It's unlocked!" I shout to Cheyenne as I let go of her hand and we part at the front of the car. She heads for the passenger door and I for the driver's side. In a matter of seconds we're inside the Jeep and locking our doors and then the backseat doors as well. I start her up, and we peel out of the lot with nobody else in sight. Still, I don't stop shaking until a few minutes later when we're pulling through the gates of the Forsaken Motorcycle Club's clubhouse.

Grady

☠CHAPTER 12☠

WE'RE AROUND THE table and about to vote on what to do with Junior. We just got through a waste-of-time rundown of what happened at The 101 Club. We've figured out that we don't got shit—no car, no witnesses, no evidence, and no fucking tracks. Which is just goddamn wonderful if you ask me. We didn't catch the car that was used to get away when some prick fired a couple of rounds into the place. Didn't even get a glimpse of it, like it's a fucking ghost.

Jim brought it to the club to talk about moving Junior out of the safe house and into someplace more permanent. We've talked about this twice now, and moving him has been voted down both times. I already asked him if this was Ruby holding his dick again, or if this was his idea. The old man swears it's his idea, but I fucking doubt it. For every ounce of support and loyalty she's shown that man, he owes her, at the very least, giving her his ear every now and then. I only fucking wish he had the fucking spine to tell her no once in a while. One more call from his Old Lady, and I'm gonna call to patch her ass in. Apparently she's running this shit anyway.

Speaking of chicks that think they're running shit, I'm about to have to have a "Come to Jesus" moment with Holly about how she's avoiding me— again. The situation was ridiculous two weeks ago. Now it's just pissing me the fuck off. Guess she doesn't realize that the more she tries to run, the more intent I am on catching her, especially after she showed me what she's made of behind all of her arrogance and indignation. I've been by her place enough times. She never answers the door. Her roommate, Mindy, thinks Holly and I are in the middle of a messy break-up, which is a good thing. It means she does know how to keep her mouth shut. Now, if only she'd let me make good on my end of our bargain, and take the fucking cash. The crazy bitch threw twenty-five grand out of her car window, so I'm pretty sure she won't accept it, but that's just too fucking bad. At every turn she's shown that she can handle her shit and she can handle mine, so fuck that. We're just going to keep playing this dance until she gives up.

"I'm telling you, the kid may be a Grade-A asshole, but he's got some theories on Mancuso's next play," Duke says from across the table. He takes a drag of his cigarette, holds the smoke in a moment, and then blows it out like it's the best goddamn thing he's ever had his lips on, and that's saying something since I know the bitch he has in his bed. Nic's hot—a little young for my taste—and she used to be a real party girl, but now that Duke's dumb ass went and knocked her up, she's all about nobody smoking around her and being healthy and shit. It's the right thing to do, but now this asshole has to get his fix in Church. Wouldn't bother me if he could just stop looking like he's just shot a load into his jeans while he's doing it.

"We're not moving him," Ryan says from my left. His voice is strained, and his muscles are tight. He's really not having any of this conversation, but too bad for his bitch ass, we each get a vote. Ryan can't see past his hatred for the guy, and while it's understandable, we really need him to get his head in the game and to start voting smart, not angry.

Some months back, Jim called in a marker he'd put in with the club decades ago. His Old Lady, had a couple of kids—twins—that were taken from her. Jim promised her that even though she didn't have custody of the kids, should they ever need it, he'd keep them safe. It was one of those things he agreed to and then forgot about, but then just before summer, he had to call in that fucking marker. And as if rescuing a teenage girl from the Italian fucking mafia on their own turf isn't stupid enough, we ended up rescuing a teenage girl who ratted her own father out. My word is my word, so I went and did my thing. It was a club vote, and the club voted that the girl is family, so I kept my mouth shut, played my part, and let it go. But then Ryan had to go and fall for the bitch, and now shit's all fucked up again.

"He's of no use to us as long as he's living in that shithole," Duke says, leaning in toward Ryan. "I get that this is personal for you, but you gotta let it go, brother. Princess has." Ryan's head cocks to the side just slightly, and he narrows his eyes. Ryan has an itchy trigger finger because Junior beat the shit out of the girl, Alex, until she had her ribs busted up and she could barely see from her swollen eyes. Can't say I'd let that shit go, either. If Layla had taken a beating like that, the motherfucker would be dead. Even if he was my own brother, I'd gut him and let him watch me tear his intestines out of his body.

"Do I?" Ryan says.

"Yeah," Duke says like it's the most obvious thing in the world.

"Like you let it go when Darren tried to rape Nic? Like you handled that? Is that what I should do?"

"That's different, brother," Duke says. "That piece of shit fucking raped her more times than your dumb ass can count and then he tried to rape her with *my* baby inside of her. *Mine.* He hurt her, and he made her think she was shit. Princess took a couple of pops and walked away from it. Nic's still trying to figure her shit out. Do *not* fucking compare the two."

"Hey!" Wyatt shouts. "Neither of those situations should have ever happened. The club failed both of them. The last thing I want to think about is how we let a member's kid get raped...again and a-fucking-gain...and how we let a member of our family be kidnapped from under our noses. So let's move the fuck on, already, shall we?"

With that, the bickering comes to a halt and we take a vote. It comes back tied with 5-5, and it all starts up again. We've moved past the bitching about what Junior did to Alex, and now we're onto figuring out where we would even put the kid if we did vote to move him.

Heavy thuds sound at the solid wooden door. I peer up at the door, over my brothers' heads, and try to bite back my anger. The prospects and the lost girls know better than to interrupt us during Church. Something better be on fire, or somebody's head is about to fucking roll.

Fish jumps up and goes to the door. When he opens it, one of the prospects barges in. He's got a cell phone to his ear and his face is pale white. He's a short thing, and stocky, but he's built as fuck. We call him Squat and, until about five seconds ago, he was one of the ones I thought we'd patch in. *Stupid fuck.*

"Mancuso got to Miss Priss," Squat shouts and turns around back out the door. My stomach sinks as my worst fears are realized. Miss Priss is the name Ruby gave Cheyenne when she was a toddler. Despite her raising, Chey's always been a girly girl. My brothers waste no time getting on their feet and rushing out after him. I launch myself from my seat and push to the front of the crowd. Every thought I have vanishes as I go on auto-pilot.

"She's holed up at the high school in the office with one of the employees," Squat says as he moves out of my way. My brothers and I grab our phones and guns from behind the bar in the main room and rush out the front door into the parking lot. Our bikes are all backed up in an orderly line against the side of the building. I'm two feet away from mine when a familiar white Jeep barrels into the parking lot, past the open gates. The vehicle comes skidding to a halt, and before it's even fully stopped, the passenger side door swings open and Cheyenne jumps out.

I'm stone still for a moment as I force myself to check back in. Chey's here, and she's safe as long as she's within these gates. Her lips are parted, and her chest heaves with panic. Her eyes flash from the left to the right and back again before they settle on me. She lets out a deep breath and runs at me so fast that when she reaches me, I have to take a step back from the impact.

Instantly, I wrap my arms around her and crush her to me. The rush of fear, and then the gratitude of having her here and safe, is practically unbearable. I squeeze her small body until I feel her tapping out on my lower back. It's something she's done since she was in grade school, which is apparently when my hugs got too tight and started to smother her. I can't help it. The more independent she becomes, the tighter I want to hold on to the little girl she once was.

"Can't," she whispers and takes in a shaky breath, "breathe." I loosen my grip and let her go.

"Sorry, sweetheart," I say. I give her a moment to calm down before I find out what's going on. My eyes lift to the Jeep just as the driver climbs out. It's Holly Mercer, and she looks more than a little uncomfortable being here. As she should.

"You," I shout and point at Holly. Her jaw slacks, and she lifts a finger, pointing at her own chest. I nod and crook my finger to order her over to me. She tightens her jaw back up, and straightens her back as she walks over. Finally, it seems she's learned to follow a fucking order when she hears one. It's about damn time I found something that knocks her off her game. She's one hard-headed bitch.

She goes to open her mouth, but I shake my head. "Don't."

Yanking my cell out of my pocket, I dial Ruby's cell and wait for her to pick up. She answers on the second ring. "That was quick."

"Chey's at the clubhouse," I say, hoping to give her some peace of mind.

"Are you shittin' me?" she says in disbelief. "I told her to keep her ass at the school."

My eyes cut to Holly. Guess I gave her too much credit for following orders. I say a quick thanks to Ruby then hang up the phone and shove it back in to my pocket. "What happened, Chey?" I ask.

"This scary dude was leaning on my car when I left football practice. He said he had a message for you," she says. She waits a beat before saying, "I ran into the office and told Holly."

"Why didn't you call me?" I ask as gently as I can.

"I did. You didn't answer," she says quietly. That sinking feeling returns. We don't bring phones or guns into the chapel – with rare exception, –so of course, I wouldn't know she called. Doesn't matter though. My kid needed me and I wasn't there. Nothing else can make me feel as low as being unable to help Chey does.

"What did Holly do?" I ask Cheyenne. Holly's mouth opens, and I put my finger in the air to silence her. I'll hear from her in a minute. I want to hear from Cheyenne right now.

"She ran outside and told the guy to leave," Chey says with her eyes sliding over to Holly. I take my eyes off my daughter and scan the parking lot. My brothers are all standing around and listening. They're smoking and keeping an eye on the open clubhouse gates. I catch Wyatt's gaze and nod toward Chey. He's at her side in a minute, leading her inside for a soda and to chill out. Once she's out of earshot, I look to Holly and signal her to follow me as I walk into the clubhouse. She follows close behind as we walk through the main room and down the hallway, and practically bumps into me when I pause at the door to my room. I doubt she'll talk openly in front of the club, but maybe if I get her alone I can get a few things out of her besides insults.

I open the door and let her in first. She walks in cautiously, her eyes everywhere but on me. She's different from how she normally is around me—mean and bitter. Right now, she's quiet and compliant. It's good to know she's not a raging nut case all the time— not that the raging nut case doesn't get my dick hard. She starts going off and gets me torqued up and acting irrational and shit, and that's good for no one. I haven't met anyone who could piss me off as bad as Holly Mercer can, and that's saying something considering the assholes I share a patch with. Every time we're in the same space shit gets explosive. We're all trying to keep a low profile on behalf of the club right now.

As it is, I've got Detective Gonzales all over my ass to come down to the station to answer a few questions about the recent assault on a local named Darren Jennings. Apparently someone saw a van that looks similar to one the club owns in the neighborhood the night Jennings's body was dumped in his dad's driveway. As if we don't have enough shit to deal with, now we get to deal with the cops crawling up our asses because Duke had to be a prick. Not that Darren didn't deserve what he got.

"Ruby told you to stay put," I say. It's the first thing that comes to mind. Not the most important thing to be focusing on, but I want to know what the fuck she was thinking when she drove my kid through town while one of Mancuso's men is here. And at Chey's fuckin' school no less.

"That was terrifying," she says as she folds her arms over her chest. She's seething mad. Her eyes are narrowed, and everything her gaze lands on receives a dirty fucking look if I've ever seen one. That natural pretty shines through even her pissed face. She sucks in deep breaths that go in steady and blow out unsteadily. My eyes catch sight of her chest rising and falling and I'm back to thinking about bending her over shit.

"I don't even know what that was about, but I *never* want to be sucked into your club's crap like that again."

Now I'm glad I brought her in here. I can deal with a little sass behind a closed door, but in front of my brothers? We'd have a real big problem. I should consider it a problem even in here without any witnesses, but there's something about this woman that just makes me not give a shit that she's throwing me attitude. I haven't had anything new in a while and might as well see what I can do. I haven't been fucked proper in a while and even an uptight bitch with a smart mouth and a nice ass has me forgiving shit I shouldn't.

Going soft is one of the reasons Ruby wants us all settled at home. You don't got a steady woman, you go soft on all of them, she says. I guess she's right.

Women like Holly are nothing but trouble, and trouble is the last fucking thing I need. Still, she's hot and fiery and God help me, but I like it. Still, I'm chalking up my interest in her to a temporary bout of insanity. I was all emotion last week, but as much as I enjoyed having my hands all over her like that, I really shouldn't entertain the idea of letting this shit spiral out any further than it already has. I lock my shit down and focus in on what I need to take care of for right now.

"Tell me what happened," I say and lean against the door. She paces for a moment with her thumb in her mouth. She bites down hard enough to wince and then pulls it out. When she swings around, her eyes are wild and her hands shake at her sides.

"I don't even know," she says. "I was at my desk. Cheyenne came running in saying there was a weird man at her car who had a message for you." Her words come out quickly, but the last one has a bit more punch than the rest. Yeah, she's real unhappy with me right now. "I went outside and told him he couldn't be on campus, and I told him to leave Cheyenne alone. He didn't like that much, and he told me that Mr. Man—Mancini, I think—his business partners are here and they need to meet with you."

"You mean Mancuso?" I ask. Before I can get the word out, she's snapping her fingers and nodding.

"That's it," she says then starts pacing again. "Anyway, he

said they need to talk about an acquisition and something about a hostile takeover, and then it was weird. He said something about the club not wanting to give up some assets. It didn't make much sense, but then he said something about aggressive tactics. I just, I can't do that again. Look at me, I'm shaking," she says and lifts a shaking hand up to my face.

Shit.

"Anything else?"

"I asked him why he couldn't go to you himself, and he said he wanted to check on Cheyenne," she says and trails off. She places her hand over her mouth and gasps. Whatever she's thinking about is frightening her, which is putting me on edge.

She rushes up to me, places her hands on my chest and says, "He threatened her. He said he'd hate to see anything happen to her, and when I started to freak out, he asked me to not make him hurt me."

Everything in the room comes into focus. Even the tiny imperfections in the paint job where the wall meets the ceiling are crystal clear. I can hear everything around me. Forcing myself to be hyper aware is the only way I can shut down the straight-up panic attack I'm about to have. It's rare that I find myself losing control and turning into a madman, but fucking with my kid is sure to do it every time. Cheyenne is the only good thing that came of my marriage to Layla, and she's worth every goddamn headache and heartache I've had over her bitch mother. I can't live in a world where my kid doesn't, and even the faintest suggestion of losing her is enough to make me shut down entirely. But I can't go there and let that happen. People depend on me. Letting them down can get them killed. My brothers deserve better than that. So instead, I let myself slip into autopilot where I can just take care of shit without thinking too much about what I'm doing.

"You and Chey are both safe," I tell her and reach up and awkwardly place my hand on her shoulder. She's not calling me an asshole or screaming at me, so I try to do what I can to keep shit calm. Her eyes drift to my hand and, very slowly, she removes her hands from my chest. Something doesn't sit right with me with the way she removes her hands, but instead of thinking on it, I file it away for later. I'm never going to figure this woman out, and there's no reason I should want to. When I take my hand off her shoulder, she backs up. I push off the door and then open it with every intention of walking out without saying anything else. But the look on Holly's face is so pathetic that it stabs at something in me, and I find myself trying to comfort her. "You trust that I'm going to keep you safe?"

She gives little more than a non-committal murmur that I don't understand, but as I stride out of the room she whispers so low I shouldn't even be able to hear it, "I want to."

On my way down the hall and into the main room where my brothers are all sitting around and talking strategy, I let that tiny bit of confidence Holly has in me push me to make good on my promise. My kid is safe as long as she's with us—which is where she's going to stay—but I have no clue what I'm going to do with Holly. I doubt she'll be gung-ho about staying with me until this shit blows over, and I can't lock her up in the basement for her own safety. Although, it would serve her right for being so fucking difficult. Regardless of what I end up doing with her, right now I need to get Ian and one of our prospects to take her and Chey to the house to be with my mother, who should be home right about now. I need them safe with a few of my brothers so I can focus on finding this asshole and demonstrating why his little stunt is the last mistake he will ever make.

☠ CHAPTER 13 ☠

WE DON'T HAVE any fucking clue where this guy is, let alone *who* he is!" Duke shouts from across the table. We're in Church—again. I'm starting to think I should just move into this fucking room with how many club meetings we've had lately. This shit is necessary, and I need to keep my head in the game, but I can't stop my foot from tapping on the floor in a show of impatience. I just want to get home to Chey and make sure she's okay. I still need to figure out what to do with Holly, and I need to calm my mother down. No doubt she's half past crazy right now.

"That prick isn't going to help us. He's just going to lead us around by our dicks," Diesel gripes from the far end corner of the table. Beside him is Chief's empty seat. If he were here, he'd know what to do. Having to sit and stare at that vacant space makes it hard to trust in what we're doing.

We're back at it about Michael. Especially now that this Italian cocksucker has shown up and targeted my girl, it's even more important that we get better intel. When we got back to the clubhouse half an hour ago, every one of us looked totally defeated and mentally wiped. We rode around looking for that asshole for a good hour before giving up.

Fort Bragg isn't big enough to spend any longer than that looking for the guy. He sticks out enough that when we asked local business owners if they'd seen him, a few of them were able to confirm that they had. The last time we had some asshole walking around in a two thousand dollar suit it was when Junior swung into town and tried to kill his sister for information on the club. So far we got Mr. Hill from the hardware store on the look-out. That old man is nosey as fuck and one of the best locals to have on your side if you need anything. Loyal as he is stubborn.

"Anybody think to run this by Lank?" Bear says from beside Diesel. Lank is Thomas Lankershim, a dirty cop who's had his mouth on our dicks for the better part of a decade. I shake my head and lean forward.

"Lank is out of touch right now, got it?" I say. Diesel and Bear exchange a confused look, and Fish shakes his head. Only Duke seems to fucking get it. "Not to beat a dead horse or nothing, but we got the FBPD inspecting our balls right now over that Darren shit. For *some* reason, they have witnesses that place our van at the scene."

"We got it, Knuck," Wyatt says, using part of my club nickname. "Let that horse die."

"I'm just saying," I say, completely unable to let it go. "We have to be more careful about the shit we're pulling out there. We got too much going on to make mistakes."

"For the last goddamn time, that was not a mistake," Duke

snaps. I go to open my mouth when Jim slams his gavel down and screams. His face is bright red, veins stick out at his temples, and he is shaking with anger.

"Enough!" he says. "All this bullshit is getting us nowhere. We're just spinning our wheels. If you assholes don't have anything else constructive to add, go home and get your dicks sucked."

Duke scrubs at his face and slams his hand down on the table and says, "Fuck." I look over the empty chair beside me and find that, for once, Ryan is calm. He's our resident hothead and the guy most likely to lose his shit or shoot someone. I can only surmise that without Ian at the table, he doesn't have anyone to keep him in check so he's having to watch his own ass for once. Maybe I should send Ian off on missions more often if this is how Ryan is without him here to cool him down.

Jim dismisses us. After a few words with Wyatt, I head down the hall to get home to my kid. Ryan rushes up beside me, gives me a hard look, and says, "Can we talk?"

"What about?" I ask, hoping it's not about his bitch again. The last time we went over the shit with Alex it didn't go so well, and now is not the time for him to be coming to me about this crap.

"Miss Priss," Ryan says. I stop dead in my tracks and stare him down. Whatever it is, it better be good. He and I are on thin ice right now, and while I don't think he's going to start something, I never can be totally sure with him. Ryan's always been a loose cannon, but he's also always looked out for Chey. Back in the day he used to keep an eye on her when Layla would unexpectedly drop her off at the shop while I was busy. He's barely twenty-five, and only eight years her senior, but in a way he's like the big brother she never had. Whatever my personal feelings are about the shit with Alex, I could never totally turn my back on a guy who has done right by my kid.

"I might have a lead," he says and looks around to make sure no one else can hear.

"And why am I just hearing about this now?" I ask.

"Not up for a lecture from the king," he says and nods in the direction of his father. I lift my chin and raise my brows to let him know that I'm listening. "Guy who deals blow in Mendo, he's got a cousin who's hard-up for street cred down in Richmond. The cousin works for Homeland Security. Word is he's been taking bribes for years, only his clientele dried up with a couple of RICO sweeps. He has access to passenger manifests for pretty much every airport nationally."

A slow smile spreads on my face. Ryan may be a Grade-A asshole, but he's slick, that's for sure. The guy's formed connections with every kind of loser you can imagine. Sometimes, like now, it pays off. Having access to a motherfucking Homeland Security employee with proper access to passenger manifests is going to come in handy. I almost don't give a shit what we have to do to get this guy in our pocket. If he proves useful, I'll even let the guy suck my dick as a thank you present.

"What does he need?" I ask. I was hoping to get back home soon, but that looks like it's going to be a no-go.

Getting an identity on this asshole is priority one.

"His grandma lives near the docks. Her house has been broken into twice this month. Two other women have been mugged and had the crap beat out of them. Dude needs to know his grandma is safe, but he can't afford to pay street rent anymore. Shit started when he stopped paying."

Typical. Places like Richmond are riddled with crime, and the cops don't have enough staff in the county, let alone the city, to stop it all. Street gangs have taken over and made it a place nobody actually wants to live in, but they can't afford to move out after they've paid protection money to the gangs. It's total bullshit. And some people think *we're* assholes.

"We're already stretched thin, and Richmond is a five hour ride from here," I say. "We don't have the manpower to bust into the barrio and swing our dicks around."

"You trust me?" Ryan asks.

I don't even pause to think about it before saying, "Yes."

Just because we don't always get along doesn't mean I don't trust him. He's my brother, and that shit runs deeper than any beef I'll ever have with him.

"Then let me handle it. Go home. Tell Miss Priss I say hi," he says and slaps me on the back as he walks away. I stand in place and watch Ryan walk away. I let myself have a single moment to consider that maybe Alex has been good for him. He's always been a bastard, but he's a good guy to have watch your six. All the bullshit he causes sometimes makes me forget that I actually almost like the guy.

The street is dead quiet with few lights on inside the

sparsely-set homes. The neighborhood hasn't changed much since I bought my house back when Cheyenne was a toddler. A few of my neighbors have remodeled their homes over the years, but by and large, everything looks the same. With so much changing so often in my life, this kind of steady is exactly what I need.

At the end of my street, there's a large clearing. I bought the house that butts up to it. The closer I get to my split-level, the more at peace I feel. There's a part of me that's always on edge, has been for the better part of twenty years, but here—in my home—sometimes I can take a deep breath and not tense up that it's going to be my last.

I swing my bike into the driveway and give a nod to Ian, who's sitting on the front porch, his feet resting on the railing and his hands in his lap. I can't see it, but I know he's got a piece resting on his legs. I park my bike in front of the garage next Ian's and Jeremy's, and don't bother covering her up. If it starts to rain, I'll put her away later. Once my helmet is off and she's resting on her kickstand, I set my helmet on her handlebars and give Ian a nod.

"Alarm's on for the perimeter except here in the front. Baby Boy's been doing sweeps of the backyard every ten minutes. So far we're clear," Ian says and stands from his position. In his right hand is a stun gun. In his left is a semi-automatic with a suppressor attached to the barrel.

"Good," I say. "Thanks for hanging out, but I got it."

"I don't mind. I can stay, brother."

"Your sister needs you," I say and slap him on the back. The guy's already going through some serious shit, and I don't need to be adding to his plate. Ever since we brought Alex to Fort Bragg, Ian's been having to deal with some fucked-up shit. I know it eats away at him. Knowing you have twin siblings out there somewhere is one thing. Being confronted with them face to face the way he is, is another story altogether. Ever since we found Alex, bloody and beaten, at the hands of her twin brother, Michael, Ian's been more distant than usual.

"Yeah, she does," he says and waves me off. As he turns, the light catches the scar that runs from his ear to his mouth. I wonder if he forgets it's there, if it's so much a part of him that he doesn't feel it when he shaves. Or if every day he can feel it, the bumpy, cracked skin that never healed properly.

Inside the house, all is silent. The front room is empty, as it usually is. There's no television in there, so we have little reason to spend time in that room. Still, the light is on. Bypassing the main hallway, I walk the perimeter rooms, starting with the kitchen. The light is on in here, too, as well as the family room before me. The kitchen is a large, open space that oversees the family room. When my mother moved in about twelve years ago, she told me to expect a lot of home-cooked meals because a kitchen like this deserves to be used. I don't eat here much, but she and Chey make doing dinner together a regular thing. Still, despite the open space, I can't see a single person. Reaching into the back of my jeans, I pull out my .45 and hold it down at my side.

With my eyes wide open, I walk slowly and cautiously through the dining room and into the family room. Still nothing. Movement catches my eye from the back porch. I raise my gun up and creep toward the sliding glass door. Just as I reach the glass, I lower my gun and blow out a frustrated breath.

On the back porch, leaning over, with their arms resting on the railing, are Jeremy and Cheyenne. They're facing one another, and she's smiling. Wide. She's giving him the same smile she gives me when she tries to convince me she's going to bring her grades up in time for the end of the term. It's the same smile she gives her grandma when she makes Chey's favorite dessert. Now I raise my gun for a whole different reason. I don't care if she is seventeen. Jeremy Whelan does not deserve her smiles, and he certainly doesn't deserve the giggle she's giving him. He's not patched yet. I could shoot him, and my brothers couldn't say much about it. Except for Duke. He'd catch hell from Jeremy's older sister—Duke's woman, Nic. But she's not my bitch, so it's not my problem. I *could* shoot him.

In the reflection of the glass, I can see my mother standing several feet behind me. She places her hands on her hips and says, "Oh, for heaven's sake. They're just talking. Put down the damn gun."

I turn around slowly, put my gun in the waistband of my jeans, and roll my shoulders to release some of the built-up tension. She's been giving me crap about letting Chey date for years. It's not that I won't let her date. She's more than welcome to date. She just chooses not to more often than not. I guess she doesn't like to go through the hassle of trying to ditch my tail and failing anyway. I'll give her credit for trying, though. She's definitely getting better at that.

"You hear about today?" I ask her.

"You'll find him," she says. And that's my mother. She doesn't answer questions if she's certain you already have the answer. "I want to know why he targeted my granddaughter."

"You and me both. Ryan's working a lead right now. We got eyes and ears in town working in our favor. We're gonna find him, Ma."

She sighs heavily, and it's one of those rare times that her age shows. Her mouth turns down, smile lines become more apparent, and crow's feet spread outward as she narrows her eyes. Her dark brown hair has fewer grays in it than mine does—thanks to Violet at the salon she goes to with Ruby every six weeks. She's not intimidating in size like Elle is, but when she gets going there's no stopping her. Disapproval from Lisa Grady is almost worse than being on the business end of an enemy's gun. The woman should have been born Catholic the way she throws around guilt trips like they're fucking antacids. And I can tell, just by that single sigh, that she's about to deliver up a doozy.

"What's going on?" she asks. "I know Ruby's daughter is here, and I know why. Don't pull my leg with vague answers. Just tell me how bad it is."

"A fucking mobster showed up at your granddaughter's school today. How bad do you *think* it is, Ma?" I snap and instantly regret it. She has every right to her concern, and here I am being a dick about it.

"We've been over this, son. You pull that macho crap with everybody else, but need I remind you that I am your mother? I choose to be here for Cheyenne. I don't *have* to be. Now, start talking."

Ball buster. She's a fucking ballbuster, but I'd be lost without her. Layla hasn't spent more than a night under this roof in the last five years and no more than a few months in the last ten. Always in and out of rehab and then out drifting. I'd be fucked if my mom wasn't here to do all the domestic shit with Chey. A guy like me has to go when he needs to and not worry about finding a babysitter.

"Ruby's ex wants his daughter back, and he's got his men coming to get her. He's not too pleased that we turned his house into Swiss cheese, and he's probably pretty ticked off that we got his son now, too, and took down a few of his men in the process. It's going to get worse before it gets better, and I don't know how many men he's got coming out here. All I know is that shit is not safe. If I had the manpower to cover you, I'd send you and Chey down south to stay until it all gets sorted out, but I don't. So I need you to do as you're told so you don't put yourself or anyone else in any more danger than you're already in."

Like the old hand that she is, my mother agrees and listens intently as I spell it out for her. No going out alone. No answering the door for anyone. No talking to or about anyone involved with this shit over the phone or outside of this house. The list is extensive, and by the time I get to the end, her eyes are glazing over. It's not like we haven't been through this before. It's just that this time it's not some petty beef about territory and clientele. This time it's about revenge and family loyalty—two things that will always stir

REV

up dust in ways that nothing else can.

A floorboard creaks from the hallway. In a split second, I have my gun out and pointed at the noise. My mother moves behind me and curls into my back. There's another creak and then an earth-shattering scream. Shit. Holly.

With everything going on, I'd totally forgotten that Holly would be in the house. I move in to find her sliding down the wall in the hallway. Her hands are up in front of her, waving me away. They shake just slightly in their movements. The sliding glass door rolls open and slams against the stopper, creating another commotion. From my side, Jeremy rushes into the room with a gun I didn't know he had pointing out in front of him. With his other hand, he's holding Chey behind him, blocking her. He's shielding my little girl, and while his head is still on the chopping block, I think I'll let him live for now.

"It's okay," my mother says, raising her hands to Jeremy and Chey. "We just scared Holly, that's all." Baby Boy lowers his gun and places it in the waistband of his jeans. Fucking kid didn't even put the safety on first. Either that or he didn't unlock the safety before he stormed in here.

"Who the fuck gave you a gun?" I ask. When we let Jeremy prospect at seventeen, he didn't know how to drive a car, much less ride a Harley. He's also still in high school—for now—and has zero experience handling a gun. The day he received his vest, he also received one of my old bikes to learn on. He's been riding for a few months now and is getting pretty good at it. Still, we agreed no guns until after he turned eighteen.

"Trigger," he says. I should have fucking known. Ryan got the name Trigger because back when he was learning to shoot, he'd shoot anything that moved. Unfortunately for his grandfather, Rage—a retired club member—Ryan's first real shot was at the old man's foot.

I motion for him to hand me the gun then check the safety. Sure enough, the safety isn't on. I click it on and shake my head. "You're gonna blow your fucking dick off." I cast Chey a quick look to see that her eyes are on Jeremy. She's got this look on her face like she thinks he just saved Tokyo from Godzilla or some other fucking amazing thing like that. I turn the safety back off and hand the gun over. "On second thought, go ahead and blow it off."

When I turn back around, Holly is standing and rubbing her eyes. She looks from me to my mother to Jeremy and Cheyenne and then back to me. "I can't handle having one more person pointing a gun at me today," she says and blows out a shaky breath.

"What do you mean," Chey asks. "Did that man at school have a gun?" Her voice rises with every word, and she's growing panicked as the seconds pass. I don't like to lie to my kid, but I can't bring myself to tell her that all mobsters carry guns. The world hasn't jaded her yet. She stills sees the good in people, and I don't want to take that away from her. The rest of the world will do that for me soon enough. I don't miss the sly admission from Holly though. She didn't tell me the bastard pulled a gun on her earlier. We'll have to talk about that, just not where Chey can hear.

☠CHAPTER 14☠

ALL IT TAKES is my mother saying the words ice cream and Chey is wondering off to the kitchen. I don't miss the way she bites her lip and bats her eyes at Jeremy when she asks him if he wants any. And I definitely don't fucking miss the way he says he'd like some of her ice cream. That prick isn't eating anything of hers. He's eating *my* ice cream. I don't remind him whose house he's in only because of the look my mother is giving me. I already know my protectiveness over Chey is, apparently, a little unhealthy. And I'll work on that one day. Just not today.

"That asshole at the school pulled a gun on you?" I ask Holly. Her hair falls over her shoulders and stops just a few inches down her back. It's a messy rat's nest right now, which is sexy as fuck. The doe-eye blinking thing she's doing, and the stuttering as she tries to get the story out, and the hair… I'm not twelve anymore. I shouldn't feel like I have to go into a bathroom and rub one out just to have a conversation with a chick.

"He didn't exactly point it at me, but it was in a holder thing on his hip. He showed it to me," she says. In a matter of seconds she goes from scatter-brained to annoyed, and she's scowling at me. "I want to go home."

I had a feeling she'd get here at some point. She wants to go home, but I'm not sure that's the best place for her right now. I doubt Mancuso's guy has anything on her, but I can't be so sure. He had enough on me to get to Chey, and while he didn't actually hurt either Chey or Holly—and he certainly could have if he wanted to—it fucks me up to think about either of them out on their own. The guy's clearly got some resources, and until I know what they are, I don't know that I'm good with letting Holly leave.

Wyatt suggested I let her go home and have one of the guys sit on her, but I don't think we have enough resources for that. As it is, we're stretched to the limit. We got guys watching the roads in and out of here during high traffic times, and we got guys watching Alex at Jim and Ruby's. We had ten patched members, but that was before. Now we're down to nine. I can't see pulling anyone off of Alex. If I let Holly walk, then she's going unprotected. And I still don't know if I can trust her to keep her mouth shut.

"Follow me," I say and turn around. When no movement sounds behind me, I pause and turn back to find that she's standing in the same place with her lips pursed and her arms folded over her chest. Out of all the shit I could do to this woman—shit so depraved that she probably can't even fathom it—and how goddamn patient I've been, she still doesn't trust me.

"Fine," I say. I let my feet carry me away from the kitchen and toward the far side of the house past the guest room. It's not until I'm already in the garage that I hear her footsteps. When she appears in the doorway, it's just her head and hands as she grips the frame and peeks around. Layla doesn't enter rooms like that. She just kind of floats in. Always has. Elle doesn't just enter a room. She fucking owns it. But not Holly. She's not a part of my world, and I try to remind myself of that for the fiftieth time. I can't expect her to know how shit goes when she's never been a part of anything like this.

Ignoring her, I tag a couple of beers from the aging refrigerator in the corner near my bench saw and crack them open. I give her a brief glance over my shoulder and head over to the mess that takes up an entire car bay. Set atop a work blanket, I have most of the parts of the 1972 Shovelhead that I've been working on for the last few months. It's a slow project, but one day I'll get her upright and racing. Right now she looks like nothing more than a pile of crap—all dirty and scratched up—but she's going to be a beauty when I'm done with her.

Taking a couple swigs of my beer, and setting the other one on the wooden chair beside me, I sit myself on the floor and get to cleaning the old oil out of some of the smaller parts. I hate cleaning this shit up, but the prospects never do it right. I keep telling them that to make something work well, you have to take care of it, and when you're building a bike that means making sure her parts are in the best condition possible. But they're all young and impatient and they have yet to learn how to give care to do something right.

"What are we doing in here?" Holly asks from behind me. I can't tell where she is in the room, and that puts me on edge. I should be able to track her movements. Having spent years honing my senses, I should be capable of following the subtle hints that tells me where she's gone and when she goes. Little things like the scent of her perfume drifting past me, the quiet little murmurs of clothing as pieces brush against each other, and the careful pitter patter of her feet against the cool concrete floor. But her voice feels so close and yet so far at the same time. It's like she's closing in on me and dulling my senses.

"Building a bike," I say then clear my throat to rid my voice of its hoarseness. "And having a beer." I clear my throat again, but still, it sounds so gravelly and unnerved even to my own ears. What the hell is wrong with me?

"I don't drink beer," she says. Her voice is closing in now, and her jean-clad thighs swish as she approaches. It's the wrong visual—now I have the image of Holly, spread bare and tossed over the open tail gate of the bed of my truck that takes up the second bay of the garage. I've never been all that patient, and I've always struggled with being told no. Once I want something, I have a hell of a time not having it. And the more time I spend with this woman, the more I want her, and the less I'm willing to accept that she won't let me have her. Until I can see for myself, her thighs will haunt me.

But more importantly, who the hell doesn't drink beer?

"Why's that?" I ask, opting out of bullshitting with her and just being direct.

"I just don't like it," she says, her voice even nearer now. She sounds so serious with her words not so much clipped as they are decided.

"Wine?" I ask. My mother keeps wine on-hand with the excuse that Chey and I are too much of a handful not to imbibe once in a while. Holly shakes her head no.

"I don't drink," she says in a small voice.

When I hit Gonzales up for a profile on her, she practically shit her pants. Didn't want to give it up, and didn't want to even look into her. Miss Holly Mercer is the favorite niece of Harry Mercer, a half-genius sergeant for the Fort Bragg P.D., who happens to be Angel Gonzales's supervising officer. Angel's done a lot of shit for the club over the years, and she's never complained about it, but this favor cost me more than I'd like to admit.

Despite the cost, when Gonzales got me the intel I needed on Holly, it told me everything from her GPA upon graduation from high school—3.1 average—to her brief stint at Humboldt State, her subsequent departure, and then her relocation to San Francisco. Somehow Gonzales even managed to find out innocuous things like Holly's preference for vanilla over chocolate and her fear of butterflies. I can't even process what the butterfly thing is about, but every little piece of information in that report did more than just give me a snapshot of who I'm dealing with. It told me a story of a woman who is neither a goody two shoes nor a hard ass. In the short time I've known her, she's shown herself to be neither fearful nor particularly brave. By now I'd normally know everything I need to about a person of interest, but with Holly, the more I know the more I realize I don't know. Like how she apparently doesn't like to drink—at all.

"That a court-ordered deal?" I ask. She comes around and sits down with her legs crossed beside me. Her proximity practically suffocates me. She's all soap and sweet smells. Not over-powering like my mother and Chey, but just right. Inviting. It's a welcome change from all the body odor and oil and cigarette smells I get from my brothers. It serves as one more reminder that even an asshole like me could use a little sweet in his life.

She looks down at the fuel line insulator and pile of bolts and washers I have set aside to build the carburetor. Horror fills my gut as she reaches out and picks up a bolt and a washer. It's not the end of the world, but I like to lay out my work area with all clean parts before I get started.

"I asked you a question."

"And I didn't answer," she says. She slips the washer over the bolt and watches as it slides down catches on the head. She's got a quarter-inch bolt with a three-quarter-inch washer that is far too large to fit properly.

"There a reason you won't cooperate?" I ask, set down the part I'm holding, and grab my beer. I should be angry with her, flat-out angry that she is being difficult. From the moment she came to in my guest room, she's been a pain in my ass. I've tried to bully her into submission, and it didn't work. I tried to threaten her, and that didn't work. She doesn't lash out, and she doesn't cower. Gentle didn't work and neither did mean, so all I have left to work with is being real and hope she responds to that.

"Is there a reason you haven't asked me what I want?" she says, clutching the bolt and washer in a closed fist. With a shake of her head and a heavy breath, she turns her body toward mine. It's a simple gesture, the turn of her body, but it's enough. She's talking. I can work with that.

"How much do you know about my club?"

"I know enough," she says. Only, with that kind of answer, it's clear that she doesn't.

"I know you don't like my methods, and you don't understand our ways, but you need to understand this—what we do as Forsaken is always in the best interest of the club. We're no different than your Uncle Harry and his boys. I will always protect my brothers."

"I guess that makes me collateral damage then," she says, nodding. Her shoulders slump in resignation, and she hunches forward just slightly.

"Yeah," I say. "I got a job to do, and you're making shit difficult at a really bad time."

"I'll take the money then," she says without taking her brown eyes off of mine.

"Good," I say and toss back half of my beer. I should leave it be, but I don't. It's that niggling desire to figure her out that forces the next words from my lips. "Why don't you want it? Someone in your position should be clawing at the chance to get their hands on that kind of money."

"It's not worth it," she says. Her eyes follow my beer as I

lift it up and finish it off. When I set the empty bottle on the concrete, she keeps her eyes glued to it for a moment before rolling her shoulders and looking everywhere but at me. "That kind of money would help, sure; but it's not worth what I'd have to give up."

"You're not answering any of my questions, and I'm losing patience," I grit out. My muscles are tensing. There isn't enough beer in the fridge to keep shit calm if she keeps this up. I haven't had to listen to anyone give me the runaround in conversation since the last time Chey missed her curfew. It was all one big web of excuses and no actual answers. Unfortunately, I don't think I can ground Holly for not being straight with me—not that it works so well when I try to ground Chey. I would, however, like to spank her again.

"Hey," she snaps. She leans forward and slaps at the ground with her free hand. She's close, so close I don't know if she intends to or not, but she's in my space. If I thought her presence was insufferable before, I was wrong. I breathe in her scent, and it's so strong this close. Undiluted. Her lips part, and her tongue sneaks out to lick her bottom lip. I glance down for half a second to watch, but it's too late. Her mouth forms a hard line, and I return my gaze to her eyes.

"I said I'd keep my mouth shut and I have. That short guy you got following me everywhere can tell you that I've kept my word. I don't want your money, but it's not because I'm going to rat on you. That's all you need to know." Her eyes are narrowed, and she's breathing heavy. It's sort of hot the way her chest heaves and her cheeks flush. I wonder what she would do if I just leaned over and told her I was going to fuck her until she couldn't argue with me anymore. But I don't. Women like Holly have expectations, and they're a complication that I refuse to bring into my life. I did it once, and I won't be doing it again.

She's mouthing off—it should be pissing me off.

But it's not.

Because, like with every other time I'm around her, I'm off my game. The only thing that's pissing me off right now is that she caught Squat following her. Stupid fuck isn't going to earn his top rocker at this rate.

"Why don't you drink?" I whisper. My eyes quickly glance down at her lips again. I'll bet she tastes as sweet as she looks.

"Why won't you let me go home?" she whispers back. The anger in her voice fades and is replaced with a soft murmur.

"Why don't you drink?" I repeat.

"I have enough trouble with making poor choices without alcohol, okay? Now, why won't you let me go home?

"Because we're building a bike," I say.

"Bullshit," she says. There's a defiant little bite to her tone that brings a smile to my face. She scowls at me, but it's more confused than angry. "You want me to be honest, but you don't want to be honest with me."

"That dickhead at the school today? He'll kill you." I've never had a problem with keeping my mouth shut before, but I told myself I'd be real with her. Real is an uncomfortable territory for me. It's my job to protect my brothers and safeguard our secrets. Part of that is keeping club business within the club, but the other part is information management. I haven't done such a great job at managing Holly so far, and if I don't get it under control soon, someone is going to start demanding that I take more drastic of measures to seal this shit off.

"But," she protests and retreats. Her eyes are wide, and she looks scared. I need her scared. Fear is the great motivator. Before she can get very far, I lean forward and grab the back of her neck and pull her close to me. Her nose is but an inch or two away from mine. Her body tenses up from the close proximity. She could consume me at this distance. Everything about this woman could suck me in and spit me out, leaving me confused as fuck for God only knows how long.

"That's his job, you know," I hiss. "He's from New York, and he's been sent here to kill his boss's daughter. Make no mistake that you mean nothing to him. He will slaughter you and sleep like a baby afterwards. You are inconsequential to him."

"Don't," she whispers. A single tear rolls down her cheek, and her lips tremble. "Don't tell me this."

I ignore her plea and continue, tightening up my grip on her neck so she knows I'm serious.

"I don't have men to put on you anymore. You're not a priority to the club. He kills you and that ties up our loose ends—that means if you leave this house, you're unprotected, so you might as well go home and decide which outfit you want your mother to bury you in, that is, assuming anyone finds your body."

☠CHAPTER 15☠

SEVERAL MORE TEARS fall down her cheeks but she doesn't take her eyes off mine. She keeps herself steady despite her fear, and that's something I can admire. She sucks in a shaky breath and fights off the wail that's about to escape.

"Shh," I whisper. I keep my voice gentle as I lean in and say, "It's okay." She sucks in a deep breath, her eyes widen, and she huffs. She lifts her fisted hands and pushes at my chest. Frustrated screams slip from her lips, and she closes her eyes as she tries with all her might to get away. It's not enough to loosen my grip, and when she realizes this, she starts throwing her fists into my chest with no more success than before.

Maybe I went too far, or maybe I went just far enough. I don't fucking know. But now she's freaking out with no sign of calming down. I wrap my free arm around her waist and pull her to me and crush her to my chest. Her head rests on my shoulder. I've had my share of women in my bed. I've even cared about a few of them, but I can't remember the last time I held one in my arms and comforted her.

She quiets instantly and stills in my arms, caught off guard by my actions. And then, she relaxes. She's not the only one. This whole situation is just getting way too fucked up. I should have let Fish or Ryan fuck with her just enough to put the fear of God into her ass. But now, now I have no fucking idea what I'm going to do with her. I've already shown myself that I can't hurt her, and I can't seem to bring myself to scare her like I should—even if it is for her own good—and with her refusing to cooperate, I'm in a difficult position. If I'm going to be honest with myself, I have a pretty good idea why I'm struggling with this situation.

She pulls back just slightly and looks me in the eyes. It's just a moment—one single moment in a hundred or so that we've shared. Her eyes mist over in the corners, and her chin shakes. She's vulnerable, and here, and I'm able to do what it is I wanted to do last week. So I don't waste any time. I tighten my grip on her and lick my lips. Her chin stops its movement, and she sucks in a shallow, nervous breath. She's gorgeous like this. I start to move my face closer to hers, about to take what I want so desperately.

Her arms reach up and wrap around my neck, and she's dragging her nose along my cheek. The sudden forwardness of her actions takes me by surprise. She's breathy and quiet and needy when she says, "This might be the worst idea I've ever had, but I don't care. I'm going to kiss you, and you're going to kiss me back."

I have to clear my throat to get the words out, and even

then it's rough and they practically get stuck in my throat. But I want this, possibly more than I've wanted anything in a long time, and for just right now I'm going to let that be okay. I'm a father, a brother, a soldier, but I'm also a man. "You sure you want to start this?"

"No, but you make me stupid," she says. Her eyes dart down to my lips. Half a second later, she's pressed up against me. Her lips ghost over mine, teasing me. I let her have her fun for half a moment before I pounce. With one arm cradling her and the other hanging onto her neck, I crawl over her and gently lay her on the floor beneath me. Resting my pelvis on hers, I create slow circles with my half-hard dick into her center. Our lips move together in an intense frenzy. At first it's all tugging at flesh and hard pecks at the corners, and then finally I'm slipping into the heat of her mouth. She's smooth and hot and wet and everything I expect and want from a kiss. Her pushiness and desire urges me on. My dick goes from semi-hard to practically fucking steel. She wraps her legs around my waist, but half a second later, she stops. I gave her plenty of warning, and now that we've started it, I'd like to fucking finish it. In an attempt to get her legs back where they were, I buck into her twice, but she doesn't move. Her kisses slow, and she untangles herself from around me. As she pulls back, panting and gorgeous, she says, "What about that short guy you have following me?"

I let go immediately, pull back and sit up. If she's going to play it like this, I'm fucking done now. I won't torture myself by trying to convince her to wrap her lips around my cock and suck like her life depends on it.

She scrambles to do the same. I don't want to stop what we're doing, nor do I want to let her go, but the mood is kind of broken at the mention of Squat. She shouldn't know that Squat has been following her. I thought he would have been able to handle it when I assigned him the task, but I obviously overestimated his dumb ass. I only put him on her to begin with because I trusted that he wouldn't fuck it up. He won't be able to earn his cut if he can't do something as simple as tailing someone without getting busted, and I'm not thinking too favorably of him since he's the reason I'm willing myself to go soft. The kind of business we handle and the risks we take require that the men who wear the Forsaken patch be able to blend into a crowd. Holly never should have been able to figure out that she was being followed. Not that it matters now, since Squat is being reassigned. I don't know who I'm going to put on Cheyenne, but it won't be that fuck up. That's a risk I won't be taking with my kid.

"You thought I didn't know?" she asks. Of course I thought she didn't know. I would've thought that an eager asshole like Squat wanted his top rocker enough to do the job right.

"Had to make sure you were keeping your mouth shut," I say. She doesn't say anything for a few minutes. She's all nervous glances and heavy sighs with her lips smashing together and then pushing out. It almost looks like she's making one of those stupid fish faces that Cheyenne likes to do when she's getting her photo taken. But it's more than that—she's not trying to look cute or sexy. She's working through something silently, and I think I spent enough time around her by now to know that she won't speak until she's ready.

"I told you that I won't say anything. You won't take me at my word, so if I have to take the money to get you to believe that I'm not going to do anything to get you or your club into trouble, then I will." And that's exactly the problem. We deal with a lot of shady as fuck people in our line of business. I learned two things in my last twenty years with his cut on my shoulders: number one, everybody has a price; and number two, that there is no such thing as getting something for nothing. And the fact that she won't take my money makes me think she's going to take my freedom. Only, she doesn't seem to be malicious or deceitful. If I didn't know any better, I would think that she really just wanted to be left alone. Which is a damn shame because the more time I spend around her, the more aware I am of her presence.

"Stay here," I say. She is an adult and responsible for own fate, but I can't help the bad feeling that I get from the idea of letting her walk. She hasn't told me what exactly went down between her and Mancuso's guy, but from the way she avoids the topic altogether, I'm starting to worry that it was more than she's letting on. And if he has taken an interest in her, then she's screwed.

"No," she says. She gives me a small shake of her head, and then her shoulders rise in the air, stay for a beat, and fall. "I was an idiot for thinking that it could be a good idea to let

Cheyenne think that were sleeping together. Now my boss is asking questions and even Mindy thinks I'm hiding something from her. If I stay here, it's only going to make everything worse."

"You won't stay here because people are asking questions, so you would rather be murdered to avoid a few uncomfortable conversations?" I don't even know what the fuck to say about this shit anymore. I've tried my best to get it through her thick skull that getting dead is a very real possibility here. She shifts in place and looks down at her lap. Her fingers work at the hem of her blouse.

"The more time I spend with you, the more that guy is going to think I matter. It's better for you and Cheyenne that I stay away. If he thinks we know each other then he can use me as leverage. You have enough to worry about with Cheyenne and your club. You don't need to worry about me as well."

"Stay," I say again, quieter this time.

"I don't fit in here."

"Yes, you do," I whisper.

"But, I don't."

"You're insane, and ballsy, and you handle your shit. You fit in here alright."

I sound like a pussy.

Her silence is unnerving. She doesn't react to my fucked-up attempts at getting her to stay for a long moment, then she says, "But I don't *want* to be those things."

I don't give her anything for a good minute or so. I've nothing to give. She doesn't want this and I won't force it.

On one hand, she makes sense. Her staying here could make it look like she means something to me, which she doesn't. Well, more than I want her to, anyway. Still, that doesn't address the fact that she's already had words with this guy and apparently the asshole pulled a gun on her. But she's made her choice, and I'm not the kind of man who begs.

I can walk away from this.

"Fine. You've made your choice. I just hope it doesn't come back to bite you in the ass," I grit out.

She stands to leave and says a few words on her way toward the door. Things like thank you and other bullshit pleasantries tumble from her mouth as she closes the door behind her. The air in the room changes, no longer charged and now kind of empty. I hate that she's even partially right about Mancuso's guy seeing her as a bigger threat if she stays here. On the other hand, it doesn't sit right with me to let her go and not know what she's up to. It's fucking insane, and what she does with her time is none of my goddamn business. But for the last few weeks Squat has kept me up to date on her comings and goings. Everything from what kind of takeout she orders to where she shops and how often has been logged, in code, in a palm-sized notebook that he carries around in his back pocket.

Innocuous little details like knowing that she and her cousin Mindy eat at Sea Salt Pizza about twice a week, and that she's stopped by Early Bird Hardware twice in the last two weeks, but has only purchased something once, have left me wondering about all of the other dumb shit she does that I don't know about. Squat hasn't been able to figure out what kind of pizza she orders at Sea Salt yet, but he did get her coffee order for me. I should have paid attention when I ran into her there, but I was much too focused on pissing her off. I would be a liar if I said I had no idea why I want to know what kind of pizza she likes or what kind of coffee she drinks.

The last few minutes I spent with Holly Mercer make me realize something that I'd rather not admit: I like her. But it's more than that. It's deeper. She's infuriating and pushy, and she doesn't give a shit that I wear this cut. She is who she is, and fuck if that ain't some kind of beautiful stupidity.

I don't want to like her, and I don't want the complication of trying to insert her into my life. But it's there, and I don't think it's going to go away anytime soon.

The door creaks as it opens, and there stands Elle. Her long black hair cascades over her shoulders and falls the top her old, worn brown leather jacket. Like always, she's wearing white jeans and a fitted top that stretches at her perfect fucking tits. She sees me notice the curves of her body, and a smirk appears at her lips. It's easy between us. We both know what we're after, and neither one is interested in fucking that up, and right now my dick couldn't be more thankful.

After her father's death, it took me some time to shake the feeling of guilt that crept in because I'd been fucking my best friend's little girl for years and lying to him about it. I don't know that he would be pissed because one of his brothers did him like that as much as he'd be pissed that the asshole hadn't made Elle his Old Lady.

"You look tired," she says. As she walks into the room, she lets the door close behind her and twists the lock into place. There is only one reason she would lock the door. She doesn't move fast or anything, but it feels like one moment she's across the room and then she's right on top of me. First, she shrugs off her jacket and tosses it on top of the washer and dryer nearby. Then it's her top, and then her shoes. Her jeans slip down her long legs slowly, and finally she's just in her bra and panties. I crook my finger, and she drops to her knees. Her gorgeous fucking rack is in my face and her hot pussy just a foot away, I let out a heavy breath. My muscles tighten as I lean forward and move onto my knees. She places her hands on my shoulders and presses her tits into my chest. Her nipples are hard as they press into my cut. It's always good between us, and I'm more than up for a guaranteed orgasm, but tonight I just don't feel like doing any work.

"Long day," I say. I don't give her anything else—if I do, she'll ask too many questions. She and Chief didn't have the best relationship for a few reasons. Him leaving her mother for her stepmother, Barbara, left a tear in their father-daughter bond. But what created the furthest distance between them was that Elle never understood that club business wasn't any of her business. It's only been a few times that I've had to remind her that I don't shoot the shit about my brothers. Period. But even a few times is a few too many. So instead, I reach around to her ass and give it a squeeze. She's soft and supple, and the purr that escapes her lips is enough to get my dick hard. There's nothing better than a nice quick fuck at the end of the rough day.

When I slide my hand into the leg hole of her panties and assault her clit with my thumb, she grips my shoulders tighter. With my free hand, I undo my belt, pop open the button of my jeans, and slide down the zipper. She's quick to grab my dick through my boxers and slide her hand from the base to the tip and back again. It's a matter of minutes until we are both grunting and moaning. Just before she falls over the edge, she uses my shoulders as leverage and lifts herself up. And then slowly slides down my needy cock. I hold her at the waist to guide her movements. I let the day and all its bullshit wash away with the blissful fucking feeling of hot, wet pussy.

Nothing else on this planet can make all of the bad shit disappear like pussy can. And pussy like Elle is hard to come by. Gorgeous fucking light brown skin, dark eyes, dark hair, and a whole mess of attitude. But no drama, no expectations, no commitments. Perfect fucking pussy. I'm not as young as I used to be and the exertion of holding her up like this begins to wear on me. All the booze and bud through the years has taken its toll despite my time in the gym. I suck in a deep breath and, even though I wasn't all that close to coming, it's like my orgasm is fast tracked and I'm losing myself in the soapy, sweet air around me.

Only, it's not Elle. It's Holly that I'm picturing in all her perfect fucking infuriating glory.

☠CHAPTER 16☠

THE FLOOR CREAKS beneath my feet as I make my way into the small cabin that we use as a safe-house. Junior's been here for weeks, and at some point we're going to have to see about moving him, but a few of the guys won't sign off on it yet. It's moved on from being a safety issue to a personal vendetta. I'm all for righting wrongs, but eventually something's got to give. This is just one more thing that's splintering the club from the inside out, and if I were the worrying kind, I'd fear for our future. We're a brotherhood. If we don't have each other's backs, then we don't got shit and these patches that I'd lay down my life for don't mean a goddamn thing.

The cabin is long and narrow, reminiscent of a shotgun style house. The kitchen was long ago gutted, and the bathroom is nothing more than a half-working sink and toilet. Junior's lucky that he's family—even though we haven't let him out of this shithole, he's enjoyed daily home-cooked meals from Ruby. Like the one I have in my hands right now—fried chicken with mashed potatoes, and corn on the cob all wrapped up in aluminum foil and put inside a plastic Tupperware container that fits nicely in my saddlebags. I don't usually play Meals-On-Wheels, but Duke's been bugging me to give the kid a chance. He seems to think the intel the kid has is legit and that he really is interested in helping us.

In the corner of the room, Junior sits on the old stained mattress that we've used for interrogation more times than I can count. His legs are bent, and his arms are slung over his knees. His body jumps slightly at the sound of my entrance, but he keeps his head steady. After he recovered from the shit-kicking that Ian gave him, his entire demeanor changed. When I first caught sight of Ruby's boy, he was fucking manic. He kept screaming, "He'll kill her!" and fighting us at every turn. He wasn't very cooperative during his recoup, either. But since then my brothers haven't reported anything but cooperation. This could mean he either wants to help us, or, despite his declarations, he really does want his sister dead.

"Dinner," I say and toss the closed Tupperware container at him. He responds quickly and catches it with little issue. His large hands tear away at the lid, and he dives right in. With the cob of corn in his hands and a mouth full of corn, he swallows then looks up at me. I grab the chair near the mattress and sit down.

"Who's been making these meals?" he asks. To the best of my knowledge, he's never asked where his food was coming from, so this is progress.

"Ruby," I say and leave it at that. He doesn't press. He just nods and goes back to eating. It's not my place to tell him that she's his mother—not that he'd even believe me anyway. Shit, if I hadn't known about this kid from the beginning, I might be doubting it, too. I don't think I'll ever forget the day Jim told me about his woman's fucked-up past and the babies she had to leave behind. Ruby had only been in town a few months and hadn't let Jim in yet. He'd said his promise to protect her kids was the only reason she gave him a chance. That was back when Layla had just started fucking up again, and Chey was barely two years old. That night when I got home, I woke Chey up and held her for what seemed like hours. I had to remind myself of how fragile she was at that age so that I didn't squish her.

"Heard you got some theories," I say. He finishes off the corn and tosses the cob into the bag.

"Does this mean you're willing to listen?"

"I'm listening, dude. Whether or not I think you're full of shit is another thing. Start from the beginning," I say.

"My dad didn't send me out here, my cousin did. Tony's taking this shit personally. I don't think my dad even knows what's going on," he says. I'm more than a little surprised to hear that Mancuso is probably not involved yet. All Duke told me was that the kid has some intel that I need to hear and that he's getting the vibe that it's legit.

"Tony's still recovering. He took a shot to the stomach that had him in the hospital for a few weeks. That's his bullshit excuse for not dealing with this himself. So anyway, I'd been hit in the shoulder, so when they arrested me, I went to the hospital. Some dick from the feds came in and told me that my dad and uncle were going away for life. He said my cousin was half-dead and my father's organization was done for."

"Name?" I ask.

"Agent Wilks," he says. "He was with a scumbag pig who'd pretended to play dirty and butted up to my dad. Officer Adam Davis. That's when they told me how they'd found the warehouse they arrested me in."

"What warehouse?"

"A warehouse full of meth. Tony had a beef with the guy who ran it. That's how he ended up with a bullet hole in his stomach. He was giving the guy shit about missing product or something. I'd been trying to control the situation when Al came from out of nowhere. Davis was smug as fuck when he told me that Alex gave up the warehouse. I didn't believe it until I got out on bond." His words are definitive, not like he's confused or trying to make shit up on the spot. It's also consistent with the little bits we got from Gloria, Mancuso's sister, when she called about Alex. Gloria didn't give us much. It was little more than telling us that Alex had ratted her dad out to the feds and that Tony, Gloria's son, knew. So, obviously, Alex wasn't safe there.

She shouldn't be safe here, either—on principle alone—but she's Ruby's kid. No matter how much I hate it, she and Ryan are together right now, and it doesn't look like it's going to end any time soon. The asshole was raised better than to bed a rat.

"You were surprised?" I ask. Now that he's mentioned it,

the opportunity has presented itself to get a little intel on Alex. Ruby's kid or not, she's living in Jim's house, and she's got my brother under her thumb. She's too close to this club and, until a few months ago, none of us had even met her. They all think she's just a scared kid who's making the best of a bad situation, but I'm not sure that's true.

"About my sister?" he asks. His eyebrows raise like he didn't expect the question. I nod and wait for an answer. I can't say that his vouching for her means shit to me, but if he confirms my fears then that's reason enough to urge Ryan to back off.

"Your friends tell me she's happy here," he says. "Tell me she's okay, that she's being taken care of." For some reason, we're breaking ground today. We might be able to use him to get a leg up on Mancuso's plans. Still, his questions unsettle me. I want to ask him why he's so concerned for a bitch who got him arrested, and how he can do a total one-eighty, going from beating the crap out of her to playing the concerned brother.

"Didn't think you'd care," I say honestly. Maybe I can get some insight into what I'm working with. He shakes his head and looks at the plastic container in his lap. When he lifts his head and meets my eyes again, there's an emotion behind his face that he's fighting to mask. It can't be easy, whatever it is that he's feeling.

"I lost my temper," he says quietly. "I totally lost it. I put so much on the line, and she wouldn't let me help her. I still don't get it. She should want to get away from you people." I choose not to take offense to the comment. He looks lost in thought and like he's given up every ounce of fight he ever had.

"And where would she go, if not with us?" I ask. "Because from where I'm sitting, she's a rat who fell into a pretty good situation."

"She's not a rat," he hisses. His words come out cold as ice, and his eyes are narrowed. The apathy is gone, and in its place is what looks to be flat-out hatred. "You don't know shit about my sister."

"Enlighten me," I say. His anger doesn't vex me, nor does it put me on edge. If anything, it comforts me. It's something, but it's not quite enough. I want more before we get back to Mancuso.

"First, tell me if she's happy. Tell me that she's okay," he demands. Maybe I overplayed my hand, because he looks confident now, like he's convinced I'm going to give him what he wants.

"She's settling in," I say. The first thing that pops into my head is that Alex is with Ryan. And while I'm half-tempted to put that shit out there, it's none of his business. I'm pretty certain that Ryan loves her, and I don't doubt that she loves him. When Junior kidnapped her and she wouldn't give the club up, he beat the shit out of her. Blow after blow, she refused to tell him where the club house is. It didn't matter where he hit her or how hard. She didn't back down. I don't worry about her opening her big fucking mouth as long as she and Ryan are doing well. It's when he fucks up and she gets pissed that I worry about. If she could send her own father away, then what's to stop her from doing the same to me and my brothers? Nothing, that's what. "You don't need to worry about her. Your sister ever do anything like that before?" I ask. I got shit to do, and it's starting to get late. Despite the fact that he's being chatty, I don't want to be here all night.

"The running in to break up a fight? Nah, not since we were little. The talking the cops? Never," he says. "She thought she was saving me, you know? She's always had this thing about the family. There is no gray area with my sister. For her, I'm either a part of her family or I'm part of my father's family. One of the last good days we had together, we talked about where she wanted to go with her life. She had all these big dreams of college and stuff. It was like she was in total denial or something. When I told her that I was going to get my gold gun before the end of the year, she freaked out on me. She knows, having grown up in the life, that once I take my oath, that's it. There's no turning back. So whatever she did, she did it to save me."

"Clean or not, she talked to a cop. How can you be so sure she didn't hate your daddy enough to put him in prison?"

"Because I know her," he says. "She might not like that the family demands there be no divided loyalties, but that's her blood. Gold gun or not, I'm her brother, and she wouldn't do anything to hurt me."

"You hurt her once, how do I know you won't hurt her again?" I asked. Since the club has put themselves between this bitch and harm's way, I need reassurances that he won't turn on her again.

"I'm going to have to live with that until the day I die. I

can't make that right, but I can try to help your club figure out a way to stop Tony before this crap gets out of hand and my dad finds out and gets involved. When I came here, I thought if I could make it look like we died in a fire, and let you people think so too, you would get word back to my aunt Gloria. By then, she and I would be long gone. We could have run if only she had told me where you guys have your meetings. I needed a few bodies to make it look like there was a struggle. I didn't want to hurt her."

My limbs lock in place. I give myself a minute so I don't say something that's going to put us two steps back. It's a good thing this little prick is laying all of his confessions at my feet and not someone else's. It's no secret that I'm not a fan of his sister, but so far he and I don't have any problems. I want to keep it that way. Unlike some of my younger brothers, I know how to keep myself in check—most of the time.

"This uh, cousin of yours—he's got to be looking for you. Who is he sending?" I ask.

"Only one person I can think of who Tony might be able to manipulate into doing the job. Guy's name is Leo Scavo. Tony doesn't have the rank, and he isn't likable enough for my father's men to be doing him any favors. Only reason he could get Leo is if he didn't tell him the real reason he wants my sister back."

"You know how this guy operates? His tics?"

"My father calls him the peacemaker. He's always reasoning with people, ironing issues out before they blow up, and he's a team player. Leo shows up, we're lucky. I don't think he would take a kill order from Tony, and even if he did, I want to think he wouldn't kill my sister. He and Tony are both just soldiers, so neither of them have their own crew."

"There something I should know about Leo and your sister?" I ask.

"Dad likes Leo. Started talking to him about giving him his own crew. My father is something of a traditionalist, so when Leo makes Capo, he was going to give Leo his blessing to marry Alex. That's what he calls it, his blessing. It's not his blessing, though, it's a goddamn order. As far back as Sicily, with my great-grandmother, the men in our family have been arranging marriages for the women. It's old-school Italian. The problem is, Alex didn't want any of it. She didn't want to be married off, and she didn't want to be part of the life."

With a nod, I stand and stretch my back out. It feels like we've been sitting here and talking forever. I point at the food in his hands and tell him that it's getting cold. I leave the small, decrepit cabin, exchanging a few words with the guys we pulled in from down south to keep an eye on Junior. It's darker out now than I expect it to be for early evening.

I didn't like having to pull from other charters, but I had no choice. Every time I turn around, I got one more fucking person I have to protect. We used to be a ten-man charter, but that was before Junior blew into town and one of his guys took out Chief. Now, being down to nine, and needing a detail on the safe house—and after last week, Cheyenne, too—I don't have any more bodies to keep on everybody.

I'm halfway to my bike when the sound of gravel crunching under tires alerts me to an approaching vehicle. I pull my .44 out from the back of my jeans, unlock the safety, and whistle at the guards on duty. Their heads pop up, and they ready their guns—long-range rifles—toward the narrow gravel stretch that leads down to Highway 101. From between the trees appears a slick, black Mercedes. Nobody should know this place is here. The drive up from the highway is long and windy for a reason.

The car stops, and out steps a tall man with broad shoulders in an expensive as fuck black suit. From his olive skin tone to the suit on his back and the car he rolled up in, this is Mancuso's guy. One of the guys behind me yells at the Italian to drop to the ground, but he doesn't move. He raises his hands in the air and smiles just as two men step out from the woods wearing similarly pricey suits and holding guns that match the rifles I gave my men. My stomach drops as I realize we're evenly matched and too far away from civilization for anyone to hear shots being fired.

And my evening goes from decent to fucked-up immediately.

☠CHAPTER 17☠

YOU LOOK PANICKED. Forgive me, Mr. Grady," the man in the suit says. He smiles wide and rotates his wrists in the air. "I have been sent to deliver a message for Forsaken."

The fact that this fuckhead knows my name makes this situation even worse. Having some Italian prima donna come at me is going to put me on edge no matter what. But here, at the safe house, it's even worse. My nerves are fucking shot, and I have no doubt that this is the asshole who has big enough balls to come at my kid at her school. The gun itches in my hand as I focus my attention down the barrel and on his heart. If I didn't need information out of him, I'd put a bullet in his chest right now and just take my chances on the guards having my back and taking out the other two. But taking him out doesn't resolve anything.

"Who are you?" I shout, careful not to redirect my shot.

"I am a representative of Mr. Mancuso," he says. I don't even try to get a name out of him because he's already decided what he's going to give me. The best I can hope for is that Junior hears some of this, but keeps his mouth shut. Despite our soundproofing efforts, the cabin is old, and we don't want anything inside that would tell a nosy sheriff that it's anything more than an abandoned property that's been subject to squatters.

"And the message?"

"Family is very important to Mr. Mancuso. He has requested the safe return of both Michael and Alexandra."

"Yeah, I'm sure. The last place Princess is safe is with your organization," I snap. It's not something I call Alex often—Princess—but this guy is digging himself into a deeper and deeper hole. He went after my kid, and now he's suggesting I'm too fucking stupid to know how much danger Alex would be in if we just let her go back to New York.

"Princess?" he asks. His smile falls. "So then you know how important Alexandra is to our family."

"Kind of figured it out when Junior and his friends showed up. Too bad none of them made it back to New York to tell you how hospitable we are here on the West Coast," I say. I suck in a deep breath and stand a little straighter. For the first time since he rolled up, I feel on even ground. The cocksucker may have caught me off guard, but now that I've found my footing, I'm thinking more clearly.

"It's unfortunate that you aren't more agreeable. I should advise you that I won't be leaving without the Prince and the Princess. The length of my stay is entirely up to Forsaken." His expression sours with every word he speaks.

"You will be leaving, and you'll be doing it alone. It's up to you if you do it in a pine box or on two feet."

"I was hoping we could have come to an agreement, but I see now that you're not the reasonable man that Ms. Mercer led me to believe you are. By the way, she spoke very highly of you. I hope that knowledge provides you even minor comfort in the coming days," he says.

The moment Holly's name falls from his lips, my stomach drops. I know for damn sure that he's full of shit. Holly would never call me reasonable and unless asshole is a term of endearment, she wouldn't speak highly of me, either. Still, he knows who she is and that puts me on edge. Days ago, when I let her leave my house, I knew this could happen. I knew letting her leave was a bad choice. Ice cold fear washes over me, but I say nothing. A callous smile spreads across his face, and his eyes practically dance. A man like him—one who knowingly storms onto Forsaken property with guns blazing—is dangerous and sadistic.

"What the fuck are you even talking about?" I snap.

"A beautiful woman like Holly shouldn't be left alone. I can see the appeal. She's pretty when she's calm, but it's when she's panicked and crying that she's at her best. So angry and scared," he says in a wistful way. His voice trails off at the end like he's remembering something. I try to focus on the details, but it's all getting clouded over by the way he's talking about Holly. I shouldn't have left her alone, but I did. She's not my problem—or she shouldn't be—and that's where I'm stuck. I can barely manage everything I already have going on, but at every turn I'm making her my problem. *My priority.*

"Holly has nothing to do with this," I say. My voice betrays me, the desperation showing through, and I lower my gun just slightly. I try to keep it where it was—aimed perfectly at his chest—but it's too hard. I just want to drop it and run, but that wouldn't be wise. *Holly's hurt.*

"*Holly* has everything to do with this. You stole what was supposed to be mine. Alexandra was promised to me, and you took her. Do you believe in an eye for an eye, Mr. Grady?"

"There is nothing you can do, no place you can hide, and nothing that will save you if you've hurt Holly. I will separate your flesh from your bone with my bare hands," I say. My gun falls lower as my heart rate peaks.

"She's in pain, Mr. Grady. Torn from the inside out. I'm trying to work with your club, but you've been unwilling to cooperate. As a show of good faith, I will make you a deal. I want to meet with your charter president—right here, right now. He shows, and I'll tell you where she is and how long she has left."

I give up fighting this guy. He may have the balls to come up on Forsaken property without an invite, but he's obviously calculated and in control. He's competent enough to find a way to ensure my compliance.

Lifting my hands in the air, I take my finger off the trigger, click on the safety, and drop my gun on the ground. I lift the bottom of my cut on each side and turns in a full circle so he knows I don't have another gun behind my back. I'm not stupid enough to carry my extra piece in a visible place. With two fingers, I carefully dig my cell out of my pocket, hit speed dial number five and bring the phone to my ear. It rings twice before he answers.

"Yeah?" Jim says on the other line. I can hear the television in the background and Alex playfully shouting at someone. Then Ryan's voice pops up. He's laughing and telling her to pipe down or he's going to make her silent. Jim laughs into the phone and says, "Damn kids are adults, but they sure don't act like it."

"I need the full table at the safe house. Mancuso's guys have paid us a visit," I say. Asking for a full table is how we communicate that we need every man—patched or not—and we need them fully armed. The man before me shakes his head and makes a disapproving *tsk* with his mouth. "Scratch that. I need you to come alone."

"Got it," Jim says. Asking for the full table means I'm getting the full table, even if this asshole thinks I'm not. Jim will roll up alone, but the rest of the men we can spare will be in the shadows.

"And Pres?" I say to get Jim's attention. "I need to check on Sweets."

"I'll send one of the guys by her place and have him call you once he knows something," he says. After I gave Holly the nickname Sweets last week, the guys didn't say anything about it. They just kind of picked it up without questioning me. Thank God for it, too. I don't know what I would say if they did.

I hang up the phone and slip it back into my pocket. When I look at Mancuso's guy, he's much more relaxed. His hands are clasped in front of him. I'm sure he has a gun on him, but he hasn't once drawn it.

"He's on his way," I say.

"Hopefully your president arrives soon. Ms. Mercer is a fighter, but one can only hold out so long with her injuries. She let me lay her down without much fight, but then her nerves got the best of her when I parted her legs. She was so tight, and slick, and needy. Have you not taken care of her properly?"

In an instant, I've grabbed my gun from the dirt and I'm on him. His backup moves just as quickly, and they both have their guns pointed at my head from less than five feet away. The barrel of my piece is but a few inches from pressing into his expensive suit. He doesn't flinch or suck in a deep breath. His eyes widening slightly at my proximity is the only reaction he gives. He raises his hands in the air and motions for his guys to back off. It's only now that I notice the guards are at my sides. They back up a few steps, but keep their focus and aim steady. We don't speak, nor do we move an inch while we wait for Jim to arrive. I've shut myself down as much as I can, trying to feel nothing. I can't have let it be this easy for her to get hurt.

Soon, the familiar rumble of Jim's bike sounds. He gives us a wide berth as he pulls up beside me and cuts the engine. He's totally silent as he hops off his Harley. Most of the time when I look at Jim Stone I don't see the man he is now—aged and graying. He's the age his father, Rage, was when he gave up the gavel. Rage didn't immediately retire out to Nevada when he stepped down. He hung around for about six years before he couldn't stand to look at Jim and Ruby together anymore. Once he lost Silvia, he lost himself.

"James Stone," Asshole says. Jim gives him a short nod and places his hands on his hips.

"And you are?" Jim says. I wonder how long the fucking pleasantries are going to go on for before this asshole decides to tell me where Holly is.

"I am unimportant," he says. "I have expressed to your friend here how incredibly important it is that I return to New York as soon as possible with both Alexandra and Michael, but so far he has been unreceptive to my requests."

"And for good reason," Jim says. "We made a long trip and have taken on a lot of heat to get Alex out of New York. Mancuso won't be coming within five states of her."

My phone rings in my pocket. I tuck my gun into the waistband of my jeans and step away from the crowd. The Caller I.D. tells me it's Jeremy. "Yeah?"

"Sweets and Bean are MIA. I've checked their apartment, then Bean's work, and then the high school. Nothing," he says quickly. "I'm back at the apartment now. Their cars aren't here, and there's no lights on. You want me to break down the door?"

"Stay put." I hang up the phone after giving the order and rejoin the group. When I return, Jim and Asshole have moved on from where they were. Now they're discussing history.

"A company man like you should know that you're not high enough on the totem pole to give a charter president orders," Jim says.

"You don't even know my name, let alone my rank, Mr. Stone. My place on the totem pole might surprise you," the

Italian says. The clock's ticking. I don't have time for them to whip 'em out and measure their dicks.

"Pres, you're looking at the asshole who Mancuso was going to marry Princess off to," I say, pointing to the Italian. Then I point my finger to Jim and look at Asshole. "And you're looking at the man who married Princess's mom. Now that you got my president here, you can tell me where Holly is."

"Princess's mom?" Asshole asks. He looks from me to Jim with curious eyes.

"Holly Mercer!" I scream. I can feel it in my soul—I'm starting to crack. My senses are firing off like fireworks exploding in the night sky. Jim senses it. Asshole senses it. The douchebag Italians behind him sense it, and so do the guards. My fist shakes with the burning need to knock him the fuck out. Jim's here now. It's all he asked for in order to tell me where Holly is. He better make good on his word.

He has to.

"You have served your purpose, Ster—". He places a finger over his lips to hush himself. "That's right. You're not a fan of your given name." He's playing with me.

"Now," I yell. He smiles softly and nods.

"Very well. Now, pay attention, because I will not repeat myself. Thirty-nine, one, four, one, two, seven, four, sixty-eight. Negative one, two, and three. Eight hundred and ten, zero, and sixty-eight," he rattles off so quickly I know I don't catch it all. It's not so much like he's telling me a series of numbers as he's playing a game with those numbers.

"That's not a location," I say.

"It is," he insists. "And hurry—the degrees must be dropping by now, and it's likely brackish."

I look to Jim, who nods. I take off for my bike as quickly as I can. Once resting on the seat, I dial the only person I know who's good enough with riddles to have even have a clue what all those numbers mean. Ian picks up on the first ring, to my immense relief.

"Knuck," he says, using my nickname.

"Holly and Mindy are missing. Mancuso's guy has them somewhere. Asshole gave me a bunch of numbers and said some seriously cryptic shit, but none of it made any sense."

"You sure? I got a red line on one of his guys right now," he says. Of course. I told Jim we needed a full table. Everybody we can spare is up here right now. We probably got at least four guys in those woods with sniper rifles on these assholes.

"Positive."

"Meet me at the highway," he says and hangs up. Turning the bike on and revving her up, I tear down the dirt road and make it to the highway in record time. I swing onto Highway 101, heading north. It's not even a half mile before I see Ruby's red Suburban parked off to the side. I pull up behind it and cut the engine. Ian strides over to me with a laptop in one hand and snaps his fingers together with the other.

"I caught thirty-nine, one four, and a few other numbers. Then negative one and sixty-eight, but there were a few numbers between those, too. He said to hurry because the degrees are dropping and it's brackish?" I say in frustration. I should have paid better attention so I could remember it all.

"Brackish? Like water is brackish?" he asks me. I shrug.

"Fuck if I know," I say.

"Degrees are dropping... like it's getting cold? Cold water?" he muses and starts typing something into the laptop. We probably shouldn't be getting signal out here, but some poor kid from Stanford's computer sciences department needs money for his fancy fucking university, and we need signal in places only the government technically has. It's a beneficial arrangement.

"Wait—degrees... what if it's not temperature, but like a location?" I ask. Ian's eyes dance for a moment before his brows draw together.

"Thirty-ninth parallel, do you think he could be talking about the thirty-ninth parallel?"

"I don't even know what that fucking is," I say.

"Longitude and latitude. Fort Bragg sits on the thirty-ninth parallel. They're somewhere along the water," he says in a hurry.

"How do you know that it's the coastline and not farther inland?"

"Brackish water is salty. Lakes and rivers, with few exceptions, are not."

"How the fuck do you know this?" I ask.

"I actually graduated high school, asshole," he says back with a taunting smile.

"Okay, well, we have miles of coastline. They could be anywhere. I need something more specific."

"I need you to remember the two numbers that come right after thirty-nine so I'll be able to narrow it down to a few blocks," he says.

"Shit," I say and hit the handlebars of my bike. Holly's life depends on my ability to remember a bunch of fucking numbers. Had I known this was going to be important one day, maybe I would have paid better attention in school, or maybe I wouldn't have spent a couple of decades killing my brain cells. "It was… thirty-nine, one, four, two."

"Cuffey's Cove, down in Elk," Ian says after typing a bunch of shit into the computer. I nod and start my bike. Ian rushes to the Suburban, tosses the computer inside, and climbs in. We head off south as fast as we can. The farther I get away from Fort Bragg, the less this feels right. Something nags at me, and I rack my brain trying to figure out what it is. We've been heading south for barely two minutes before I signal Ian to stop and pull over. When he does, I pull up to the driver's window.

"Coordinates are wrong," I shout over the noise of the Harley. Ian puts the SUV in park and leans over, grabs the laptop, and opens the screen. When he nods, I continue, "It's not thirty-nine, one, four, two. It's thirty-nine four, two seven." He doesn't ask, and I don't bother to explain the Mad Hatter-like rhyming the bastard was doing and how confusing it was. He just enters the numbers into the computer and nods again.

"Follow me," Ian says, and we turn around and take off, going north now. I'm not a spiritual man, but I kick myself half the ride, especially as we pass the dirt road that leads to the safe house. At some point, I've started to wonder if every fucked-up thing I've ever done is coming back to me.

Am I such a bastard that the people I care about are going to keep getting hurt?

We pass the College of the Redwoods and nearly run a red light while we're at it. Just before the bridge that spans over Noyo Bay, we turn into the parking lot for Coast RV Park. We nearly side-swipe a sedan that's backing out of its space on the way through the lot toward the make-shift dirt roads that make up the streets for the RV park. Behind the small park of maybe twenty RVs is a curved road that practically hugs the cliffs of the coastline.

He pulls off to the side of a road that doesn't look like it gets much action and hops out of the SUV. I pull up behind him and turn off my engine. All I can see is dirt and RVs and, in the distance, the college and some ramshackle buildings that have no distinctive purpose anymore and should probably be torn down. Ian strides around the SUV and looks to the water. From behind him, I can see the water perfectly. Every sharp rock, and every steep dip comes into view. I've seen enough sick shit in my time to know that the coast is prime place to dump a body. The salt water and the currents, not the mention the wildlife, do a good job at tearing up flesh. The ocean is nature's garbage disposal.

To our right is the bridge that connects the southern end of town with everything else. It's where the Noyo River spills into Noyo Bay, which eventually becomes part of the Pacific. The straight that leads the bay into the ocean is narrow and partially aided by a concrete sea wall that extends out a good twenty feet. The concrete wall is narrow and not made for lounging, but there at the very end, sit two figures.

I'm still for a solid minute until I see movement from both of them. My chest hurts from all the stress, but in this moment, it's as though a weight has been lifted. I have no idea what condition Holly will be in when I get to her, but the fact that she's moving is enough for me right now. I still won't let myself consider that he was inside of her, that he violated her in that way. Not after everything we just went through with Duke's woman and her ex. I can't go there.

I just can't.

I take off to the cliff, easily finding a path that's been worn into the dirt and rock by whoever services the coastline here. I doubt it's the Coast Guard. We don't have anything worth their interest up here. The closer I get to the water, the steeper and more difficult to navigate it becomes. Rocks become slick and sharp, and the water itself is more aggressive this close up. Ian is right behind me. He struggles about as much as I do, having to occasionally grab a rock beneath his feet in order to steady himself.

When I reach the sea wall, I breathe a sigh of relief that it's wider than it appeared from shore. It's nearly five feet wide and, though it's wet, the extra width provides me some comfort as I run forward toward Holly. The sea wall is shaped like an "L," bending midway. I slow at the turn, careful not to lose my footing, and then pick up speed again as I near the girls. The closer I get, the easier it is to see how they're sitting. Back to back, they each have their legs dangling over the edge of the sea wall. Neither one looks badly hurt.

Holly's head turns. Her mouth is covered in duct tape, and

when her gaze lands on me, her shoulders sink and her eyes water. The absolute terror that shines in them breaks me into a thousand useless pieces. Closing the distance between us, I drop to my knees and take her face in my hands. I don't know how much of it is insanity and how much is a message from a higher power, but this woman has been thrown into my life and I think it's for a reason.

I don't want the complication of an Old Lady, but it looks like fate has other plans.

For the first time in a week, I can breathe easy. Holly's here, and I know she's safe. She can fight me all she wants, but I'm here and she's stuck now.

Holly

☠CHAPTER 18☠

THE COLD WIND slices through my thin tee shirt. I knew I should have grabbed a jacket this morning, but we were running late and it didn't seem important. Apparently, I was wrong. Sitting on this slab of concrete, with the icy breeze and spray from the Pacific rushing up at us, I'm reconsidering not only my wardrobe, but all of my life choices.

I don't know that I should have moved home. The first few months back here in Fort Bragg were pretty boring, but these last several weeks have me thinking I'm going to lose my mind. Actually, maybe I shouldn't have broken up with my ex. Or the guy before him. The longer I think on it, and the farther back I go through my exes, the more depressed I feel. I go to open my mouth and tell Mindy that I've always dated assholes, but my lips aren't able to move. The duct tape pulls at my skin, so I stop trying to force out sound.

Mindy leans back and rests herself against me. My eyes narrow, and I find myself realizing that perhaps there is one more poor choice I've made in life—renting an apartment with Mindy. Every inch of my body aches, and I'm cold and tired, and she has the nerve to use me as a support system. The extra pressure sends a painful spasm down my spine. I'm tempted to push her off me, but I don't want her to get hurt, and I have the kind of luck that if I push her, she'll fall in the water and I might go with her. So instead, I take the high road and hold back the tears that form at being in this situation. I remind myself that she's in this situation because of my association with Grady, so I let her lean on me while I quash further thoughts about sending her overboard.

Noise sounds to my left, and I turn my head to see what's going on. My heart beats faster with worry that the crazy mafia guy is back. He wasn't exactly rude when he insisted that we get into his car with him, and he was pretty polite when he explained what he had to do and the message he wants me to give to Grady. He and his two men were even quite considerate as they walked us down this seawall and asked us to sit facing opposite directions. They made sure we didn't hurt ourselves when they tied us together and were quite delicate when they applied the duct tape to our faces. Still, we were kidnapped, tied up, and left on a seawall, so it doesn't really matter how goddamn polite they were about it.

Rushing down the seawall, coming right at us, is Sterling Grady. The very sight of him makes me stop breathing for a good second. His face is red, and his wavy hair whips itself across his face and covers his eyes. He doesn't let it deter him, though. My chest constricts with every step that he comes closer. I can't even begin to process how it feels to see him right now. A hundred emotions swell inside of me—gratitude, anger, self-pity, fear, relief, anxiety, lust.

Barely a foot away, he drops to his knees. My eyes don't leave his as he reaches forward and takes my face in his hands. It's a simple gesture, yet so intimate and gentle that it brings tears to my eyes. I might be losing my mind, but I need a little safety right now. Even though Grady is the most dangerous person I know, I don't feel it in my heart. Right now he looks like a man wrecked. His chest is heaving, and his eyes are turned down like he's in pain. The last time we were this close, I kissed him. I just took charge and did it and he liked it. Maybe if I had stayed then, we wouldn't be here now.

Behind Grady stands a younger man, around my age if I had to guess. He is tall and lanky, with wavy blond hair and a nasty scar that runs from his ear to his mouth. I see little else about him because I don't want to take my eyes off Grady. There's something in Grady's expression—like he's a man destroyed—that I don't understand. But it doesn't matter. He came to save us. I don't think I can let go of him. Ever.

Very slowly, he removes one of his hands and peels the duct tape off my face. It stings as it goes, but every time I jerk back, he whispers gently and shushes me into silence. He leans in closer, a pout practically covering his entire face, and says, "It's okay."

When he gets the tape off, he leans me forward and inspects the rope that binds my and Mindy's wrists together. In a matter of seconds he has the knots untied and our wrists are free. Out of my line of sight, I can hear the telltale peeling of tape, and then Mindy gasps. Grady stands and backs up a foot to make room for his companion. The man steps forward and offers Mindy his hand, which she takes and awkwardly stands. He leads her down the seawall and toward the cliff side.

Grady crouches down and grasps my upper arms with both of his hands. We stand together. I lose my footing and accidentally step on his booted foot, which sends me sideways, but Grady pulls me into his chest and holds me tight to his leather vest. My eyes close, and I pull in a deep breath, absorbing as much of his scent as I can. I've always loved the salty ocean air. It was a sign that I was home or close to it, and even though I didn't want to be here, I never wanted to be too far away, either. Only now, the last thing I want to smell is the ocean.

With my face pressed into Grady's chest, I breathe in deeply, much preferring his masculine musk to the salty air around us.

"You're freezing. Let's get you in the SUV." I nod and he releases me. I turn around carefully, and we walk the length of the seawall to shore in less than a minute. The first time I walked this wall, it felt like it'd taken at least five minutes, but before I'm even done considering it, we've reached the shore. I let out a heavy sigh and have to stop my lower lip from trembling. As we make our way up the hill, Grady takes the lead, grabbing my hand to make sure I don't slip. I try to make a joke about tumbling into the ocean after his efforts to rescue me, but it doesn't go over so well. He just gives me a look over his shoulder before he continues moving forward.

At the top of the hill, Grady's companion is getting Mindy into the back of a red Suburban. He wears a Forsaken cut just like Grady does. There's something about his face that makes me uncomfortable. I want to think it's not the heinous scar, but something else. He seems off. His brows are pulled together in the center, and his eyes are focused so intently on something off in the distance that I can't see.

"Ian's going to take you in the SUV with Mindy. I'll be right behind you on my bike, okay?" Grady says. I give him a slight nod. At some point, down on that seawall, I decided to give up trying to make decisions for myself. Every decision I make gets me into some kind of trouble no matter how well thought-out it is, so I'm done. If Grady wants me in the SUV, I'll get in the SUV. Still, a part of me would rather he be in the SUV with me or I be on his bike with him. In his presence is the only place I've felt safe lately. But I pushed him away. I just want a reason to cling to him now and to hang on until this awful fear of something else happening passes. Unfortunately, I have a feeling that if I stay in his world for too long it won't ever pass.

Inside the SUV, Mindy is silent. She keeps her gaze on her hands as they fidget in her lap. It's occurred to me that my association with Grady has brought her to this place where she doesn't even want to look at me. Ian shuts my door, and I let my head fall back against the seat. Save for the sounds of us putting on our seat belts, it's silent as Ian starts the engine and pulls away. Behind us, Grady's bike roars to life. The deep growl of the Harley keeps me company as we make our way through town.

Soon enough, we're pulled up in front of my and Mindy's apartment building. Ian parks the SUV, gets out, and walks around to open Mindy's door. Her hands shake as she unbuckles her seatbelt, but when she finally gets it, she's off like a light, Ian on her tail. I don't notice the sound of the bike until it's turned off and the silence is deafening. In those moments before Grady opens up my door and helps me out, I feel so alone and exposed that it makes my skin crawl. Annoyed with my own weaknesses, I mentally kick myself in the ass for feeling like a stupid trauma patient. The man from the mafia didn't hurt us—he was actually kind of nice about what he did. I don't think I really have a right to be as affected by the experience as I am.

Silently, Grady leads me up into the apartment, where we stand awkwardly in the entryway. Mindy is curled up on the couch in the living room, and Ian has his eyes transfixed on the window that looks down on the street below. The door shuts behind me, and Grady quickly checks out the small hall bathroom, then my room, and Mindy's. The galley kitchen is exposed to the living room, and there's nowhere to hide. All in all, our apartment is really quite modest. Grady's home, though not opulent, is obviously cared for and lived in. By comparison, this apartment looks like a place for boarders, not a home.

"Did he touch you?" Grady asks. His mood is dark and the scowl on his face is too intense for me to even consider arguing with him. Mindy scrubs her face with her hands and taps her foot nervously.

The question catches me off guard. I struggle with a response, but eventually end up saying, "No."

Relief washes over him almost immediately. Blowing out a deep breath he says, "You two need to pack your bags. You're coming to my house."

"I'm not going anywhere with you! You are off your rocker!" Mindy shouts and jumps up from the couch. With wild eyes, she stumbles over her words and is screeching about not knowing him and not being safe anywhere and having no idea what's going on and why we were just forcibly taken and that she is refusing to go anywhere. Grady keeps his expression neutral, but I think I've had enough run-ins with him to know that he's having to work at it. Patiently, he waits until she's done and has puttered off into some kind of incoherent babble. Her eyebrows are raised and she's pretty much pleading with him, but it's doing no good. I know that flat expression of his. It means that the only way you're getting out of doing what he wants is to either shoot him or overpower him. Since she can do neither, I don't hold my breath for her success. "I don't know what's going on, but that asshole was watching me for weeks. He was in the shop all the time and I... I thought he liked me. "Just, please. Leave me alone."

"It's either my house or Duke's house," he says. Having been given a choice, Mindy relaxes some and takes a moment to think it over. She looks at me and shrugs. This is the first I've heard that this guy and Mindy's coffee shop guy are the same person. She didn't say a word about it until just now.

"If I stay with Nic, will you come with me?" she asks. She looks positively desperate.

Just as I'm telling her that I will, Grady butts in, saying, "She's staying with me."

"You're staying with him?" she asks me. I look from Mindy to Grady and back to Mindy again. They both look determined and more argumentative than agreeable. I shrug and give a non-committal nod. Mindy gives a small huff, folds her arms over her chest, and looks at the floor.

"I don't know you," she says then looks up at him.

"This situation is fucked up. I get that. I wish you didn't have to go through that. But the best thing I can do right now is to keep you safe, and that means getting you to a place where you can be protected. That's not here. So you can either stay with me where Holly is going to be, or you can stay with Duke and Nic. Make a decision right now, or I'm making it for you," Grady says.

Mindy doesn't question why I'm apparently staying with Grady. She knows most of what's gone on between us—well, an altered version of it. I told her I nearly ran him off the road when I got sick while driving and he stopped to check on me and yell at me, and ever since we've been doing this kind of dance around one another. I wouldn't break my promise to Grady, not even to tell Mindy, if I absolutely didn't have to, but I had to give her something. She knew something was up, and I couldn't keep totally denying it. When I'd first returned home after being shot, I was able to keep it up for a few days before I made up the stupid car story. Then after the run-in with the mafia guy at the high school, I confessed that I'd been at Grady's house that afternoon. I did, however, leave out the whole having my life threatened thing.

"I'll stay with Nic," Mindy says. Her voice is quiet, and she sounds so defeated. I'm about to tell her that she'll get used to Grady's bossiness when I realize that, despite these scary and uncomfortable situations, Grady isn't a part of my life. In fact, the only time we've actually spent any time together is after something awful happens, and then I go back to my boring life and he goes back to whatever he does. I'm always left with the same dull disappointment that I didn't have or take a chance to get to know him better. He's saved me more times than I'd like to admit I've needed saving, and yet these rescue missions are really all we have. That and that one kiss. That explosive kiss that I almost took too far. A small, stupid part of my brain wants more.

"Go pack." Grady leans in and presses his hand to my lower back, guiding me down the hallway. I'm not paying attention and thus not very compliant, but that doesn't seem to matter. He pushes me forward gently. When I start to walk on my own, he follows behind and leans himself in the doorway of my room. The small room is pretty messy. Swiftly as I can, I kick stray bras under my bed and cover my dirty panties with other pieces of dirty laundry.

"You ain't got nothing I haven't seen," he says, eyeing under my bed, where I've kicked two bright red bras.

"That doesn't mean I want my personal items out in the open for you to see," I respond as I shove a mix of casual and work clothes into a duffel bag.

"We can come by in a few days to get more stuff if you need it," he says, eyeing the duffel bag. Like an idiot, my cheeks heat. The idea of spending days in his home, surrounded by his scent and his deliciously overbearing masculinity makes me nervous. If I were smart, I'd be afraid for my life right now and formulating a plan of action to get myself out of this mess and as far away from him as possible, especially considering it's his fault that I'm in this mess to begin with. But realistically, I know that's not going to happen, so I just shut up and go with it.

"How long will I be staying with you for?" I ask. His eyes stop wandering around my barren, messy room and land on me.

Without an ounce of humor he says, "Until you're safe. However long that is."

"That's really vague."

"I let you leave my house twice, and each time you were targeted. You don't have to like my answer, but you do have to deal with it. I will *not* let anything hurt you again. You got that?"

That nagging hope that maybe he likes me for more than a quick hump on a garage floor resurfaces and blooms in the pit of my belly. His words come out so clear and decided. He's not some young guy who doesn't know what he wants or has a tough time communicating it. This is a man who does as he pleases, takes what he likes, and doesn't apologize for it or ask permission.

And if I'm not careful, I might fall for him hard enough to not recover.

☠CHAPTER 19☠

I TENSE UP and claw at the sheet beneath me. My throat aches from the exertion of screaming so much in such a short period of time. Once I'm coherent, I close my mouth and the room falls silent. This is the third time tonight I've awoken myself in a panic. The first time I woke up screaming, Grady ran into the room with his gun drawn. Cheyenne and Lisa followed right behind him. Lisa had a flashlight and Cheyenne had a straightening iron in hand as if they were prepared for battle. They were also wearing shirts, which was a good thing, but Grady wasn't; which was an even better thing.

The bedroom door opens and Grady walks in. He reaches out and flips the light on. Still in just gray sweats with no shirt on. This time he strides in slowly and his gun hangs loosely in his hand. His free hands scrubs at his face, and he says, "Somebody better be in here trying to kill you."

"I'm sorry," I say, blinking spastically from the sudden brightness of the room.

"That's a first," he says, "you being sorry." He runs a hand through his hair, and his muscles flex. I noticed a tattoo on his ribcage. In a beautiful script, he has CHEYENNE tattooed on his left ribs. A lot of people get tattoos of their children's names, so it's not like the tattoo in itself is unique. It's just one more little thing that shows how much his daughter means to him.

I've never been involved with a guy who has kids before, and actually, until now the very idea gave me an uneasy feeling. I didn't want the complication or frustration of dealing with an ex and a kid and all, but it's different with Grady. He's all muscles and gorgeous dark hair and brilliant green eyes. And when I see his tattoo, lovingly placed on his ribs, with the name of his daughter, I don't want him to leave. It's not so much a fear of being alone as it was the fear of not getting to know him.

"Are you *ever* sorry?" I snark.

He walks to my side of the bed and looks down at me with puffy eyes that make his exhaustion obvious. "My regrets would haunt even your waking hours."

The seriousness of his response takes me aback. I find myself speechless for the first time in a while.

"Since you woke me up *again*, let's get this shit over with, yeah?" he says. He sets the gun down on the side table and sits himself at the foot of the bed. His tattoos are gorgeous. His left bicep is covered in a warrior tattoo that is adorned with skulls. On his left forearm is a woman with wings and her legs spread. I try to pretend that one's not there. His chest, right above his heart, has some kind of double-sided tree trunk with a Celtic-style branch banding around it that forms a circle.

"What's with the tree?" I ask before I can stop myself.

He looks down at his tattoo for a moment before raising his eyes and saying, "Circle of life. What ends begins again—shit like that."

"Wow, you're deep," I say with an impressed nod.

"Too easy," he says with a smile and a shake of his head. His eyes travel down to my breasts that strain beneath my tank top. "Back to business—I need to know what Mancuso's guy said and did."

"I don't want to talk about it," I say in a plea.

"I don't care," he says flatly. "I need to know."

"Fine," I mutter. "He showed up at our apartment. He said he was sorry for intruding, but that he needed us to hand over our car keys and to go with him. I tried to run down the hall, but he grabbed me and said that he didn't want to hurt either of us, he just needed to borrow us for a little while. He had two guys with him. They took our car keys, but not our house keys. He said they were moving our cars to a nearby parking lot. When his guys returned, they put our car keys in the kitchen, made us take our house keys, and then very politely ordered that we go with them."

"He didn't have a gun on you? He didn't hurt you? Touch you in anyway?"

"No. He did warn me not to yell at him, but that was it. He said he just needed to send a message to Forsaken, but that he didn't want to hurt us."

"That it?" he asks.

"He said for me to tell you that nobody is safe," I say. His expression darkens and he narrows his eyes. It only lasts a moment before he shakes it off and stands.

"You think you can let me get some sleep now?" he asks with a yawn.

"I just…" I say and then think better of it. He wants to leave and go back to bed, but I don't want him to go. Squirming uncomfortably in my spot, I reach out, but then pull away. I can't bring myself to tell him what I need. But I don't have to, it seems. He looks down at me thoughtfully.

"Don't want to be alone, I get it." He walks across the room. My heart falls a little as he nears the door. He stops a foot away, reaches out and shuts the door, then turns the lock. I watch in breathless anticipation as he cuts off the light, then rounds the bed and climbs in the other side. Slipping beneath the covers, he lies on his back and pounds his pillow into submission. Yawning, he wiggles in his spot. I turn toward him, full of nervous excitement and wonder. He's so close—close enough to touch—but I'm not certain this is something I should be pursuing. I know I *want* to pursue it, I just don't know if it's smart to.

"Yeah," I whisper. His eyes flutter closed. "Thank you for not being a dick."

He opens one eyeball and narrows it. "After weeks of avoiding me, now you want to talk?"

"We don't have to talk, I'm just too tense to fall asleep right now," I mutter.

"Okay, fine," he says in a gravelly voice. He reaches out and pulls me to him. Our bodies are flush against one another and as I tilt my chin up, I find that we're practically nose to nose. I'm stunned by his action, but beyond that, excited to be so close to him. After this dance we've been doing for weeks now, I'm about to explode just by the anticipation of it all.

His arm around my waist slides down to my hip and his hand snakes around to my ass. His commanding touch kneads my supple flesh. He bucks his hips into mine. He's already half hard. A needy whimper falls from my lips as he continues his movements. Knead. Buck. Knead. Buck. He doesn't look so tired anymore, but rather, a man driven. The last time we were here, I pulled away. I won't be making the same mistake twice.

Awake and determined, he hooks his thumbs around the waist of my pajama pants and panties and yanks them down. His movements are so quick that I barely have time to react, but he doesn't care. He slips a hand between my thighs causing me to tense up. Using brute force, he lifts my leg into a bent position where I'm left exposed at my center. Being bare before him is nerve-wracking. I look down at my thighs, which are much too thick and my belly which is slightly rounded for no reason other than my love of milkshakes and my hips, which are wider than I'd like. I wonder if I measure up to the women he's used to having sex with. This thought sends me down the path of wondering how many women he's had sex with, how many names he never got or forgot entirely, and if he'd recognize every woman he's been with or if some are just a blur.

"Don't go there," he says. His eyes drift from mine down

to my exposed pussy. He drags a single finger lightly up my center. Shivers rack my entire body. My eyes flutter involuntarily and I have to actively fight to keep my legs where they are. His finger drags back down, parting my moistening flesh, and dipping inside. He finds my nub without issue and draws smooth circles in a slow and deliberate fashion. "Whatever you're thinking about—don't. Just relax, Sweets."

His finger works faster in frantic circles. My head falls back into the pillow and I tilt from my side to my spine. Incredible waves of ecstasy take over my muscles as I slide into a puddle of blissful immobility. He leans over me, and his finger leaves my wet core for a split second before returning. One jerky circle and two fingers part me as they slowly slip into my depths. A minute passes before he pulls them out and then back in. He creates a torturous rhythm. I've broken out into shivers and a thin sheen of sweat coats my entire body. I'm spiraling into oblivion as he pulls out and pushes his fingers back inside. He hooks his fingers inside of me. My body shakes and I gasp for air.

Leaning down, he nips at my neck and whispers, "I'm too tired to get into it tonight, but tomorrow, I'm gonna let you wrap that smart mouth around my dick and swallow everything I give you."

Coming down from that amazing high, I pant wildly. I don't even have the energy to argue or shake my head. Incredible orgasm or not, I want to bring him back down to reality and remind him that I never asked to suck his dick. But I don't because now that he's mentioned it, I really do want to taste him.

He slides his fingers out of my wet pussy and draws his sweats down just far enough to free himself. He uses the wetness of his hand to aide in his efforts as he slides down his thick shaft and then back up again. He moves faster and faster in a combination of smooth and jerky movements. My lips are suddenly dry and no matter how many times I lick them, it's not enough.

"If I touch you anymore tonight, we're not going to get any sleep and I have to be right when I take care of that fucking Italian," he grits out.

"What are you going to do to him?" I ask quietly, turning onto my side. My eyes are transfixed on his straining dick as he works himself toward the edge.

"He scare you?" he asks. His movements slow just slightly as his hand is drying. Feeling brave, I reach down between my legs and use my index finger to rub my swollen and sensitive nub in fast, violent circles. My muscles lock up and all it takes is seeing Grady's eyes glaze over for me to come again. I don't give myself any time to recover. Instead, I coat my hand in my own juices and reach for him.

"Yeah," I whisper.

He moves his hand away and watches as I wrap my hand around his rock hard cock and pump him slowly. His words dissolve into a moan as he says, "Then he's going to suffer when he dies."

There's something disturbingly erotic about his comment. It feels more like a declaration or a promise. It spurs me on to pump him faster with a lighter touch and then slower with a firmer touch. A few cycles and he's shoving my shirt up off my belly. In a shaky motion, he moves my hand away and positions himself over my bare stomach. He works quickly, his breath is ragged, and his eyes snap closed as he comes on my bare skin. It's a beautiful thing to witness—him losing control like that. For a man like him, who values being in charge, it's a gift to see him vulnerable.

☠CHAPTER 20☠

LAST NIGHT WAS incredible. I'm on my fourth cup of coffee and it's not doing anything to wake me up, but I don't care. I called in sick—I could have gone in to work, but I couldn't imagine having to be there after yesterday. Grady's guest room is comfortable, more so when he's in it with me, and he assured me that I'm safe in this house, even going so far as pointing out every safety feature he's installed. Still, once he left to "take care of shit" this morning, the panic came back.

I take a drink of my coffee and let my mind slip back to that cozy place where I'm falling asleep in Grady's arms. He's just cleaned us up and I'm curled into him. The memory is short though. This morning he told me I fell asleep instantly. Suddenly my exhaustion doesn't seem so bad. Sleep is overrated with a memory like that, but I don't think I should keep going down this road while I'm at his dining room table with his daughter and mother preparing to play a board game.

To my left, Cheyenne sorts through the Monopoly pieces, and across from me, Lisa organizes the play money by denomination. One moment, I was sitting here poking through *Teen Love* magazine and realizing how old I've gotten in the last decade, and the next thing I know, Cheyenne and Lisa are coming through the front door with the guy Grady used to have following me. I've since learned that the club calls him Squat, which seems appropriate enough, and that as a prospect, he's not allowed to tell me his real name.

I find out how dedicated he is to becoming a member of the club—what Cheyenne informs me they call "patching in". Cheyenne gives the poor guy a bunch of stupid orders. He blows her off at first, but all it takes is her saying, "Don't make me tell my daddy that you disobeyed a direct order." The poor man does seven jumping jacks and quacks like a duck twice before she gives him a break and they high-five and laugh about it. Now, Squat walks the perimeter of the house, checking and double-checking the locks. Every time he finishes a round, he calls Grady and checks in.

"I want the shoe," Cheyenne says as she grabs the shoe from the pile of game pieces.

"Well, that's surprising," Lisa says. She playfully bumps Cheyenne in the upper arm and throws her a mischievous smile. Cheyenne mimics her grandmother and rolls her eyes.

"She thinks I have a lot of shoes," Cheyenne informs me. Lisa nods furiously and mutters something I can't hear. Cheyenne holds up the dog and the race car to Lisa. "Which one do you want, Grams?"

"Let Holly pick first," Lisa says as she doles starter money out to each of us.

"Oh, right," Cheyenne says. She picks up all of the pieces, with the exception of her precious shoe, and holds them out to me. Without even thinking about it, I choose my old standby, the ship. I've never chosen anything but the ship since I was a kid. She raises an eyebrow and says, "That's my Dad's favorite."

"Your dad has good taste," I say and give her a slight smile.

"Not always," she mutters and shows the remaining pieces to Lisa, who picks out the dog. Lisa gives her a sideways glance and shakes her head.

"What, I'm just saying," Cheyenne defends herself. "Holly knows I like her."

"I'm going to pretend like there's not some kind of subtext going on here," I say and take a drink of my coffee.

Just as I set my mug down on the table, the front door opens and the alarm squeals loudly. I can't see him, but I can hear Grady cursing at the alarm. The noise stops a moment later, and his heavy footfalls sound on the hardwood as he draws near. He rounds the corner into the kitchen. His arms are full with two plastic store bags that he sets down on the counter while he surveys what we're doing. Like a pathetic puppy, I perk up the moment I lay eyes on him.

"Monopoly?" he asks with raised eyebrows. Lisa stands from her place at the table and beelines for the bags on the counter. He abandons the bags and heads for the fridge, where he grabs two beers. On his way through the kitchen, he says something to his mom that makes her laugh and then comes to the table and sits down in the empty seat beside me. "Dibs on the ship!"

Cheyenne shakes her head and points her finger at him, "You're not playing!"

"You ever play Street'Opoly?" Grady leans in and asks me.

"What?" I ask. I've heard of a lot of different versions of the game before, even one that could be totally customized, but never Street'Opoly.

"Well, you're about to be schooled," he says. He takes a pull of his beer and gives me a sly smile. The attention makes me blush, but after last night, it probably shouldn't. Clearing my throat and tucking my hair behind my ears, I smile wide up at him. He smiles back broadly, the lines around his mouth and eyes deepening. He truly is gorgeous in a way that is all man and muscle and arrogance.

"You think you can teach me a thing or two?" I say in a low and breathy voice. My heart rate spikes, and I flush all over.

"Baby, I'll teach you things that are illegal in nine states," he whispers. Cheyenne makes a gagging noise from my other side. I glance at his lips then up at his eyes and back to his lips. My nerves have disappeared and in their place is pure, unadulterated lust. He dives in for a quick kiss and then pulls away like nothing happened.

"Well," I say lowly while trying to clear my throat, "you can try, but you're going to have to do it as something aside from the ship. I already called that piece."

"My house, my rules, my ship," he says. I feel his arm move behind me. The adult, mature Holly wants to think he's making a move and wrapping me in his strong embrace, but the kid in me recognizes this move. It's the same one my older brother, Theo, used when we were kids and he wanted to get his hands on something I had. Back then, Theo, Mindy, and I were inseparable. I may have fallen for this trick a few times when I was little, but Mindy and I soon learned the art of the hand-off. In my experience, every girl who's had to deal with an overbearing male in her life knows about the hand-off.

I take a chance, lean in toward Grady, and blow out a shaky breath. His arm pauses for a brief second, and I pounce, grabbing the ship from the table and handing it off to Cheyenne. Like a pro, she grabs the ship, hops out of her chair, and runs around the table to Lisa, who is dumping wings out of the plastic bags and into a glass bowl.

"That's fucked," Grady says and leans against the back of his chair. He takes a pull of his beer and shakes his head. "You're supposed to be on my team, Chey!"

"Ha! You grounded me last month for being like ten minutes late for curfew. You're on your own, dude," she says. He grumbles something about an hour and fickle memories, but doesn't make a stink out of it.

Lisa and Cheyenne bring bowls of wings and dip to the table, along with empty plates and a lot of napkins. I finish off my coffee and opt for a Coke before we dig into dinner. The entire experience of sitting around the kitchen table with this family makes me yearn for something like this for myself—a group of people so tightly-knit that they can tease one another and even argue, but it's all in good fun. I don't doubt that, like any other family, they fight and have their differences, but they're all just so relaxed around each other. I can't imagine Cheyenne doing anything that would truly shame her father. I wonder what it must be like, to know that kind of love and devotion.

Dinner ends and, as the game begins, Grady lays out the rules of Street'Opoly for me. Cheyenne and Lisa object to playing his way, but he ignores them and breezes through his explanation. In some twisted way, Street'Opoly has the extra element of gang involvement. Apparently nobody ever chooses the iron or the thimble, so he puts them to use to represent two different street gangs that seek to control the game board. The best way to protect yourself from the damage they can do to your houses and hotels is to pay one of the gangs for protection, but that gang has to make sure they can keep you safe; a task which is apparently quite difficult during times of war between the thimble gang and the iron gang. Truth be told, by the time he and Cheyenne were done explaining the rules, I thought they both needed to be committed. As if the game doesn't have enough rules, now I have to worry about The Thimbles street gang—which Grady represents—devaluing my properties. Since I snubbed Grady's gang, he's sworn to target me. Cheyenne runs The Irons street gang and promises me I'll be safe. The very fact that I'm genuinely worried about an attack from The Thimbles as we start to play is ridiculous, and I mentally take note that if Grady and Cheyenne need to be committed, I ought to just book myself a neighboring room as well. Only, I think I'd like that almost as much as sharing a padded room with Grady.

Only Lisa refuses to pay street protection. I don't know how that works, but she's confident that she can handle herself. The one thing that this crazy version of Monopoly buys me is the opportunity to hear Grady talk. Every time I ask a question, he goes to answer, but then Cheyenne cuts him off, then he cuts her off, and they end up in some kind of bickering contest until Lisa steals a move when it's not her turn and they notice her little dog is progressing on the board out of order. They don't fight it, but it does stop them from nit-picking about why the other person is wrong.

I'm the biggest idiot in the world. In the three hours it takes us to play the game, I fall completely and totally in lust with Grady. It comes on so strong and immediate that it reminds me of my first kiss in ninth grade, and the first time a boy told me he loved me. It's like being slapped across the face and punched in the gut, and it's nothing like any lust I've felt before. It's terrifying and exciting, and when Grady leans back in his chair and tosses an arm over my shoulders, I actually feel like I want to throw up. He's so much of what I've always wanted in a man—strong, caring, protective, playful—and the more time I spend with him, the deeper I'm going to get. But it can't be more than lust, a primal desire to be part of his world, even a little bit, because love doesn't happen this quickly.

I barely know him, but I'm looking to change that. I know the important things. He loves his daughter and is respectful to his mom. He's a big, scary outlaw biker who can frighten me into submission, and who's made up his own twisted version of a board game that he apparently plays with his daughter often. He's gone out of his way to help and protect me, even though I'm not technically his responsibility. And I've lost my marbles because I'm going out of my way to defend him. And he gives fantastic orgasms. That alone qualifies him for obsession status.

He did get me into these messes, but he could be a real bastard and leave me to suffer the wrath of his enemies and he done with it. His hands and the club's hands would be clean of it if he'd just let that mafia guy take me out. And I wouldn't be the kind of person who thought about things like how to take somebody out and keep your hands clean if it weren't for Grady and his club. But even knowing this, I don't want this to end. I don't want to lose the bickering and the excitement and the way his heavy arm rests on my shoulders. Even if it is temporary, I'm part of something real, and I like it. I more than like it, but I don't let myself go there.

Grady catches me staring at him a little too long and raises his eyebrows in question. A smile tugs at my lips. I raise my eyebrows in response, trying in vain to mimic the half-hearted scowl he's sporting. He hooks his foot around the front leg of my chair and, with the help of his arm around my shoulder, he tugs me closer and places a kiss on top of my head. I flush with anticipation of where this is going and hope that I'm not a complete idiot for thinking we could be something.

"You fit in here," he says. "You fit in with me—with us. We don't fit in anywhere, either. So we fit in together."

And just like that, I'm a goner.

☠CHAPTER 21☠

BY THE TIME the game is over, both Cheyenne and Lisa can't stop yawning. I think Lisa won, but I'm not entirely certain. All I know is that I definitely lost. Cheyenne is mumbling incoherent things about taking down The Thimbles street gang with a series of federal charges. I try to ask her what kind of sentence The Thimbles would get for that, but she replies with something about shooting bunnies. Lisa stands from the table, stretches her back out, and pats Cheyenne on the back. "Time for bed." They leave abruptly and when they're out of earshot, I turn in my seat and ask Grady, "Should I be worried that your daughter is talking about shooting bunnies?"

"Nah," he says as he finishes off his fifth beer since dinner. "The bunnies deserve it." My eyes widen and I can't find anything to say. What the hell does that even mean anyway?

Suddenly, being alone with Grady is too much. I want this. It just makes me nervous. I hop out of my seat and collect the bowls and plates from around the table. In the kitchen, I set them in the sink and get to rinsing them off in preparation to put them in the dishwasher. Grady follows behind and dumps the empty beer cans into the recycling bin. He hovers over my shoulder as I scrub the dishes free of food particles. Warm breath heats the back of my neck sending a shiver down my spine. He lifts my hair, drops it over the front of my shoulder, and presses the front of his body into my back.

"What are you doing?" I whisper. I don't want him to stop. Feeling his body pressed into mine, trapping me between him and the counter, makes me think I could be agreeable to just about anything—things I probably shouldn't agree to. Like going to bed with him. But he is and I am, so I can't think straight enough to wonder how insane I am. I want him, I know that. I want him more than I've wanted anything in a long time.

"Getting you to cooperate so I can fuck you. Don't think I forgot what you look like as you come." He drags his hand up the center of my spine all the way to the base of my neck. His touch is gentle. It makes me want to tell him everything about myself. His proximity is much too close– it is unnerving. I am already in way too deep for my liking. It can't be healthy for me to be this obsessed with him. I guess it's just been so long since I've been in any kind of relationship that I forgot how these things work. I force myself to be here and in the moment, and not too much in my own head. "Where do you want me to fuck you?"

Turning off the water and using my hands as leverage

against the edge of the counter, I take a deep breath and let my head fall back against his chest.

"Are you always this bossy, and does it actually work for you?" I ask.

"I'm the one asking questions here," he says. His hand comes around from the back of my neck and trails effortlessly across my collarbone and down my forearm. "I asked where you want me to fuck you."

"Is that how it usually works for you with women?"

"I don't normally do a lot of talking with women," he says. "Don't usually care what they have to say." I'm not exactly surprised, but maybe a little disappointed. It's easy to forget who he is, and what he does when he's sitting around playing a children's game with his daughter and mother on a Friday night.

"What makes me different?" I ask. Immediately I regret the question. It is stupid of me to ask, to even think that there is a difference.

"Everything, or maybe nothing. Maybe it was just the timing and the situation, but I think we got something here. Something I ain't had in a damn long time," he confesses. I don't really know what he means by that, or maybe I do, and I just don't want to admit it to myself. Last night and even during the game tonight, being with him seemed like a great idea. But I know so little about him that it's scary how little I care what big, awful things I could uncover.

"Listen, I don't do sappy shit," he says. He brings his arms up and rests his hands on the edge of the counter. "But I like you. I want to see where this goes."

Looking down at his large, rough hands, I think that maybe this could work. He's being direct with me and verbalizing what he wants, and I have a feeling that he doesn't do that with a lot of women. He strikes me as more of a do now and reap the consequences later kind of guy. Only, as silly as it sounds, I don't really know how to be in a relationship. If that's what he even means. I'm probably suffering from some sort of PTSD, or some Florence Nightingale kind of crap that makes me think that everything that is actually a really horrible idea might be good idea. But I've been down the rabbit hole of insanity before, and last time it was alcohol fueled and drug-enabled. I don't have that excuse this time.

"Mindy's an addict and an alcoholic," I say. I shouldn't be sharing this with him. It's really none of his business, but if I want to keep this, whatever this is, I should start by being honest and letting him in on this part of my life. "You asked why I don't drink, and that's why. I followed her into oblivion and I don't like who I am when I'm not sober."

I have never willingly shared that with anyone. It's Mindy's story to tell, not mine. We went through all that crap together. Only, when I was ready to move on, Mindy wasn't. "I tried to help her. I enabled her, ended up dropping out of college because of it. It was a hard two years that I don't wish to repeat."

"Few months back, my best friend died. It tore me up. Tore Chey up, too. That's why her grades suck. I wasn't tuned in enough to notice and when you called me out on it, it only pissed me off." I don't say anything out loud because it seems pretty obvious that there's nothing I can say that he would appreciate. Instead, I opt for hoping that the more I share, the more he'll share.

"Every man I've ever dated is a tool," I admit.

"I'm a tool," he says.

"No doubt," I whisper.

Grady reaches out with his thumb and caresses my knuckles. I let my eyes fall closed and the rest of my body sink against his. I never talk about what went bad with me and Mindy because it's still too painful to recall. His left arm lifts off of the counter and curls around my waist. He sucks in a deep breath at the top of my head and releases it slowly. His body grows stiff in every way imaginable.

I take my free arm and place it over his arm at my waist and squeeze. Gooseflesh appears all over my skin. He places a kiss to the back my head and then another to the shell of my ear. I have now had his lips on the back of my neck, the back of my head, and on my ear. And while each kiss is better than the last, they aren't enough.

"Kiss me," I whisper. It worked well for me the last time, so I go with it.

"I'll do more than that. I'll suck on your tits," he says. His hand at my waist travels up and ghosts across my nipple. His words are so crude that I should be offended, but they have the exact opposite effect. An overwhelming need overtakes me. "And eat your pussy."

The same hand drops to the crotch of my jeans where he drags his finger down my center. My body involuntarily locks into place and my breathing ceases for the few moments it takes my brain to process what he's doing. It doesn't matter how much attention I pay to myself, it's never the same alone as it is with a partner. Last night was proof of that.

"And I'll fuck you until you beg me to stop." He presses his hardened dick into my back to emphasize his point. I have to force my muscles to loosen and to remind myself to breathe. If ever my heart were on the verge of giving out, now would be it.

"I don't do casual," I say. Even now, in this moment, I try not to forget all the strides I've made the last few years in order to get myself back on track. Step four. The moral inventory. I've never done casual sex very well. Being with somebody intimately always leaves me expecting more, and there was a time when I took whatever they were willing to give. But I can't be that person anymore, and damn the stupid steps because they make me say and do things I would rather not– honest things. I never should have let Mindy convince me to do them with her.

"I can't do casual," he says. "My life, the club, Chey… everything. We are either strangers who fuck or you are my woman. There is no in between bullshit about dating multiple people, seeing if it's a good fit, and all that stupid yuppie shit." His words take me by surprise. A man like him, I expected some criticism for my position. I've been on an emotional cliff all night, in danger of falling into an abyss of feelings I'm not ready for. And like everything in life, I see it coming. I'm losing my footing and then before I know it, I've fallen so hard that I don't think I'll ever recover. Lust, love. Whatever you call it, I don't care anymore. This is like falling into the best thing you didn't even know existed until you almost passed it by.

"Being your woman, is that what you call being your Old Lady?"

"Not exactly. I tell my brothers that you're with me and they will treat you like family. But, being an Old Lady only happens if the club unanimously votes you in. We won't even consider taking a vote until a brother has been with his bitch for at least 18 months. It's an honor to be voted in." I don't ask what the point of being voted in is because I'm totally distracted by his use of the word bitch. I really hate that word. As scary and foreign as all of this is, it's my life for the foreseeable future. I'll brush up on motorcycle club lingo at a later date.

"I don't like that word," I say. He tenses behind me, but says nothing.

"It's the way I talk. It's just a word," he says lowly. But it's not just a word to me and it grates on my damn nerves every single times he uses it.

"You're asking me to accept so much about your world, plus the danger I've already been dragged into. Why can't you just honor this one request?"

"I'm not used to the give and take of relationships, but I'll try," he says.

"Fair enough," I say, giving in.

Taking my hand, he leads me out of the kitchen and through the living room, then down a flight of stairs. We move slowly in absolutely no rush. My body buzzes in nervous anticipation the further we get into the house. At the bottom of the stairs is a rec room on the left, surrounded by large single-pane windows. On the right is a short hall with two doors. We walk through the first door and step into a dark, masculine room. Grady flips one of the four switches on the wall and soft lights illuminate the room in a warm glow. The walls are gray and the carpet is a worn Berber. The furniture is mismatched and aged, though sturdy to the eye.

He shuts the door behind us and moves to place his hands on my hips. My breath hitches as he runs his hands under my shirt and drags it upward. We undress one another slowly, taking our time. First it's his cut and then his shirt. My pants and bra follow along with his jeans and socks. Soon, we're in nothing but our underwear.

He reaches out and cups my face in his hands then kisses me deeply. He slips in between my lips and massages my tongue with his own. His hands knead at my breasts and then my ass. He dips his hands into my boy-cut briefs and slides them off. I do the same with his red boxers and let them hit the floor.

Hooking my leg up over his hip, I wrap my arms around his neck and lift myself into his arms. He helps support me with both his hands on my ass. I push my damp pussy into the shaft of his straining cock. He moans soft, but deep at the contact.

"You on the pill?" he asks. I rub my core against him again and shiver in response.

"Yes," I admit. I have been for years, but I leave that part off.

"Do you trust me?" he asks. Looking into his eyes, I realize that yes, I do trust him. I capture his lips with my own as we devour one another. With a steady grip, he rocks me into his large cock. I swivel my hips until a steady build begins in my core.

Lifting myself in his arms, he gets the hint and uses one hand to guide himself to my entrance. He parts my folds and spreads me wide as he enters my wet center. I lower myself slowly so as not to hurt either of us and to savor the moment. He groans as he buries himself to the hilt. It's an incredible feeling, having him so deep as he claims me.

Soon, he's laying me on the bed. We're still connected, but the moment I'm safely on the mattress, he rears back and then slams into me. I gasp for breath and have to bite my lip as he brings me nearer and nearer to the edge.

Wanting to be with Grady is one thing, but having actually been with Grady is a whole different ball game. I thought I had it bad before, but now it's a hundred times worse.

☠CHAPTER 22☠

I'VE BEEN THINKING a lot lately about the differences between right and wrong. Surely, stealing is wrong. But is it wrong if you steal food to feed a child? Murder is wrong, but I suppose I could probably make a case for that as well. Morality is really subjective – at least that is what I'm going to tell myself so I can sleep at night after this.

Mr. Beck won't issue Jeremy a permit because he has a beef with the club. That seems wrong, especially in light of the fact that, when I asked Jeremy why he was so determined to work at Forsaken Custom Cycle, he said he wants to make his dad proud. While Grady is usually pretty mum about anything related to the club, he does talk with me liberally about the personal dynamics at play between the club members and their families. Some of the relationships seem a little messy, but he promises me that once things calm down with the crazy Italian guy, Jim and Ruby are going to have a big party so I can get to know everyone. They're obviously a tight-knit group that has each other's backs, and if I want to be worthy of my place beside Grady, I'm going to have to earn it.

"Next," the teller says. She gives me a friendly wave of her hand, welcoming me to her station. I recognize her as the mother of one of my students. Her daughter, Vickie, is a sophomore with a serious eager-beaver attitude. I give her my best friendly smile and push out whatever lingering guilt I am feeling about doing this. It's for a good cause, I remind myself. Even if there are some casualties along the way, I'm determined to carry this through. Mr. Beck may not be the monster that I want to paint him to be, but he's certainly not a good guy, either.

"Holly, how are you doing today?" The teller is all smiles as I set the three checks and the deposit slip on the counter. I lean forward just slightly and give her an apologetic smile.

"Oh, pretty good. You know, I just realized that I don't have the account number for these deposits. Mr. Beck was in a bit of mood when he sent me over here. I would really hate to have to go all the way back to the school." Thankfully, she doesn't push. One of the benefits of small-town banking is that it's actually quite easy to convince a teller to pull up a customer's information using just their name.

"Don't worry about it. Between you and me, Mr. Beck never remembers his own account number." With a few taps of the keyboard and a little redirect of the mouse, she's pulled up what she was looking for, grabs the pen, and gets to filling out the account number on the deposit slip. In addition to Mr. Beck's obvious agenda against the club, he has a rather liberal interpretation of what can be counted as a business expense. Unfortunately, his liberties have all been small and accounted to less than $500 in the last few years. I'm not looking to bust the guy for a few too many business lunches from questionable establishments. Call me crazy, but I don't think the school board allows their administrative staff to write off lunch at the golf course every other Tuesday, even if Mr. Beck's companion is the ever-charitable local attorney, Larry Jennings.

"Thank you," I say as the teller deposits the checks without issue and hands me a receipt. I look over the receipt for a moment and hop from foot to foot. The teller eyes me curiously, but stays quiet. Finally, I turn back toward her and give her a nervous smile. "I might be biting off more than I can chew here, but I just don't want to get in trouble at work. Are deposits like these common for Mr. Beck?"

The teller looks around and bites her lower lip. I sigh then pat her rested hand on the counter. With a nod, I say, "I'm sorry, forget I asked."

I'm about to turn around when she says, "Wait. Listen, if you're uncomfortable with making these deposits, I suggest you go to the school board with your concerns. I have nothing against Mr. Beck—he's always been good to my kids—but he has a membership at the golf course. That place is expensive. My husband is a landscaper there, and he's seen him playing a few rounds during school hours with Larry Jennings. You know that lawyer whose son was…violated?"

Pay dirt.

I force myself not to smile or show any other sign of excitement over this information. I knew Mr. Beck was up to something. His behavior has changed too much in the last several weeks for there not to be a reason for it.

"Well, my husband thinks Larry Jennings is trying to find out what happened to his son because Mr. Beck is always handing over these files and the few times Bob got close enough to hear, they were discussing troubled students. It doesn't seem right—an administrator doing something that like. It's awful what happened to poor Darren. Things like that aren't supposed to happen here, ya know?"

I nod and lean in like what she's said is the absolutely most interesting thing on the planet. "I know. That's kind of scary, but how can Mr. Beck help?"

"The police haven't made any arrests, so I'm guessing he thinks it might be someone at the school who hurt his son. Only reason Bob and I can figure why Larry has been so generous to Mr. Beck."

The more she talks, the more I realize I am in over my head. I've never done anything like this before, and the best I can hope for is that I don't end up ruining my own life in the process. But I have to know what's going on. I figured I'd find something fishy in Mr. Beck's records, but had no idea I might run across something like this. I don't even know what "this" is yet, but so far it's not looking so good for Mr. Beck, which actually helps me follow through.

"Generous?"

"I didn't say anything, and I'll deny it if you say I did, but one of our other tellers deposited a check from Larry Jennings to Mr. Beck the other day. I wouldn't have thought twice about it, but when I was balancing her station, I just happened to remember my husband griping about Mr. Beck playing golf during school hours."

"I'll keep it to myself," I say. "I'm not out to get him or anything, I just don't want to be involved with something that doesn't feel right. Gotta protect my own butt, ya know?"

She agrees, and we exchange a few pleasantries before I go. The more I find out about Dick, the better I feel about forcing his hand to give Jeremy the work permit.

Back at the high school, I stride in with shaking hands and flushed skin. I spent the entire drive over from the bank trying to calm myself down, but when that didn't work, I decided to just go with it. With purposeful steps, I beeline for Margot's desk. She looks up with concerned eyes and a frown. "Holly, what's wrong?"

"I think I may have done something that could get me in trouble," I whisper as I lean over her desk. "Mr. Beck had me deposit those checks, right? Well, please don't say anything, but one of the ladies at the bank suggested that Mr. Beck may be making more deposits to his personal account than he should be."

"I've been curious about that over the years," she says quietly. Her eyes dart around the room nervously. "It's always tiny little amounts, but it adds up. Tell you what, just refuse to run his personal errands from now on. That's what I've started to do. But for now, you have proof he asked you to do it, so even if he does get his wrist slapped for too many expenses, you're in the clear." She finishes off with a friendly smile. I give her a nod and act like her words were the most comforting thing I've ever heard. In reality, they do comfort me. They tell me that if this goes south, Margot believes me.

"I'm just going to go tell him that I think my working hours are better served here, doing the work I'm paid for, not running errands," I say quietly and straighten my back as I head down the hall toward Mr. Beck's closed office door.

Two knocks later, after a thousand knots in my belly, doubts in my heart, and the overwhelming desire to turn around and run away, Mr. Beck shouts for me to open the door. When I turn the handle and enter the room, he's at his desk with our attendance and grade tracking software pulled up. His face is a shade redder than normal, which is saying something considering he's always a little on the red side. Jeremy Whelan needs this, the club needs this, but most of all, Grady needs this.

"I'd like to offer you one more chance to change your mind about extending a work permit to Jeremy Whelan," I say as I close his office door and push the button lock into place.

"Holly, I've explained why I will not issue Jeremy a work permit, at length, to several people, and I refuse to have this conversation again. I'm sorry," he says in exasperation. I nod, and pull out the deposit slip, and hand it over to him.

Now or never.

"What's this?" he asks as his eyes try to make sense of the numbers on the small receipt.

"It's your deposit receipt," I say. I'm really doing this. I am. "This morning you sent me an email asking me to prepare three checks from the school's vendor checking account to be made payable to you."

"I did no such thing," he shouts.

I raise my now steady hand in front of my face and shake my head. "You'll find this is going to go much more smoothly if you can restrain your temper."

"What are you doing Ms. Mercer?" he asks.

"I'm letting you know that I'm uncomfortable with running your personal errands. In your email, you explained that you purchased new office supplies for yourself and you had a business luncheon as well as a dry cleaning bill that was to be charged to the school's account. I never have understood why you think the school is responsible for your dry cleaning bills, and this one was a doozy, *Dick*. Who spends over three hundred dollars on dry cleaning, anyway?"

"I didn't ask you to deposit any checks this morning. You had me sign those checks for the soda vendor, the water delivery guy, and the landscaper. I've never spent that much on dry cleaning!" He's started to scream again, but I use my hand to indicate that I'd like it if he lowers his voice. His face is a much darker red now, and he's breathing heavy.

"Silly, *Dick*. The district pays for the landscaper and the soda vendor, and Margot has already paid the water delivery guy through June. You see, I have all of that on my calendar. I wouldn't have asked you to do such a thing. Did you know I'm obligated to report suspicious behaviors?"

"This is starting to sound like blackmail. The club is

putting you up to this, aren't they? I'll have both Cheyenne Grady and Jeremy Whelan expelled for this. You'll be fired, and I'll bring charges against you for your part. That bunch of inbred felons can't buy me." His jaw trembles as he talks, his eyes are hard, and he's struggling to pull in deep breaths.

"No, the club has no idea we're having this conversation," I say. Nor should they ever find out. I suspect Grady wouldn't be too happy with me if he did. "Do you really think you have the upper hand here?"

"I haven't done anything wrong," he says lowly.

In the eleven years that he has served as principal at Fort Bragg High School, Richard Beck has only expelled seven students. One of those students actually set the library on fire—on purpose. The other six earned their expulsions the good old-fashioned way, by not showing up to class and letting their grades plummet. In addition to looking up Mr. Beck's expulsion rate, I took the liberty of pulling the former student files that we have on Forsaken family members since Mr. Beck's employment. Trying to explain to Grady the reason I needed the real names of his brothers was a huge pain in the butt. He used this really deep voice and guffawed at me as he said things like, "club business, babe," and, "appreciated, but keep your nose clean." Grady may have been adamant about not telling me when I first brought it up, but I was able to reason with him. As it turns out, Sterling Grady can be convinced of almost anything as long as you have his dick in your mouth.

Once he was able to see the value of my offer, I got to work. It didn't take me long to prove my suspicions right.

Though Mr. Beck has only expelled seven students in his tenure, he has petitioned—extensively—for the removal of twelve. The five students he hadn't been able to expel were all related to the club. From his communication with the school board, it looks like he almost got Josh Wilcox expelled in his sophomore year. But just as he asked for leniency on behalf of Jeremy Whelan, Jim Stone had gone to bat for Josh Wilcox back in the day as well. Mr. Beck's reasons for attempting to expel these kids always comes back to one thing: a concern over their violent nature. And yet, there are no disciplinary records that indicate violent outbursts.

Still, something is going on here. Mr. Beck does everything by the book when it comes to Forsaken. He certainly doesn't like the club, and he doesn't like their kids, but the last doctored petition to the school board for immediate removal was sent two months prior to Ian Buckley's graduation, and it looks like they began just a few weeks after Ian, Ryan Stone, and Josh Wilcox started high school. Ryan and Josh ended up dropping out early on in their senior year anyway. While I'm not a fan of Mr. Beck's bullshit vendetta against club, it looks like it's possible that the three boys drove him to do things he hadn't done previously.

Until now.

"I've looked up your records, and I know the score. You hate the club and everything they stand for. You detest their kids, and you've made it a point to try to punish them time and time again. It must be frustrating to be unable to do your job properly because of the incredible influence of

Forsaken."

"You won't be able to find employment in this town after this, Ms. Mercer," he says. His voice is slowly steadying, but it doesn't matter. His fingers still shake.

"Mr. Beck, this is how it's going to go. I need something from you, and you need something from me," I say, taking a play right out of Grady's playbook. "I refuse to owe anybody any favors. You can keep your job and the two grand that was just deposited in your account if you just sign Jeremy Whelan's work permit and back date it to this past July. If anybody should ask, you gave Jeremy permission to work while you prepared the permit, and of course, you're so very sorry for any inconvenience your lateness may have caused."

"You're going to destroy my career if you go through with this."

"That's one thing I'm good at, Mr. Beck, destroying things. But that's worst case scenario. This doesn't have to play out like that. Consider this an investment in your future. You don't ever have to say a word to the club about this. You just get to look like a compassionate soul who had a change of heart. You issue that back-dated permit, and I'll be sure to keep both Jeremy and Cheyenne reasonably in line until their graduation."

"And if I don't?" he asks.

"Then I'll be in tears when I show up at the district offices telling them that you threatened me when I told you I wasn't comfortable depositing checks to your personal account anymore. I'm certain that when they investigate your personal finances and they see you've received payments from Larry Jennings with no reasonable explanation as to why, that they'll dig further. They'll probably even find out that you two like lunch dates at the golf course when you're supposed to be here, serving the students of Fort Bragg. What is going to happen to you when the entire town discovers that you're selling your students' personal data to Larry Jennings so he can conduct his own investigation into his son's assault? Even worse, how do you think my uncle will like it? You've made some poor decisions recently, and it's up to you how you're going to pay for them."

His glare deepens, and it takes him a moment to move. He turns back to his computer and pulls up the work permit template. He works diligently to prepare the permit, but I notice the date isn't quite right in the EFFECTIVE DATE field. "Change that to August 26th, will you?"

His fingers stall on the keyboard, and he blows out a frustrated breath before he fixes the date. "This permit won't be valid before today without a letter explaining my error."

"Yes, and thank you for signing the letter yesterday," I say, unable to hide my budding smile. I'm grateful for Dick's ineptitude at times. He never looks at the stuff he signs, and this time, that's come in handy. He shakes his head and plugs away. Soon enough, he's printed Jeremy's permit, signed it, and handed it to me.

"Thank you, Mr. Beck. I'm going to be heading home early now. I assure you that you've made the right choice," I say and slink out of his office. Back at Margot's desk, I shake Jeremy's permit in her face.

"How in the hell did you get him to do that?" she asks. I

shake my head from side to side wildly.

"I just confronted him about the checks and told him that I'm uncomfortable with it. He said he understands and he doesn't want to make me uncomfortable. Then he just churned this out and told me to give it to Jeremy Whelan."

"That sounds suspicious," she says.

I shrug and say, "I think so, too, but what do I do? Do I tell the school board or do I let it go and let the kid have his permit?"

"That's a hard one," she says. "I can't tell you not to let the school board know about your concern, but Jeremy seems to really need that permit."

"I know," I say. "As much as I'm not comfortable keeping this quiet, I don't think I can punish the kid for this, ya know?"

And that's why I'm doing this—to prove to not only Grady, but myself, that I can have his back as well as he's promised to have mine. The club is important to him, and Cheyenne talks about the members like they're blood to her, so I have to do something to help preserve Cheyenne's family. If helping Jeremy helps Cheyenne, and that in-turn helps Grady, then I don't really have a choice. I haven't known them very long, but they're my family now. I can't go back to stiff dinner conversation and bullshit faux polite concern about which direction my life is headed in.

I tried to be good—tried to be what my parents wanted. I tried to live up to my older brother's example, but I was miserable. It wasn't until I ended up dealing with Grady's crazy ass that I started to feel alive again. My parents, Mindy, and even Uncle Harry can take their disapproval and stick it up their perfectly tight butt holes.

☠CHAPTER 23☠

MARGOT AND I spend the next few minutes discussing Mr. Beck's behavior. I agree that he's acting strange and I drop a hint that I might not be the only person in town who thinks so. I let her think that she talks me into putting Jeremy's needs of my own concern for Mr. Beck's shady dealings. Sure minds me that I was just following orders given to me by my boss and that she has run a personal errand or two for him in the past as well. After all, she says, what does the school board expect us to do? Still, I express concern over being involved in something questionable. I just want to be proud of the job that I do here, I say.

If there is anyone that I feel guilty about involving in all of this, it's Margot. She has nothing to gain if Jeremy gets his permit, nor does she have anything to lose if I choose to go through with reporting Mr. Beck to the school board. I trust that the advice she gives me is based purely her concern over the welfare of Jeremy Whelan and his family. Margot can be a little lax and her time management skills can certainly use some improvement, but her heart is solid. In talking with her, I wonder if she would ever be the kind of person to do something like I just did. I have my reasons for doing what I have; but if Margot knew the truth would she understand?

Those thoughts plague me as I make the drive across town to work Grady's house. When I enter the house, I'm more than a little surprised to see Jeremy and Cheyenne sitting on the couch, far closer than I think Grady would like, both zoned out with their attentions focused on the television. It's the tail end of another news report about Darren Jennings.

"Who would do something like that?" Cheyenne says, almost absentmindedly. Jeremy's knee bobs and he gives her a sideways glance.

"Maybe he deserved it," he says. There's something different about Jeremy right now—something throwing me off. I just can't put my finger on it. Maybe it's just his comment that's unsettling me. I try to make nothing of it, but something is off about his response. The teller at the bank already made the suggestion that it could have been one of the students who banged the guy up, though I have no idea what a college senior home for the summer could have done to a high school student that would warrant the kind of violence he suffered.

Cheyenne, too, is surprised by his comment. She turns to her side and looks at him with her brows drawn together. "What do you mean?"

"Nothing," he says quickly and turns his attention back to the television.

"Oh no you don't," she says and elbows him in the ribs.

"Do you know something the cops don't?"

"I don't know anything the cops need to know," he says cryptically. It takes me a moment, but I look him over and realize what's different about him. He's wearing a leather vest with a few patches on it. Forsaken patches. A memory from that night, weeks ago, when that Italian had shown up at the high school resurfaces. I was here in Grady's house and walking down the hallway. I didn't know he'd be home just yet, but then as I was entering the living room, the shadow of a man with a guy had scared me. I screamed and both Grady and Jeremy had shown up. My brain didn't make the connection then—maybe it just didn't want to—but now I feel like an idiot. I should have known.

Jeremy needs his permit so he has an excuse to be on club grounds. He's prospecting—a term that Grady taught me—to become a fully patched member. I can't believe I didn't see it before, but it all makes sense now. Jeremy telling Grady I was at the pharmacy. No wonder he's been able to know when I leave campus during the day despite the fact that he doesn't have a guy in the parking lot save for when I show up to work and when I'm ready to leave. Not that it's any of my business, but I'm not entirely certain how I feel about the idea of a teenage boy prospecting to be a part of the club. I know Ryan and Josh joined the club when they were young—right after turning eighteen, in fact—but Jeremy isn't *even* eighteen yet. He has like another month to go. How can a seventeen year old boy make a choice like this?

I just want to make my dad proud, he had said.

Of course. His dad's in prison, I knew that. His mom is gone and his sister is his only means of support. Of course he's prospecting for the club. He's trying to earn a living the only way he knows how. I feel like I've been lied to. I try to remind myself of what Grady had told me about the club. If the club is the federal government, then our relationship is the state government. We can function entirely separately and on our own terms unless I ask shit of him that forces him to choose between me and the club. He'll choose the club. I respect it, but I don't know how I feel about knowing that I'm automatically on the losing end of a fight I didn't ask for.

"Does my dad know what happened to that guy?" Cheyenne asks. I stay still in my spot several feet behind them and try to go unnoticed. Thankfully, I've had a lot of practice and neither of them turn around. Considering the fact that Grady never bothered to tell me that Jeremy is prospecting for Forsaken, even after I'd asked all those questions in order to help him get Jeremy's permit, I'm willing to bet that if I ask Grady the same question that Cheyenne just asked Jeremy, he'd ever tell me the truth. I could have a stack of evidence against him, but he'd still lie about it—or worse—he'd tell me that it's club business. That means that it's none of *my* business.

"No," Jeremy says in all seriousness. Only, I can tell that he's lying. Cheyenne seems to pick up on it as well. She chooses not to say anything, and instead opts for turning her attention back to the television, but she doesn't lean in as close towards him as she did before.

I wonder if it's always like this, with club members, that the only people can truly be close to them are the ones who share their patch. So much of what Grady has told me about club life is shrouded in secrecy. That's the trade-off I suppose of being with a man like him. Never before in my life have I ever felt so free to be myself. It's not like my parents are so awful, even though I tend to think that they are, as much as it is that they are the kind of people who are only searching to make themselves better. They do community service because they don't want to be selfish, they go to church because they don't want to forget that they are not the center of the world, and they would rather let go the wrong done to them than to retaliate in any way and possibly regret it later.

So much of my insecurities about where I am in life what I've done and the choices I've made are tied up in the fact that I don't think I'll ever get their approval – at least not the way Theo does. My older brother makes both Mindy and I look like a couple of lame ducks. He never did go to university like my parents wanted, but he did complete the two-year water treatment program at Redwoods College here in town, and he now has a good paying job with the city. Theo is not as straight-laced as my parents are, but he's definitely one of those people who feels bad if he misses church on Sunday.

"Hey," I say as I approach the pair. They both turn around and give me a smile. Jeremy gives me a head nod and his eyes fix on the piece of paper in my hands. "So, here's the deal. Mr. Beck made an exception to issue this work permit to you." In a second, Jeremy's on his feet and in front of me. For being just a teenager, he is awfully tall and broad shouldered. I can see what Cheyenne finds appealing about him. If I were his age, my heart would be in serious trouble because he's all smiles when he likes you, scowls when he doesn't, and the body mass to match his temper. The more I look at him, the more incredibly stupid I think I am for not assuming he wanted to be a part of the club to begin with. He even fills out his leather vest nicely

"Are you serious?" he asks, eyeing the permit in my hands.

"Yeah," I say. He reaches out to grab it but I pull my hand back and shake my head. "Sit down. We need to talk before I hand this sucker over." Ever the obedient one, he makes me wait a minute before he decides not to argue, and then reclaims his seat on the couch.

"I had to promise Mr. Beck that in exchange for issuing this that you both would be better behaved from now until graduation."

"Why me?" Cheyenne says. She hooks her thumb in Jeremy's direction. "He's the one who needs the permit." I rub my temples and take a few deep breaths before I figure out how to respond to that. What the hell does she mean by that? We've been at this for months. For the most part she's compliant and at least pretends interest in staying out of trouble and bringing her grades up, but every once in a while something like this comes up.

"You're trying to give me gray hairs, aren't you?" I say. A devious smile appears on her face and she gives Jeremy a sly look before returning her attention back to me.

"Hey, then you and Dad would match. You'd be such a cute couple," she says. "At least then people wouldn't think my dad's girlfriend is my sister." The compliment isn't lost on me. I give her a smile but shake my head.

"Blatant sucking up aside—both of you need to make a better effort to behave. Please. I promised my boss that I'd take a personal interest in seeing that you make it to graduation without incident."

"But, Holly, you're amazing. You've taken such a personal interest in my welfare that you're even sleeping with my dad," Cheyenne can barely get through the end of the sentence without giggling. Both of them manage to keep a straight face despite the intimate nature of the conversation, whereas I end up with red cheeks and hot ears from embarrassment.

"Okay, I'm done with you two," I say and hand Cheyenne the permit to pass on to Jeremy. "Speaking of your dad, where is he?"

"Club business," Jeremy says and turns back to the television. I bite back the comment that almost comes flying out of my mouth. I really hate the dismissal, especially from a kid, but fighting with him isn't going to do me any good right now. Cheyenne, however, sees no problem with starting an argument.

"Not cool," she says and stands up from the couch. She folds her arms over her chest and shakes her head. "He's at the clubhouse. Uncle Rig just got in from Detroit. They're having a party."

"Uncle Rig?" I ask. I assume Rig is a club name and not

his birth name. I don't really care who Rig is or isn't, the fact that Grady is at some kind of party without me hits me right in the gut. He told me before that he would always be as honest with me as he could be, barring club business that he couldn't discuss. It's not something I'm used to—being with a man who has such strict boundaries when it comes to sharing and privacy. Normal couples share things with each other. I already know the answer, but I feel the need to punish myself and ask anyhow.

"Is there a reason I wasn't told about this party?"

"Old Ladies don't do parties at the club house. Members only," Jeremy says. Grady told me what it means to be an Old Lady, and I understand some of it, but not all of it. The emphasis on loyalty, I get. It's the idea of being loyal in the face of disloyalty that rubs me the wrong way.

Jeremy fixes me with a hard stare, something that I suspect is supposed to convince me to drop the conversation. But I can't. I put so much on the line this afternoon that I can't lose him. I can't lose what we have together. But if Jeremy is saying what I think he's saying, can I really just sit here while Grady's out doing God-only-knows-who.

"It's not as bad as it sounds," Cheyenne says. "The only women there are super sleazy and not important at all. They just hang around for the guys who are single."

"So there *are* women at the party?" I say. I already have the answer, but I feel the need to keep talking before I lose my temper and do something insane like driving down there. "Just not the women they're committed to."

"It's just the way it is," Jeremy says. "Get used to it."

All the stories I'd heard about the club and the way the members behave—in and out of relationships—bubbles to the forefront of my mind. I'd never asked Grady if we were exclusive. I had just assumed. He told me he wanted me in his bed and by his side every night when he comes home. He'd said that when things calm down, he wants us to take a trip, just the two of us. We talked about the future with such certainty that I didn't consider that I'd end up at home playing house with Cheyenne and Lisa while he was out doing whatever the fuck he wants.

And with every passing second, my temper rises more and more. I find that I'm breathing heavy and my heart's beating in my chest. My muscles strain and my hands ball into fists at my sides. Jeremy loses his interest in me and once again refocuses his energy into the television.

Cheyenne though, she doesn't take her eyes off of me. Her face is turned down into a pout and she whispers, "Holly."

But I'm already gone.

☠CHAPTER 24☠

I'M TURNING OUT of the driveway by the time Jeremy notices I've moved. He's on the front porch with his phone to his ear. It's maybe five minutes door to door at the most, but every block feels longer than the one that came before it. The sun is setting now and the Forsaken Custom Cycle lot comes into focus under the brilliant orange hue. The gates are open halfway but manned by a couple of prospects who I've learned are referred to by their stature—Tall and Squat. The parking lot is almost full. A few pick-up trucks and sedans take up the spots on the far side of the lot while there's a line of more than twenty motorcycles butt up against the brick exterior of the clubhouse.

I pull my Jeep into an end spot and barely remember to put it in park and shut it off before I run across the lot and into the clubhouse. I can hear my name being called by one—or both—of the prospects. Grady said there was extra security because of the Italian guy—whose relationship to the club I'm still fuzzy on—but I have a feeling they're not after me because I've shown up without a prospect. No, they probably have orders to keep the girlfriends at bay.

I pull open the heavy doors to the clubhouse and immediately find myself embroiled in a thick fog of sticky-sweet smoke with loud music thumping heavily from high-hung speakers. Directly in front of me sits a pair of men with leather vests. They have a bottle of vodka between them and a couple of shot glasses. One of them has a joint in his hand that he brings to his lips and takes a hit. Is this what Grady wanted to keep from me? That they're sitting around getting high?

The men don't pay me any attention as I walk further into the room. I wish I hadn't. One woman is on another's lap and she's not wearing a single stitch of clothing, not even a pair of socks. The man at the table with them has another woman on his lap, straddling him. Her hands work furiously in his lap. I easily imagine she's got a hold of his dick. The further I get into the depths of the clubhouse and the more obscene it gets. It isn't until I see a woman on her knees who is actually giving a blow job out in the open that I turn around. Familiar faces dot the scenery. Ryan is watching some chick rub her own nipples. He watches but never reaches out and touches her. It's an interesting sight considering the reputation he earned for his sexual prowess in high school. I seem to remember rumors that he'd screw anything that moved, but then again, maybe she's not his type these days.

Just as I turn around, I'm faced with a gorgeous woman,

who is surprisingly, fully dressed. She has dark skin and long black hair with large dark brown eyes. She's got light stone washed blue jeans and a black tank above high heeled black boots.

"You look out of place," she says. I give her a moment to continue, but she doesn't.

"Have you seen Grady?" I ask. She eyes me from head to toe before smiling softly.

"He's around here somewhere," she says and shrugs her shoulders. "But you shouldn't be here."

"Who are you?" I ask.

"Elle," she says. Her stare turns flat, "And you're Holly. Like I said, you shouldn't be here. Go home and play house. The shit that goes on in this place is nothing Grady wants you to see."

"I don't know you, so please forgive me if I'm not too keen on taking orders from you," I say. If Grady has some random woman telling me to get lost, I should assume that I shouldn't be here. Not because I don't need to know what he's up to, but because if it's bad enough to be warned away, it's likely nothing I want to see anyway.

"Well, I know Grady," she says. "*Intimately.*" Of course she does. Of-fucking-course she does. There's a tirade going off in my head, but only one word that sticks out and repeats itself again and again until I'm consumed by it.

Whore.

"Is there a reason you're telling me this?" Being a woman, I already know the reason. We're territorial creatures and we don't like to lose a man to another woman. The only thing I can't figure out is if she lost Grady to me or if I'm losing him to her.

"Wow, you're slow. Grady is a particular man. He likes his women separate from his club," Elle says. Her eyes lift over my shoulder and a devious smirk spreads across her face. I sense his approach before I see him. Elle is far too pleased with herself for it to be anybody else. I pull in a deep breath and do the best I can to stay strong in the face of this stupid drama of my own making.

"Hey," he says from behind me. I turn around and come face to face with not only Grady, but four other club members as well. Ian, the guy who was with him when he rescued Mindy and I from that seawall is there, standing to his left. To his right is a huge bulking man with shoulder-length light brown hair, a strong brow, and a full beard. His leather vest has a patch that reads, V. PRESIDENT. Behind him and off to the side is a man with a shaved head and off to the other side is Josh Wilcox.

The smile on Grady's face nearly splits in two as he lunges forward, wraps me in his arms and pulls me tight against him. Everything around me fades away and it's just he and I. Elle, a woman who I don't even know but surely dislike already, isn't behind me. The loud music fades away as I bury my face in his neck. Breathing in the mixed scent of his sweat and the whiskey he's obviously been drinking. I love this man, but he's kind of a grouch. The only times I've seen him this happy are when he's either three sheets to the wind or he's scaring the crap out of Jeremy. Even when his muscles tense and he's losing himself inside of me, he doesn't look this happy.

"What are you doing here?" he says as he pulls back and cups my face with his hands. His warm, whiskey-laden breath washes over my face. His eyes are slightly unfocused and that stupid grin is still on his face. I give him a small smile in return. It's the best that I can manage right now.

"Can we talk?"

Josh comes around the side, let's the bottle of beer to his lips and knocks it back. He gives a disapproving shake of his head and walks away. Though Grady doesn't seem to be mad at me for showing up here, I'm guessing with this Rig guy just getting into town, the boys want to party, and even I can admit to any time a woman says she wants to talk, it's almost never a good thing.

Without another word, Grady leads me through the crowded, smoke-filled room, and down a long hallway. Double wooden doors with a fine inlay are at the very end of the hall. I've only heard a little bit about how the club works because I don't really ask many questions, but whatever is beyond those doors must be important. All of the other doors for hallway are basic would without any frills. The way I figure it is that what I need to know Grady will tell me and then everything else is not my business. I didn't get with Grady because of the bike he rides, or the leather on his shoulders – if anything, I got with him in spite of those things. Maybe one day I will be more interested in the way the club works, but for now I'm just trying to figure out how Grady works. Still, there are a few things I would like answers to. And I know I need to ask, even if I'm terrified of the answer.

Grady holds the door open for me. I step into the room and immediately feel unsettled. There's a queen-size bed in the corner of the room with two wooden chairs and a table on the other side. On top of the table is Grady's aftershave and deodorant. I recognize that they are the same brands and scents from his bathroom at home, so I can only assume they belong to him. As the Sergeant of Arms, I'm guessing this room is his. Why he would need a room here, I don't even want to imagine. But I can't help thinking about it. Wives and girlfriends don't belong here. This place is only for the whores.

The door clicks shut behind me and finally, we are alone. He closes in and grabs me by my waist. His large hands knead at my supple curves. All of the tension, frustration, and fear start to dissipate. It's always like this when he's touching me. His right hand reaches around and unbuttons my jeans. He drags the zipper down slowly and slips his pointer finger into my panties. With light pressure, he rubs my center and creates a firestorm of need almost instantly. Falling into him and his touch is almost glorious. He consumes me in ways I almost fear and have trouble reasoning, but I welcome it. I welcome the slow build of tension in my belly and thighs. I welcome the strained, panty breaths and the way my fingers twitch as he applies more pressure.

"You weren't supposed to be here," he says and bucks his hips into my back. He's already hard and I know that unless I put up a big fight we're going to end up naked and breathless and totally lost in each other's bodies. Jeremy's cut, blackmailing Mr. Beck, and the secret party I wasn't supposed to know about are all reasons I shouldn't be giving in to him. But I do. I let him greedily dip his fingers into my swelling pussy. I don't object to the rough thrusts of his fingers as he penetrates me. My skin erupts into a million tiny bumps just seconds before my limbs lock in place and every part of me goes numb except for my core. It's there, at my center, that I feel everything. Every drag of his finger tips along my sensitive walls. Every ragged breath on my neck. Every shaky movement of his thumb at my clit. And I know it's only a few seconds, but it feels like forever that I'm lost in that place between being alive and dead.

I want this with him more than I want anything else. I used to want to make my parents proud, and I wanted to get my life on track. I wanted to make something of myself. But with Grady, all I want is to exist. With him, I'm okay just being; content to live in the moment and not worry about what the world thinks and whether or not anyone thinks I'm a failure. Because if this man can love me as I am, then I'm determined to love myself as I am and not as I think I should be. I want a life with him and all that means. I want the chaos and the smart mouth teenager who I adore. I want his baggage and his hopes and dreams. I want his future and I want a little person that looks just like him and has a temper to match. I want sleepless nights and that permanent connection of sharing a child. I want him— all of him— and I want to give him all of me.

When I come back down, I'm panting like I've just run a

race. I love it when he brings me to the edge quickly. It's like being hit by a truck at high speeds. It happens so fast I almost don't see it coming, but then it's on me and the world melts away. He throws me off balance in a way I'm never prepared for.

But I came here pissed off for a reason. Not being told about the party, not being told about Jeremy prospecting for the club, and what that means for us are still a problem. If he's not telling me these things, then what else is he not telling me? I don't want to fight and I know from experience that we can fight for days. It's almost never-ending. So instead of pushing him off me, I turn around and take control of the situation. My hands are on his chest as I walk him back to the wall.

"Why am I not supposed to be here?" I ask. I drag my hands slowly down his worn tee shirt beneath his cut and then let them dip to his belt where I work to undress him.

"Jeremy tell you I was here?" he asks. Through the whiskey fog he's in, he seems to be taking my surprise arrival better than I expect he would have had he been sober.

"Why aren't you answering my question?" I say. "Is there a reason you hid this from me?"

He reaches up and unbuttons my top slowly, but his eyes don't leave mine.

"I got brothers doing shit in this place that I didn't want you to see. Married men fucking two whores at a time, sadistic fuckers who get off having their dick sucked in front of their brothers. It's crowded, not just my brothers here tonight, but a whole mess of guys from around here— some of them I don't know, some of them I do— but I don't trust any of them to treat you like they should."

His honesty takes me aback. I expected some kind of macho shit about having a boys night and me minding my own business, but not this. He finishes with the last button and licks his lips at the sight of my breasts straining against the fabric of my bra.

"Because I'm your girlfriend?"

"No, Sweets," he says on a whisper. Chills run up my spine by the intensity of his gaze. "I'm too old to have a girlfriend, but you belong to me."

"I'm not an Old Lady," I say. "I have to be voted in for that. I know that might not happen."

"My brothers are going to like you. Once shit calms down, they'll get to know you like I do. They'll see the man I am because I have you by my side, and they'll accept you because of that."

"You belong to me," I mumble. "I want everything."

"You have everything," he says. His hands slide down my sides and pull my jeans down to the floor. He crouches down in front of me, leans in, and places a soft kiss on my hip. Watching him, waiting for him to move next, I realize that for this to work, there can't be anything between us. I have to tell him what I've done. I have to have him know everything I'm feeling and why it's important to me that he be honest and communicative.

"I want more," I say. He drags his stumbled jaw over my lower belly and places a kiss to my navel.

"What more could you possibly want?" Grady lifts my

right leg out of my jeans and then my left. His fingers hook around the sides of my panties and he drags them down to the floor. I crouch down in front of him and get on my knees. For a moment, we just stare at one another. No matter what comes out of his mouth, I know the truth in his eyes. He'll give me this, what I'm about to ask. He loves me and we're solid. He isn't like other men I've dated. Grady doesn't fear what we have and he doesn't reject it.

"I want permanency. I want a piece of you. I want to consume you the way you consume me," I say. I slide my top off my shoulders and let it fall to the floor behind me. I reach up and remove Grady's vest and gently place it on the bed beside us. Next is his shirt, and then I finish with his belt and let them both fall to the floor.

"I won't make you a widow," he says with pain in his eyes. He gives me a slight shake of his head as his hands come up to cup my face. "The shit I told you about Mancuso—that a business deal went bad—it was bullshit. The closest thing I ever had to a father died a few months ago. He was shot in the chest by one of Mancuso's guys. There is a very real possibility that more of us will die before this is over. I won't promise you forever when I can't even guarantee you a year."

"Why is this happening?" I ask, barely able to control the shake in my voice. I should have known there was more to it when that guy showed up at the school, and I should have run for the hills when he so politely left me and Mindy on a seawall. If I was smart, I would have kept my distance. But I'm not smart and I signed up for this—with him—no matter what it brings. I can't run away now no matter how much it's scaring me because the only thing scarier than staying amid the chaos is to leave and wade through the broken pieces of my soul.

"Because a man stole a woman's children and thought he would never answer for that."

"You make no sense," I say quietly. Club business is something I've avoided, and honestly, would rather to keep avoiding. But his talking right now is important. He's giving me a piece of himself that doesn't fully belong to him—it belongs to all of them—and I'm going to be strong enough to help him shoulder the burden of his secrets.

"Mancuso's guy takes Chey, what do you do?" he asks. His face is down-turned and his expression so solemn that it's almost painful to look at him. He's imagining losing his daughter to that psychopath in the expensive suit. I want to tell him not to worry, but I can't. The guy proved that he can get to her and he can get to me. He can get to anybody, I think. None of us are truly safe and if Grady can stay on his game by feeling every ounce of that fear, then his pain has some use.

I've known her less than a year, and on a personal level even less than that, but the thought of losing her churns my stomach. She's funny and smart and the very best of Grady with hints of a woman I've never met, but who doesn't deserve Cheyenne because she's not here and she doesn't get to see how awesome her daughter really is. And I kind of hate her for creating that void in Cheyenne's life.

"He takes Chey, Sweets. What do you do—if I'm not here, what do you do?"

The words come out instantly and without any thought. I'm not sure where they come from. I only know that when I say them, I mean them with every fiber of my being.

"He dies."

"He dies," he says with a nod. "How?"

"Any way possible. You won't lose her. I promise."

He finishes undressing himself and leans over me. I arch backwards and lay myself gently on the floor as he cradles the back of my head. His lips descend on mine with such passion that I think I might explode from the kiss alone. But then his hands get to work and he brings me back to that place where I'm hanging between being here and being lost in a sea of feeling. I fight the urge to let it overtake me. I want to be here, in the present as I say this.

"Marry me," I say. It's not much of a request because I won't take no for an answer.

"Told you," he says as he slides into me, igniting delicious sparks of need. A loud groan escapes him as he buries himself to the hilt. "I won't do that to you."

"You'll give me this," I say in a breathless whisper. "I need this from you—the security—and you'll give it to me because you know you're wrong."

"I'm not wrong," he says as he slides out and then back in with a slow, shallow thrust before rearing back and this time impaling me with all his might. My back arches and my legs twitch with the force of him.

"You are," I say as my jaw shakes and I break out into shivers. We move together slowly, neither of us with any desire to rush this. "Because you're not going anywhere."

"You can't know that," he says in broken words. He blows out a deep breath and pulls in a shaky one. I lean up and nip at the corner of his mouth. We're nose to nose with his strong arms supporting my new position. The friction is incredible like this and I wonder why we'd never tried it before. "Chief died."

"You're going to marry me and when everything calms down, I'm going to give you a son."

"You'll change your mind," he says as he picks up the pace. His jaw tenses as he gets closer to the edge. I don't know where the word-vomit came from, but in this moment I want him to know everything about me. I want him to have every hope and dream because he's clearly worried about what's going on with the club. I'm not stupid enough to try to dissuade his fears.

"No." I whimper. "You're scared."

"I love you," he says as he bites his lip to fight back his impending orgasm. He stills and takes a deep breath then moves slowly in and out, in and out. I fall apart around him and a moment later, he loses himself in me as well. I manage to mumble out a pathetic "I love you" as I'm coming down. We lay there like that, connected, for a while. Eventually, he places a kiss to my forehead and says, "You ambushed me with that shit."

"You're still going to marry me," I say as I drag my hands up and down his back.

"Yeah, Sweets," he says as he kisses me. A drop of sweat falls onto my hairline near my ear. His voice is pained when he says, "I am."

☠ CHAPTER 25 ☠

WHY DIDN'T YOU tell me Jeremy's prospecting for the club?" I ask. We've untangled ourselves from one another and we're dressing. I fix the last of the buttons on my shirt and turn back to Grady who's shoving his feet into his black motorcycle boots. Aside from the cuts, the boots are the closest thing the club has to a uniform. They all wear them and it's obvious they're not a special occasion shoe. Lisa made a joke last week that Grady's laundry is now my responsibility. I hate to break it to her, but Grady's laundry is Grady's responsibility. I don't care how many other women he has wrapped around his devilishly long, flexible fingers, I'm not doing the man's laundry. It goes against everything I believe in.

"Would you have understood?" he asks. "I tell you before I got you hooked that I got a teenager prospecting for my club—how's that go over?"

Here it is—another indication that he's scared to tell me things. I want to set the record straight for him—for us—that I'm here and nothing he tells me can make me go away. Pulling a hair tie out of my jeans pocket, I lift my hair into a messy bun on top of my head and secure it as tightly as possible. I close the distance between us and place my hands on his chest. He turns his chin down toward me and wraps his arms around my waist, pulling me flush against him.

"It doesn't matter if I like it or not. You can't hide things from me. You can't only tell me what you think I can handle. Give me a little bit of credit here, will you? You think I'm stupid enough to believe that you earn a living changing oil and fixing flats? Please, this is my home. I know what the club does, and I know you're part of every bit of it."

He turns his face away and stares at the wall over my shoulder. His jaw ticks, and his touch loses that loving softness it had just a moment ago. He lets his arms drop to his sides. He's noticeably unhappy about my response, but I don't know why.

"Go ahead," he says. Looking my way, his face is hard. He's shutting down emotionally. "Tell me what you think of the club. Tell me we're criminals, that we're bastards. Tell me how it feels to fuck an asshole like me. Tell me you like slumming it."

"Oh, stick a sock in it," I say in frustration. My face heats, and I tense up all over. I can feel my temper about to rear its ugly head. "You want to know why I didn't want the money? Because I've spent my entire life cutting corners and doing things the easy way." My voice is louder than I intend for it to be. I'm basically screaming in his face now, but still, he doesn't react. "My parents don't approve, neither do Uncle Harry and Aunt Claire. Hell, even when Mindy had a fucking needle in her arm she worried about me making poor choices."

"So I'm just another one of your poor choices, huh?" He leans in with cold eyes and warm breath. His words leave his tongue on a hiss as he says, "That's what this is, isn't it, Sweets? You like to rebel. You want to pretend to be wild for a while. You talk about marrying me and having my baby, but you're going to get over this faze and you'll want to go back to your cookie cutter life."

"I didn't mean it like that," I grit out.

"But you did," he says. He cradles my neck in his hand and with a hard grip, he forces me to give him my full attention. I pull away, but his grip only tightens as he jerks my face closer to his. My neck throbs, making me wince. His eyes flick, registering that he's causing me pain. He's going to lighten up, I think. But he doesn't. "You think you know who I am, but if I told you the things I've done, you wouldn't want me, and I can't blame you for that."

"Is that what you really think?" I whisper. "That I won't love you if I know who you really are?"

"Yes," he says. His chest heaves, and his eyes are so focused and steady. If I didn't know better, I'd think he was losing control. But I do know better. He's never more in control than when he's being mean. It's like he's in his element or something. I think of all the ways I can explain to him that he's getting mad for no reason, but the irrational part of my brain that controls my mouth takes over and instead of telling him what's in my heart, I snap.

"You're an asshole," I shout in his face. His grip on the back of my neck tightens in a painful vice. Tears pool in my eyes and I blow out a shaky breath, telling myself to suck it the fuck up. *I will not cry.* "But newsflash—I love you for and despite that fact."

"You're too good." He lets go of me with such determination that I stumble backward and nearly fall on my ass. Everything has shifted between us. Just a few minutes ago, we were lost in one another and now we're staring each other down and mad as hell about it.

"You should go," he says. "And drop the marriage shit. I just want to enjoy you before you leave me, but if you keep it up, one day I'm going to say yes and that's going to make shit real complicated when it's time for you to bail."

Everything I've done to help him and help his club comes rearing into the front of my mind. Everything moment I spent in that office with Mr. Beck today, where I blackmailed and threatened him. Every goddamn lie I told to the teller, spreading this disease of bullshit all in order to help a kid who I thought needed to feed his family. It's so clear now, in hindsight. I should have seen it sooner, but I was just so focused on helping Grady. Incredible panic settles into my chest and drops to my gut. My belly aches from my growing nerves and my jaw shakes though I refuse to let a single tear fall. If I don't figure out a way to make us better, I'm going to cave in on myself and then be done for.

Rushing at him, I slap furiously at his chest. I'm barely aware that I've done it until I'm already on him. He doesn't move to stop me or to shield himself, not that I'm strong enough to actually hurt him. I grab at his cut and pull myself up against him. Yanking on the worn leather in jerky motions, I tip-toe as close to his face as I can get. Still, he doesn't move.

"I got Jeremy's permit for him," I say with a shaky voice, still clawing at the leather. Grady's eyes bore into mine curiously. "Mr. Beck didn't want to, but I made him. You think I'm so good and so normal? I blackmailed a man today— could ruin his career. And it's so fucking easy. Justifying what I've done. It's like this switch I just turned off."

"What the fuck are you even talking about?" he barks out. Finally, he moves. His hands squeeze at my upper arms so hard that my skin heats from the pressure. My pulse races. If I stop panting so hard, I'd be able to actually hear the beating in my ears.

"It's always been like this. I just do things that aren't exactly right but they're not entirely wrong either. I don't know!" I'm shouting now. "I just needed to help!"

"You got any fucking clue what kind of charges that shit brings?"

"Does it matter?" I ask. "It's on me, not you." Mr. Beck won't say anything. He has too much to lose and no proof, or so little, that he would be taking a huge risk to even mention what I did to someone else. I made sure of it. If he talks, it's going to end him. Grady must see that. He has to. We're safe, and Jeremy's safe now. It was the right thing to do.

"Holy shit," he says quietly. His eyes are full of disbelief, narrowing slightly and then relaxing. His jaw is slack, lifting just enough to make an effort to speak, but he doesn't make a sound. He appears to be slipping into some kind of circular thought process that's rendered him speechless. "You did that for us?"

"You don't get to be the only one who puts their ass on the line here," I whisper.

"Seven," he says. His eyes divert from mine, but otherwise he's still. I'm not sure what seven means, but it's important for a reason I don't think I'm going to like. If I'm going to live in this world with him, I'm going to have to hear it.

"Yeah?"

"Men. Seven men," he says. I think I stop breathing with the next words out of his mouth. They're quiet, but it's all so foggy. "The first wasn't the hardest. He shot at me first, so I just shot back. The second pulled a knife on me, got a few slices in before I took him out. With my bare hands. It's how I earned the nickname Bloody Knuckles. I remember every single one of the men I killed. Two were during a bar fight with another club, and one was a junkie who Layla had hooked up with. He'd beaten her for taking more of his blow than she was supposed to. He broke her arm. The others are inconsequential. Now, how do you like my world? How do you like me? Is *this* the man you want fucking you every night? Is this how you want to live?"

Now I'm the one who's speechless. I can barely process what he's said, let alone let it sink in. This man who plays Monopoly with his daughter and takes her out for pizza even though she ignores him half the time is a killer. The first place my brain goes is to sorting out what to make of the information he's given me on each kill. They sound like they were done in defense and out of protection, but what do I know? I think I can justify anything, because I'm not running. How else do I explain the fact that I'm not afraid?

"You should run," he whispers, but he doesn't let me go.

"No."

"I'm going to end up destroying you. I learned that shit with Layla. She fucked up, I fucked up. It got ugly. I don't want that for you."

"Destroy me," I say with the saddest, most faint smile. "Just don't leave me. Love me even when I do stupid stuff. Please."

His lips crash down on mine and he hoists me up into his arms. With every passing moment that he lovingly assaults my senses, the more secure I feel. Our frantic kisses fade into soft pecks with each of us whispering that we love the other. It makes no sense, not that it has to. Love never does.

There's a knock on the door, surprising me. I pull away, despite his urges to ignore it. The rapping gets louder and louder until I hear Tall's voice from the other side. "Sarge," he shouts.

With me still hoisted in Grady's arms, he walks to the door, unlocks and then opens it. Tall scratches the back of his neck and looks down the hall. His voice is rough when he says, "You told me not to leave without telling you first, but I have to pick Mindy up at work."

"Mindy doesn't work today," I say in confusion. Grady

kneads his hands into my ass, which gives me ideas about slamming the door in Tall's face and getting busy with my Old Man again.

I like the sound of that—my Old Man.

"No ma'am, but she's covering for Nic." I feel kind of crappy about how wrapped up I've been in Grady and Cheyenne lately. Even Jeremy has been monopolizing my attention, and I haven't checked in with Mindy in a few days. Since the day at the seawall, she's been uprooted to Duke and Nic's house, and yet I've only been by once. She's been to Grady's house three times, but Cheyenne spent most of the time talking about school and the boys on the football team and even culinary school again—which is a good sign—but it made it difficult to check in with my cousin. Grady chose not to tell Cheyenne about the seawall incident because it wouldn't do her any good to know. I wasn't hurt and that's what is important.

"Got it," Grady says. Tall turns down the hallway, and Grady moves to close the door.

"Wait!" I shout and bounce in his arms. Grady raises an eyebrow, brings his hand on the still open door back, slaps my ass, and kneads my stinging cheek. Squirming in his arms, I let out a breathless laugh. Tall reappears in the doorway and bounces from foot to foot in obvious discomfort.

"I wanna go," I say to Tall. Grady gives my ass another slap, this time softer, and levels me with a hard stare.

"You just got here," he says. He keeps his voice quiet, but his words are said in earnest. "And we still need to deal with that little thing you did."

Leaning in and whispering in his ear, I say, "I'm going to go hang out with Mindy, but I'll be home soon and you can show me all the ways in which I was a very naughty girl."

"You are one crazy bitch," he grits out and brushes his rough chin against my cheek. I straighten my legs and shove at his chest with narrowed eyes. He sets me down and blows out a frustrated breath. A devious smile spreads across his face. "Okay, you're one temperamental bitch. Is that better?"

I point my index finger in his direction as I back up toward the open door. "You're gonna pay for that."

His smile grows wider. "Can't wait."

☠CHAPTER 26☠

TALL AND I walk down the hallway toward the front door in silence. Somehow, Cheyenne charmed Tall into telling her that his real name is Aaron, but that's something I'm not supposed to know. Grady's made the prospects' role in the club very clear. They're supposed to be treated like lackeys so that by the time the club decides whether or not to vote them in, they already know how dedicated the guy is to the patch. I get it, but it doesn't stop me from feeling bad for the kid.

Once we're in the black SUV and pulling out of the lot, he relaxes in his seat. I've noticed this with the prospects. They're all business in front of the club, but once the brothers are out of sight, they chill out some. The fact that I'm up to date on Aaron's dating life is a secret I don't plan on telling Grady about.

"Baby Boy's got a big mouth," he says with a smirk on his face. "Sent me a picture text of his permit. Says you did good."

I stir uncomfortably as we turn off of Main Street and down onto Laurel, where Universal Ground is located.

"Hey," he says. "That risk you took? Pretty big. You're definitely a keeper."

"You want to tell my Old Man how awesome you think it is? Because I'm not sure how impressed he is right now."

"Ha, no." He laughs. "Until I earn my top rocker, I don't have an opinion about shit. I'm just saying, between us, you saw an opportunity to help the club and you did it. That's solid."

"Thank you, Aaron," I say softly. He nods and swings the SUV into an empty spot in front of the shop. We climb out and stride inside just two minutes before closing time. Mindy is nowhere to be seen in the small space, which must mean that she's in the stock room.

Old Man Hill sits at one of the tables with an open newspaper. He lifts his head as we enter and gives Tall a nod and me a smile. In the few times I've seen Mindy in recent weeks, she's told me that since the club can't have a man on her during her entire shift, a few locals have switched off helping cover her, especially when business slows just before closing time. I have no idea how Mr. Hill got involved, but I'm thankful he did. He may not look like much and he sure is paranoid about safety, but anything so Mindy doesn't have to be alone makes me feel a little better.

Mr. Hill stands from his seat, grabs his newspaper, and walks out without a single word. At the front door, he turns the lock and lets the door close behind him, locking us in. Tall looks to his watch and jerks his chin to the back of the shop where there's another entrance. "I'm going to go check the back. When Mindy comes out, let her know where I'm at?"

"Sure thing," I say and lean over the counter in an attempt to get a view of the stock room. "Minds!"

She comes out a moment later with a broom and dustpan in her hands and a huge smile on her face. "Hey!" she says. "You okay?"

With a confused look, I survey my body and reflection in the espresso machine to make sure I don't look totally fucked. Because I was, and even though it happened in the dirty ass clubhouse, it was incredible. "Yeah, why?"

"Because two-thirds of you is missing," she snarks.

"Ha ha," I say. "I'm sorry if I've been MIA lately."

"If you've been? Girl, I went from seeing you every day to being lucky to get a weekly drop-in. I get it, the relationship is new and you're living with him right now, so I'm chopped liver. But anyway, I just want you to know I'm only kidding and if you've gone all wackadoodle obsessed over him, it's okay." She's rambling, but the smile on her face looks like it could split in two. I can't help but smile back just as large and to take a moment to just be thankful that we're here and that we survived crashing and burning those years ago.

"I'm gonna marry him," I say. Mindy sets the broom down, grabs a rag and a spray bottle, and starts to wipe down the counter top.

"Yeah, Jeremy says this is getting serious," she says. Since she's been staying with Nic and Duke, she's had the opportunity to spend some time with Jeremy as well. She looks around the shop with narrowed eyes.

"Oh yeah, Tall's in the back," I say hooking my thumb in that direction. She relaxes a bit and goes back to cleaning the counter top just as Tall walks out. He jerks his chin at her and gives her a smile, which she returns.

"Hey Aaron," she says. My eyes widen and I look from him to her and back again. I'm not sure how much she knows about the club, but she should definitely know to call him by his club nickname. Then again, we seem to make an exception for Jeremy, so maybe Grady's riot act was a little more dramatic than need be.

"What'cha need, Bean?" he asks her. Again, I'm left more than a little confused about this. Bean? Since when did the club give her a nickname? This entire trip has shed light on why I've been a crappy best friend lately. I have no idea what's going on with Mindy or what her daily life is like now.

"I need to do a full mop-down. Can you stack the tables in the corner? They're kind of heavy."

"You got it," he says and starts to systematically stack the tables in the corner in a manner that tells me he's done it several times before.

I open my mouth to ask her how close she and Tall really are, but I'm silenced by a loud crash and the shattering of one of the front windows. Glass flies everywhere in a violent burst. Mindy ducks behind the counter and I drop to my knees, shield my head, and pray that I've covered myself in enough time to avoid getting glass in my face. I'm barely crouched down when Tall's heavy body slams into mine. He wraps his arms around me and doesn't loosen his grip for what feels like forever, but is probably just a moment.

"You okay, Sweets?"

"Yeah," I say. Everything is silent and still until Tall stands, draws out his gun, unclicks the safety, and carefully approaches the shattered window. His boots crunch over the glass as he heads for a small object in the center of the mess. With his gun trained on the window, he slowly bends, picks up the object and walks back to me. With his body shielding mine from the window, he directs me to stand and both Mindy and me toward the office. I don't waste a moment following his orders and round the counter and rush inside the tiny office. It can't be more than seven feet wide on either side. Mindy is already disappearing into the office when I make it around the corner. Thankfully, there are no windows in here and no other doors. The lack of glass makes me feel more secure, though I won't really feel safe until Grady's here.

"Are you okay?" I ask Mindy and lunge into hugging her. She wraps her arms tight around me and squeezes.

"That was scary," she says into my hair and lets go.

Tall enters the room and shuts the door behind him. He sets the object down on the desk and pulls his phone out. The conversation is short and a moment later he's hung the phone up.

Eyeing the object, I realize it's something hard wrapped in a piece of white, torn paper. Tall reaches out, but I'm faster. I grab it up and immediately recognize its size and weight as a brick. Separating the brick from the paper, I hand him the brick and unfold the paper. It looks like some kind of medical report, but I can't make much of it out. Words like internal hemorrhage stick out, but the paper is worn and some of the text is unreadable. Tall shakes his head and grabs the paper from me.

"It looks like discharge papers," Mindy says as she peers over his shoulder.

"Shit," he says loudly. Folding up the paper and sticking it in his pocket, he pulls at his hair. "Fucking hell."

"What is it?" I ask, starting to freak out. He levels me with a hard stare and shakes his head.

"Club business," I say with a nod. Being with Grady, or more correctly, being associated with the club, has a few obvious disadvantages, and this is one of them. Not knowing certain things and being embroiled in the middle of something that's obviously dangerous scares the shit out of me most of the time, but I try not to think about it. I was in danger well before I fell for Grady, so it's not like I can even blame my relationship with him for this. No, this is somebody else's doing.

"Of course it is. This is ridiculous," Mindy says. "I'm tired of the club messing up my life." She's moved past scared, and now she's getting mad. Maybe I shouldn't have said anything about the club. I know how she feels about them, but I had thought that maybe spending some time at Nic's house she'd lighten up a little. From what Grady says, the club got wrapped up in this stuff because they were trying to make something right for someone who needed it. I have to believe that, despite everything my uncle and father would want me to believe about Forsaken, they must not be that bad. I only wish Mindy could see Grady the way I do—loving and protective. Maybe then she would have a little faith that the club isn't awful, they just do things a little differently.

"I'll be in the hallway. You two stay put," Tall says. He pulls his phone back out of his pocket, puts it to his ear, and draws his gun up in front of him. With his phone tucked between his cheek and his shoulder, he slowly opens the door, steps through the frame, and then shuts it behind him.

"The guys will be here any minute," I say to Mindy. "Then we'll be safe."

Mindy just shakes her head and gives me a disapproving glare. "Who are you? I mean, really? What happened to getting your life on track and making this your fresh start?"

Every muscle in my body tenses up, my temper rises, and I fold my arms over my chest. How dare she say that shit to me? "Who am I? I'm the idiot who spent two years cleaning up after your messes. I'm the moron who thought she could pull your out of your own filth, that's who I am."

"Great, so now it comes out," she says. Her mouth forms a pout, and tears well in her eyes. "I knew you would throw that in my face eventually. I just knew it. Go ahead, Holly. Tell me how I ruined your life!"

"You didn't ruin it," I snap. Even angry, I can't bring myself to say the things that are flying through my brain. "I made my choice. I stayed when I didn't have to, I know that. But do me a favor and just get off my back, okay? I don't tell you how you fucked up at every turn, do I?"

"No," she bites back. "I don't need your reminders. I feel it every single day. I'm a fucking junkie. My feet are so tore up that I can't even wear sandals anymore. I have tracks in places you can't even imagine sticking a needle. So no, Holly. I don't need your judgment or your reminders."

"Mindy," I whisper in a plea. A tear falls down my cheek, unable to stay in any longer. This has been coming for years, but I'd hoped to continue to avoid it for a little longer. The old Mindy curses, but the new Mindy says silly things like wackadoodle and silly goose. The harsh words that fly out of her mouth scare me. They're one big red flag that the old Mindy isn't so deeply buried as I thought she was. "I'm so sorry."

"Please just drop it," she whispers and folds in on herself.

Time feels like it drags on and I start to worry for Tall. He hasn't returned yet, and even though I have no idea if it's been two minutes or twenty, I'm far too restless to stay in here like a sitting duck. Mindy says nothing as I grab the brick and creep to the door. Slowly, I open it and take a step out. Tall rounds the corner in that moment and shakes his head.

"Get back in the office. What the hell are you doing?"

"I was worried about you!" I defend myself and take a step back.

"Don't worry about me," he orders. A shadow casts on the wall at the end of the hallway and a strange man enters. He's of average height, but his face is all sucked in and his eyes are wild. He raises a gun at the back of Tall's head. I scream out at the loud bang. Dark red liquid coats my face and clothes as Tall's eyes go blank and his body drops to the floor. Blood pools at the back of his head and he's so still. I close my eyes to try to ignore what I've seen.

☠CHAPTER 27☠

IN SHOCK, I can't move or scream anymore. I feel Mindy move behind me and let out a loud scream. The man at the end of the hall is joined by another, who also has a gun in hand. They advance on us, shoving us further into the little office. The man who shot Tall points his gun at my head, forcing me into the corner and to the floor. I hide the brick behind me, hoping he doesn't see it. The second man has his gun on Mindy. She is still as a board and her face is blank. I know this look—she's shutting down. And who would blame her? She just saw a man die—a man who was her friend on some level.

Tall's dead.

I force myself to not feel what's going on around me. I've never dealt well with blood, so I block it out the best I can. It's water. It's just water that's on my face and arms.

These men don't look like the smooth talking Italian that stuck us on the seawall. No, he didn't use a gun or violence. He just asked for a favor in a way he knew neither of us could refuse. It was either cooperate or be hurt, so we cooperated. These guys look and smell filthy. A rich body odor emanates from them, and their movements are jerky. Neither looks healthy, and both remind me of Mindy when she was at her worst. My stomach rolls from the reminder.

"Nicole Whelan," the second man says looking at Mindy.

"No, I'm not—" she says and shakes her head in confusion, but he isn't having it. He lifts the gun and pops her across her cheek with the butt of it. "Shut up, whore. I didn't say you could talk."

Instinctively, I move forward, but the guy shoves the gun into my temple, making me freeze in place. They think Mindy is Nic. I open my mouth to try to correct them, but I don't dare speak. The man with the gun to my head pulls out a cell phone and pushes a few buttons, then brings it to his ear.

"I got your bitch and Grady's bitch here," the man says. His speech patterns are all over the place, and the gun shakes as he speaks. They may not know who Mindy is, but they obviously know who I am. My chest constricts in panic.

"Nicole is going to pay for what you did." There's a beat of silence before I hear shouting on the other end. It's Josh, and he's flipping out, which is to be expected. Whatever is going on is clearly personal. These guys want Nic, not Mindy, but if they know she isn't Nic, they might just kill her. The man at my side didn't waste a second killing Aaron, and they have obviously done their homework if they know Grady and I are together, just not well enough to know they have the wrong blonde. "You let us do our job and we'll leave, but if you come in here, they both die and your baby dies with them."

The man on Mindy puts his gun on the nearby filing cabinet. His eyes roam Mindy's body, and he licks his lips. Reaching out, he slaps her across her face twice and then grabs her head and pulls her face into his. She whimpers, but doesn't move to defend herself. His lips smash against hers, and he walks her back into the wall behind her. She doesn't move her mouth, she just squeezes her eyes shut as he bucks his hips into her. I close my eyes, refusing to watch what I fear is about to happen.

"Open your fucking eyes," the man next to me says. I force myself to look up at him. He shoves his phone in my face and makes me grab it. "You're going to tell her Old Man everything my buddy does to his woman."

With the phone at my ear, I shake my head and whimper, "Please no."

The butt of the gun pops me across my mouth just hard enough to hurt like hell but not so hard that I lose my grip on the phone. My mouth fills with blood.

"Just do what he says, Holly," a familiar voice says from the other end of the line.

"Okay," I whisper.

"Tell him!" the guy shouts. Not wanting to, but knowing I don't have another choice, I turn my head back across the room. The man has his hands on Mindy's breasts and is kneading them. Her arms are down at her sides and her eyes are closed. Her cheeks are wet with tears. She is dead still. As painful as it is to watch this, I can't even imagine what she's going through.

"He's touching her breasts," I manage to say through the panic that's closing in around my lungs.

"Holly, it's Ian," the voice on the other end says. "We know you're at Universal Ground. We just have to see if we can get in there without getting you two hurt even worse, okay?"

"Okay," whisper.

"So just keep talking," Ian says. "We know Nic is safe. She's with Ruby."

The man on Mindy wraps a hand around her neck, squeezes, and then slams her head against the wall behind her. My gut lurches as she opens her eyes and cries openly. He reaches down and yanks at the button of her jeans, then pulls down the zipper. She jerks away and shoves at his chest, dragging her nails across his skin. Spots of blood appear in the scratches, but she's not able to stop him. He punches her first in her stomach, causing her to double over, and then right in her nose. Blood sprays out and coats her chin and T-shirt.

"He's hitting her," I say as steady as I can. My body shakes violently.

"More detail, you fucking cunt," the man with the gun says. He uses his free hand to strike me across my face then grabs a rough hold of my breast and squeezes. I cry out in pain, but don't move to stop him. Everything is just getting worse and there's nothing I can do to stop it. He lets go and brings his hand across my cheek. "Or I'm going to fuck your face until you choke on my dick."

"More detail, Holly," Ian commands. His voice is a mixture of pain and anger. "Just tell me."

The guy grabs Mindy by the back of her neck and shoves her face down onto the desk in the center of the room. Her arms splay out to break her fall as she claws at the corner of the desk to get away, but he grabs at her unbuttoned jeans and yanks them down to her ankles. She screams with such pain that I break out into uncontrollable sobs.

"He's got her on the desk and he's taking her pants off," I cry into the phone. The man looks up at his buddy by my side and smiles wide.

"Gorgeous pussy. You should see this, dude," he says and shoves her legs apart. He unzips his fly and pulls his dick out. Mindy scrambles to get away, but he brings his closed fist down onto the center of her back. Her entire body jerks in response, and she screams louder than before. He pulls her back by her hips, and with one hand, he pushes himself inside of her.

"He's raping her," I wail. My eyes close involuntarily and I scream out.

"Fuck," Ian says. His voice is rough, and he clears his throat. "Hang in there, Holly. We're coming in, we just have to be quiet."

"Watch, you fucking slut!" the man with the gun screams in my ear. "Tell him, tell her Old Man!"

"Open your eyes," Ian says. I do as I'm told. The man rams into her harder with each thrust. My stomach rolls from the sight of it, and I try to focus on Mindy, not the man violating her. Her strawberry blonde hair is mostly covering her face, but I can see that her eyes are closed and she's gritting through the pain. Her jaw is locked, and her teeth are bared.

I reach forward and wrap my hand around hers. She jerks away, but I hold her hand tighter. Her tear-filled eyes open, and she gasps in agony.

"I'm here, Minds," I say through my tears. "I love you, and I'm here."

She says nothing in response, but she lets go of the edge of the desk and grabs my hand. She squeezes it hard and sobs into the desk.

Finally, the man stills and lets out a relieved sigh. He grunts and then blows out a breath. Mindy cries quietly on top of the desk. She's holding onto me and the desk so tight that her knuckles have turned white.

"My turn, dude," the man at my side says. The other guy zips up his jeans, and the men trade places. The man who killed Tall hands the gun over to his friend then moves to stand beside Mindy. He grabs one of her legs and one of her arms and yanks her onto the ground. She falls on top of the fallen desk accessories and screams out in pain. A cracked cup of pens is crushed beneath her face, and a tray of paper clips and other various small items is under her forearm. A sob escapes her as snot drips down her face and onto the carpet below.

"They're taking turns," I whimper into the phone. "Mindy's on the ground."

Sweat trickles down the face of the man beside me. He licks his cracked lips and gives me a satisfied smile. In a soft but menacing voice he says, "Tell him his baby is going to die. Go ahead."

"He says your baby is going to die," I mumble through my hiccups and sobs.

Ian's voice in my ear is kind and encouraging, "There is no baby, remember that, Holly. We're almost in the shop, so just hang in there." He keeps his voice quiet and steady, though the longer this goes on, the more pain I hear from him. I know they're coming, they have to. It's just not fast enough. Mindy's already so hurt. I don't know that she's going to survive this even if we make it out of here alive.

The man surveys the room before he finds something he likes. On the wall beside me is a miniature bat trophy that's affixed to a diamond-shaped placard. He yanks it off the wall and pulls the bat off its base. Mindy sobs on the floor quietly, her face in the carpet. He throws the placard down, grabs her by her hair, and kicks her in her stomach. Then again and again.

"Stop," I scream. "Please!"

A rough hand reaches out and closes itself around my neck. He squeezes just enough so that I can't breathe.

"What's happening, Holly?" Ian asks. I try to tell him, but it's impossible. All I manage is a squeak. The man shakes me, shoving my head in to the wall behind me. My ears ring, and everything gets really blurry, but I manage to keep hold of my consciousness. He lets go, and I suck in a desperate breath.

The man moves behind Mindy. He lifts her hips, takes the bat, and shoves it inside of her. Her screams are deafening.

My stomach churns at the sight. I can't take watching this anymore.

I throw the phone down and shove at the guy beside me. This is too much. They're going to kill her. I have to do something to at least distract them. The man beside me pushes me back into the wall and onto my butt. I hit the brick and scream out as the pain shoots up my spine. The brick. If I can get a hold on it, maybe I can do something to help instead of just sitting here and doing nothing.

"Keep her in line!" The man with the bat shouts. His eyes are increasingly wild, and he's taking on even jerkier movements. He pulls the bat out and throws it across the room. It hits the wall. A Streaks of blood splatter across the paint. Mindy's cries quiet, and her body goes still. She just kind of stops everything except for shallow breathing. He hurt her, and I did nothing to stop it.

I did nothing.

The man with the gun cocks it and shoves it into my cheek. His friend grabs Mindy by her hair again and forces her onto her knees. He stands before her and unzips his jeans. Her face is scratched up from the pen cup, tiny streaks of blood drying in place. Her arms are bright red from carpet burn. I don't dare look down at her naked lower half. I can't go there. This is bad enough. But bright red streaks draw my attention to her exposed thighs. The front of the man's pants are splattered in blood, and his bright red hand stains her blonde hair.

He pulls himself out of his fly and leads her face toward it. With one hand around her neck and the other at the back of her head, he forces her to take him in. Her nails dig into his thighs as she tears at his flesh, but he doesn't stop.

"And don't bite him, or I'll blow a hole in your friend's face," the man with the gun says. Mindy's eyes turn my way, and she bursts out into tears again, but the man redirects her head and slams himself into her mouth. It happens twice more before her body involuntarily seizes and she hunches forward as she chokes on him. Vomit pours from her mouth, but still he doesn't stop. He slams in again and again, not giving her a chance to recover. She gasps for air, but more vomit falls out. Her throat closes up, and her body shakes violently. He's assaulted her in every way possible and it's in this moment that I don't give a fuck if they kill us anymore. In fact, I hope they do. I don't want to live in a world where I have to have seen this happen.

It's painful, what he's doing to her—making her choke on her own vomit around his dick. I grip the brick under my ass and eye the man with the gun.

"Take me," I say. "Just stop hurting her." Tears fall down my cheeks, and my chest rises and falls in a frenzied state. I move the brick to my side opposite him. "Please, take me. Hurt me, just stop! Stop! Please!"

He moves the gun and reaches down for his zipper. I lift the brick and slam it inside the side of his face. He falls back and drops the gun. With unsteady feet and shaking arms, I climb on top of him and throw the brick into his face one more time.

The door to the office bursts open with such speed that it hits the wall behind it and bounces off. A gun goes off, but I can't tell from where. A second later, the man in front of Mindy lets go of her head. She pulls back and falls to her side as he crumples to the floor. Vomit and saliva pour out of her mouth. Her body shakes and she tries to expel the rest of the contents onto the carpet.

The man beneath me has stopped moving, though his chest rises and falls with shallow breaths. Grady and Duke rush into the room with their guns drawn. The moment I see him, I fall apart all over again. Sobs rack my body and I let out a scream so violent it tears at my throat on its way out. Grady doesn't move. He just stares at me in abject horror. His mouth turns down and his eyes are wide.

The man beneath me twitches. His arm moves toward the gun. I take my eyes off Grady and look at the man, whose face is covered in blood and caved in on one side. He's alive. I can't.

I can't let him go. He doesn't deserve to live.

It feels like forever ago that Grady told me about the men he's killed. Every one of them must tear at his soul. He says he remembers them all, and I know that, given half the chance, he'll kill this man, too. That's just another burden for him to bear.

Seven men he's killed, but none of them just because he could. They all died for a reason, but it doesn't matter. It weighs on him. My man does what he has to do to protect his brothers, the mother of his child, and me. I want to be good for him. I want to show him how much I love him and that I can handle this world. I want to be strong enough to take care of myself and to take care of my man. That means not letting him shoulder anymore burdens than he has to.

I won't let this man be number eight.

The brick is heavy in my hands as I grip it with all my might and bring it down onto the guy's face. I pound the brick in so hard and so many times that his bones crack from the impact and his features cave in. Blood coats my arms and clothes in a way that would have made me sick to my stomach just yesterday. The pungent smell of iron is everywhere, but I don't stop until Grady crosses the room and pulls me off of the guy. The brick drops onto the man's chest and it's only now that I really look at what's left of his face. There's little more left than a swollen eyeball that's been forced out of its socket and the opening of his mouth, though I can't see any teeth through the blood and torn flesh.

"Stop looking, baby," Grady says and shoves my face onto his chest. I wrap my arms around his neck and lose myself in a sea of tears and screams. I did what I had to do to protect my man, but the sight of what used to be a man's face eats me alive. I killed him. I took a man's life, and, even though I can't say I'm sorry I did it, the sight of all of the blood and destroyed facial features won't stop assaulting my brain.

His number is seven.

My number is one.

Grady

☠CHAPTER 28☠

EVERYTHING IS SILENT here. Nobody is speaking. Even Tyler, who normally comes out and chats with me, has been distant. As the owner-bartender at The 101 Club, he's a staple around here. He's gruff at first, but once you get to know him, he's good people. But today he's barely come out to check on us, even though we've been here for over an hour.

Granted, he's probably not used to having such a large crowd of respectable looking individuals in his establishment mixing with the outlaws. I grab a French fry from Chey's plate and dare her to say anything about it. Her eyes widen as she stares at me from across the table, but with a quick glance to Holly, she calms down. My right arm is stretched out over the back of Holly's chair. My fingers lightly rub her shoulder blade, which seems to help keep her calm. On her other side is Ian, who, unlike most of my brothers, is only too happy to help my woman get over her shit. The rest of them show up and eat their food.

They're kind to her and they treat her like she's one of us—because she is. But Ian's the one who makes sure they stay quiet as they eat. He's the one who demands they respect her wishes. My woman wants quiet, and I try to give it to her, but when I get tense, she starts to panic. So Ian has my back when my brothers are around. I don't really get it, but when things get noisy, she whispers twisted shit like the number one and the number seven until things quiet down. But Ian gets it. If anyone knows about being fucked in the head, it's him.

On my opposite side is my mother, Ruby, Jim, Ryan, and Alex. Alex won't meet my eyes when I look her way, but I wish she would. So much has been destroyed in the past six months. I don't have the energy to worry about her and Ryan, nor do I think it's worth it anymore. She's sent Ryan over with homemade soup and pasta so Holly could have a home-cooked meal without us having to cook it. Normally my mom does that stuff, but with Holly being so skittish, we've resorted to eating take out almost exclusively. Certain noises just set her off sometimes. She'll be fine and then something happens—it could be anything—and she retreats. I fucking hate it.

Across the table is Nic—who's gained a little weight everywhere but is basically all belly—Duke, and Jeremy. Baby Boy has scooted a little *too* close to Chey, who is on his other side, under the guise that his sister is annoying him. Duke, who normally would handle that shit immediately, just laughs. He knows Baby Boy's game just as well as I do. I just hope he doesn't mind me taking out his future brother-in-law if the idiot gets the balls to actually make a move.

Chey is sandwiched between Jeremy on one side, and Naomi Mercer—Holly's mom—on the other. Between Ian and Naomi are Edgar—Holly's dad—and her brother, Theo. Sweets wasn't sure about inviting her family to dinner with us, but they had been calling every day to check on her. Naomi mostly talks to my mom when she calls, as Holly isn't much for shooting the shit with her mom these days, but we're making progress. Chey seems to like Naomi well enough, but then, Chey likes everybody when she's in a good mood. Edgar keeps glancing nervously at his daughter, though he doesn't say a word. Sweets has managed to talk to her dad and brother on the phone at least once each since it happened. Her family doesn't seem the least bit comfortable in our company, but they're going to have to get used to it.

Family is important and one day their daughter is going to take my last name and it'll be my baby that makes her waddle and gives her stretch marks. I never thought of knocking a woman up the way I've thought of it with Sweets—not even when Layla was ready to burst with Chey. Didn't think anything of it when Sweets mentioned it before everything went to hell, but after? Fuck. I'd shred my own flesh to give her a little happy and to stop the panic attacks.

One of the reasons this is Holly's first trip out of the house is because the entire town knows what happened at Universal Ground a few weeks back. Incorruptible cop Harry Mercer's sweet daughter was brutally raped and beaten during one of her shifts. Her friend Aaron Lennox was killed trying to protect her. For such a straight arrow, Harry

Mercer sure didn't ask many questions about how one guy ended up with a bullet in the back of his head and the other's face was smashed in by a brick. Can't blame him. His daughter is fucked up in a deep way. She's only just been released from the hospital last week and has refused all visitors.

Because he's too close to the case, his involvement is unofficial, but that hasn't stopped him from coming by my house three times in the last two weeks to talk to Holly about what happened. Every time he tries to bring it up, she goes to that fucked place where she's destroying that guy's face again. It takes hours to get her back to a safe place where she isn't seeing blood everywhere. Needless to say, Uncle Harry's visits have been stopped for the foreseeable future.

She's just not ready to talk about it. I don't know if she ever will be. She cries in the night, waking up in a panic, but last night was the first night she didn't ask me to call Ian. I'm always on edge and worried as fuck when I call him for her. She has him repeat much of the same things he said on the phone that day.

Hang in there, Holly.

We're coming, we just have to be quiet.

He seems to break the sobbing by asking her to tell him what's happening. That always shuts her up and calms her down. She's beside me now with her face shoved into a Mendo burger. This is our first trip out of the house together since that shit went down at Universal Ground. She almost didn't come today, but Ian talked her into it. They bonded during that phone call where those sick fucks forced her to verbalize Mindy's assault. As much as I want to be the one to fix her, I'm slightly eased by the fact that Ian is so patient with her. My woman needs kindness and patience while she tries to pull herself out of her dark hole.

There's some shit I don't think I'll ever get over. Like seeing Layla give birth to Cheyenne or the first time my girl walked without falling on her diapered butt. Even her first day of school –all memories that are forever etched into my soul. But it's the fucked memories that keep me up at night.

Like seeing my woman straddling some half-dead tweaker. Her eyes were wild, her face was covered in tears, and she had a bloody brick in her hands. She looked at me like I wasn't even there. Her jaw shook, and her chest heaved. With one look down at the man beneath her, she slammed the brick into his face. Not once. Not twice. But again and again until I had to pull her off of him. She fought me, screaming and pushing at me. I still don't know everything that happened in that room. I know enough—for now. The rest is a nightmare she relives every fucking night. One I can't save her from.

Another half an hour and there's light chatter, but they all keep it quiet. Even Ryan keeps his volume at a respectable level, but when a car backfires outside, Sweets curls into herself and grabs onto me for dear life. I give Chey a nod, and she stands with us. The others stand and spread out. Holly recovers quickly, wipes her tears, and laughs at herself, mumbling, "sorry."

On our way out, Naomi wraps her in a gentle hug and

promises to come by in a few days' time. Her dad, who's given me two disapproving looks, and has managed to mutter a single, "hey" wanders over to us. He gives Holly a hug then reaches out for my hand. I clasp my hand with his and give him a nod.

"Take care of my girl," he says stiffly.

"Always," I say.

Holly and I walk across the parking lot to my bike, Ian stands back in the distance. He has the SUV if she chooses to opt out of riding with me. I rub her back and place a kiss to her temple. "You don't have to do this."

"I want to," she says with more determination in her voice than I expect.

"She's loud," I warn her. Sweets knows my Harley is noisy—all ours are—but I don't want to scare her. I grab our helmets from the handlebars and hand hers to her.

"I know. I'll just pretend it's you snoring next to me," she quips. For a moment, *my* Holly is there. She's snarky and raising an eyebrow. A smirk plays at her lips, and her brown eyes gleam. Placing a kiss to her cheek, I leave her where she's at and swing my leg over my bike. We're still new and because of everything, Sweets has yet to ride with me. Today will be her first if she follows through with it.

With my helmet on and my eyes fixed with Holly's, I bring the bike to life. Holly jumps in place, but doesn't retreat. She straps her helmet on her head and awkwardly climbs on behind me. Her arms wrap around my waist, and her helmet rests against my spine.

"You good?" I ask.

"Yes!" she shouts. I need no further instruction as I rev the engine and we bolt out of the parking lot. I want to take a scenic route, or even just say fuck it and make a day trip out of it. But that would be pushing it and I don't want her panicking on the highway. So I take us straight home. We sail through the wind and down the streets just like I always do. It's nothing I haven't done a million times before, but it's different with her behind me. Her grip is tight, and I can feel the worried pattern of the rise and fall of her chest, but she doesn't complain. Despite the horrors inside her head, she's strong and refuses to let the demons get the best of her.

We roll up to the house, and I cut the engine. Nobody else has made it home yet, and that suits me just fine. I need a few minutes alone with Sweets anyway.

On our way inside, I notice that she's less twitchy than she was at the restaurant. She doesn't like to be alone, but too many people don't sit well with her, either. She insists that she's ready to go back to work, but I keep making excuses to keep her home. She's just not ready yet. She needs more time to heal. She can't see it, but she's still a disaster.

We set our helmets down on the kitchen counter. She moves for the living room, but I reach out and grab her hand. Turning back, she stares at me curiously.

"Come here, baby," I say quietly. For the first week we didn't have sex once. I just jacked off in my bathroom like a fucking kid. I can't blame her for not wanting to do anything sexual after the shit she saw. In the last week, it was twice. Both times were slow and easy. Still satisfying, just not what I'm used to. And as much as I'd love to bend her over and drill her from behind, she needs gentle. She needs me to be the man she deserves, not the asshole I'm used to getting away with being.

So instead of putting the moves on her, I pull her against me and step to the side. My hands are on her hips and she tosses her arms around my neck. She fumbles awkwardly before moving to the side as well. I do it again, and again she follows in confusion. By the third step, she finally catches on and the smile that spreads across her face is so fucking beautiful.

"We're dancing," she whispers. It won't last, but she's so carefree. I want to remember this for the next time things go bad.

"Keep your mouth shut about it," I say. She smirks.

"Where did you learn how to dance?"

"Bee Scouts with Chey. Only people who know I took her to that dance are Chey, my mom, and now you."

"You'll do anything for her, won't you?" she asks.

"I'd do anything for you, too, Sweets. If I could, I'd take away all the fucked up shit that swims inside your head."

"No," she whispers and stops in place. "It's okay." What does she mean by that? It's absolutely not fucking okay. Not on any plane of existence is it o-fucking-kay. The shit she went through is not okay.

"I'm going to work through this. I will. I just did what I had to do. I'd do it again," she says.

"What are you talking about?"

"I love you," she says. Her eyes search mine for acceptance, I think. Leaning in, I cup her face in my hands and kiss her deeply, but softly.

A knock sounds at the door, causing her to jerk away. I let go of her and turn for the door. Checking the window, I find Duke standing on the porch. He's got his hands shoved in his pockets and a thoughtful expression on his face.

"What's up?" I say as I open the door. He gives me a nod and looks over my shoulder then back at me.

"Can we talk?" he says. I nod and step out onto the porch with him and shut the door behind me. He paces back and forth a few times before he speaks. "I don't think that shit was on Mancuso."

"Who the fuck else would it be?" I snap. Wyatt's got Junior at his house now, and has since the day Leo Scavo showed up at the safe house. Wyatt's getting tired of playing babysitter though, so I don't know what we're going to do with him next. Leo Scavo has been missing since that day, when apparently he and Jim swung their dicks around until they both got tired and gave up.

Duke and his theories are getting old, but Mancuso's silence has been unnerving. He may have been right about Junior, but that doesn't mean I want to listen to this shit about Mindy's attack.

"Larry Jennings," he says. He pulls a plastic hospital bracelet from his pocket and hands it to me. I take it and inspect the information on the label. Sure enough, it belongs to Darren Jennings.

"Where'd you get this?" I ask, feeling my temper rise.

"Someone left it on Nic's car the morning of Chief's funeral," he says. "Didn't show it to anybody because I wasn't sure it meant anything."

My temper gets the best of me, and I lunge and shove him backward. My words come out in a fierce scream. "Guess what, asshole? It fucking means something."

Everything comes together and makes sense all of a sudden. The fucking tweakers talking to Mindy as if she were Nic. Them calling Duke and telling him that his and Nic's baby was going to die. I know my brothers have been spending more time figuring out who was behind this shit than I have, but I don't know if anyone else besides this fucktard in front of me has put two and two together.

"I fucked up. What do you want me to say?"

I shake my head. "There's nothing you can do unless you can unfuck my woman's head. You should have brought this to the club months ago."

"Yeah, I should have," Duke says. "What do we do now?"

I toss the wristband back at him and rub the back of my neck.

"Make sure it's Jennings who orchestrated that shit, and then he suffers worse than his pussy son did. I want that entire fucking family dead," I say with gritted teeth.

☠ EPILOGUE ☠

I NEVER THOUGHT I could love someone as much as I love Chey. Layla didn't come close. She'll always have a part of me, but that's my past. The insane, hormonal woman who can't sing to save her own life beside me has ownership of my soul. She's just two feet from me, but it's too far. I'm one lucky motherfucker because now I know what it's like to love someone with every fiber of your being four times over.

"And the wheels on the bus go 'round and 'round, 'round and 'round," Holly sings along with the horrible fucking kid's song that's coming out of the car speakers. She's seated in the passenger seat of our Tahoe with the visor flipped down and the mirror flap open. Her tired brown eyes are trained on the backseat through the mirror at the little disaster who's kicking her feet in the air and trying to pull her shoes off.

At eleven months, Charlie is a handful. Her dark brown hair and big brown eyes remind me so much of her older sister. She's more mobile than I remember Chey being, but what the fuck do I know—I rarely had a sober day back then. Layla didn't really give a shit what I did. Chances were good that whatever I was into, she was doing it, too. That was also twenty years ago. Shit, I'm fucking old.

"Babe," I say, keeping my eyes on the road. My shoulders are stiff and my back hurts. I fucking hate staying in hotels, but even worse than that, I hate driving in the city. San Francisco traffic can go fuck itself with an itchy dick. Holly doesn't hear me—either that or she's ignoring me, which is something she's a goddamn expert at—and she keeps on singing. I'd take a bullet for Sweets and all, but that doesn't mean I'll listen to this lame shit on repeat. Besides, Charlie doesn't like this crap anyway.

"Babe," I say again. I peek to my right and catch sight of her rolling her eyes in the mirror. She purses her lips and cuts off the stereo. I breathe easy for the first time since we got into the car over twenty minutes ago.

"You interrupted our song," she says in mock annoyance. Or real annoyance. Fuck if I know. Charlie scrunches her face up and grabs a hold of her foot. Her face is bright red. She yanks at her little brown boot and becomes furious when she can't pull it off.

"Can't yank it off, can ya?" I ask her with an evil laugh. My eyes meet hers and for a brief moment, she smiles. Her little hands yank at her boot again and the smile vanishes. "That's right. Dad knows how to tie that shit. Ask your sister."

Her little face gets impossibly redder as she glares at me, shakes her chubby little fists and then opens her mouth. I regret taunting her immediately. She's screaming and crying. Fat tears fall from her eyes and cover her cheeks. Even in tears and wailing at full volume, Charlie is the fucking awesome. It'd been so long since Chey was a baby I'd forgotten what it was like to have a baby in the house. I love my kids and all, but shit. Thankfully, she's finally old enough that I can start to do shit with her and her personality is becoming really pronounced.

"Good job," Holly says. "You just had to piss her off."

"Just wait, Sweets," I say as I pull the SUV into the parking garage and find an empty spot. "Few months, it's gonna be even. No more unfairly ganging up on me."

Climbing out, I round the back of the vehicle quickly. Charlie is *still* wailing in the backseat like her world has ended. Sweets gets pissed if I don't get to her quick enough these days. Fucking temperamental. No wonder our daughter is so prone to throwing temper tantrums. Holly's door is open, and she's facing me when I walk up. Sliding forward to the edge of the seat, she finds her footing on the side running board. She takes my hands and lets me shoulder the burden of the extra weight as she steps down. Her rounded belly bumps my gut as she finds her footing.

"Careful with this thing," I say and place my hands on her stretched flesh just inches above where my son rests. I won't officially meet him for another few months, but I'm already planning on us leveling the playing field. Leaning in, I give her a quick kiss and a wink. Holly's hormones are all over the place these days—even so much as a wink can set her off, and do I ever enjoy the rewards when they set her in the right direction.

I retrieve Charlie from her car seat and expertly get her

stroller out with my free hand. She quiets her screaming, but kicks against my side. Now I *know* Chey was not this difficult as a baby. I can only hope that Charlie's teen years are less dramatic than Chey's were. There's a learning curve and it takes some maneuvering, but now that I'm used to having a baby in the house again, I'm like a fucking superhero. I can do just about anything with one hand and three hours sleep. Good thing, too, because when baby James is born, I know I'm going to be functioning on a lot less.

Holly grabs the diaper bag from the floorboard and shuts the door behind me as I stick the scream queen into her stroller. She grabs at the handles and pushes her way through the crowded parking garage. I let out a frustrated breath and shake my head. Jim should have been here today. Asshole. Everybody else made it. Just about. Obviously Chief couldn't make it.

We take the elevator to the lobby of the hotel. Right when we step off, a large sign directs us to the grand ballroom where graduation's being held. I couldn't be more proud of my girl today. She's graduating from culinary school with a degree that specializes in desserts and shit. It's been two long years that she's been here in the Bay Area. Even if she does make it home every chance she gets, it's just not enough. She was a great kid and a fun teenager, but now? She's incredible.

She only has one flaw.

He's six-foot-three with brown hair and navy blue eyes. He's a fucking asshole who gets worse with every passing day and the cut he wears only enables that behavior. I'm proud to call him my brother, but fuck if I don't want to call him my son. And he's standing in the doorway to the ballroom wearing dark blue jeans, a gray short-sleeve shirt that shows his tattoos, and his Forsaken cut. He's started to grow out a goatee, but it's not much yet. The shit he's done for the club reminds me that he is man enough to care for my girl. I'm just bitter about the fact that she's old enough to have a man who's not me care for her.

She loves him.

It's been rocky, and he's fucked up in ways that—I think—entitle me to take him out.

But she loves him.

"Deep breaths, baby," Holly says from up ahead. "Either that or your brain is going to explode."

Baby Boy gives me a nod as he bends down to poke Charlie in her belly. She lets out a loud laugh and kicks her feet. Even she likes him. Traitor.

"Grady," he says. "Can we talk?"

No.

"Yeah," I say. Holly looks back real quick, but then turns around and keeps walking into the ballroom. There are rows and rows of chairs in front of a small, elevated stage. If Baby Boy is here, then the rest of the hooligans must be here as well.

We walk down the hall and out onto the street. He flexes his jaw a few times and blows out a breath. He's nervous. Good. Asshole.

"Wanna do it right this time," he says.

Prick.

"She's pissed," I say.

He nods his head and says, "I know."

"I should have water-boarded your ass for that shit last time."

"You'd of had the right to," he says. "Happens in the future? Do it."

I don't know when this cocksucker grew a spine, but he did. The club's good for a lot of things, and unfortunately, one of those things is teaching mouthy boys how to be men.

Goddamn it.

"I got your blessing?" he asks.

Yeah, he does. But fuck if I'm gonna make it that easy on the motherfucker.

I reach out and grab him by the back of his neck. He doesn't fight me nor does he blink. He's a rock, just like his dad. That old bastard should be around here somewhere. I squeeze as hard as I can knowing I'm going to leave a nasty bruise. I hope it lasts for at least a week. His jaw tenses, but that's the only indication that I'm hurting him. Leaning in, I shove my chest against his. My words come out as a hiss.

"I don't give a fuck how much shit you've done for your patch. Doesn't matter how many people you've seen suffer and die, no matter how much vengeance you've dealt—you ain't seen or experienced shit until you've hurt my little girl. This is your one fucking chance—your last fucking chance. Be the man she needs. Anything less and you're dead."

"Yes, Sir," he says as steady and cool as can be. Only two reasons a man in his position isn't angry or flustered by this. He's either completely insane, or he's completely in love.

And fuck me if I'm not grateful that if this shit has to

happen, it's with him. Not that I like the prick or anything.

I release him with a violent flip of my wrist. He stumbles a bit, but then straightens his back and lifts his chin. We walk back into the ballroom and join our family. Basically is here—most of us have been in the city for a day or two now since it's quite a trip. Duke and Nic stand with Holly. Their daughter, Robin, who is two now, stands in front of Charlie's stroller and is talking with her. I never know what the fuck they're trying to say to each other, but I'm damn sure they're conspiring. Alex and Ryan are close by. Took him long enough, but he finally told her she's gonna marry him. Guess she said yes, judging by the size of the rock on her finger. Ian is talking to Ruby, and I think Elle's supposed to show up at some point. She said she might have to work, but I can't keep track of her schedule. Diesel isn't showing, which is fine. Jim not showing chaps my ass, but what the fuck am I gonna do about it? Asshole. Wyatt is already seated with Mindy by his side and Butch a few chairs down. My mom is on Mindy's other side, but when she spots Holly, she taps Mindy's shoulder and they get up and go to love on the babies. Women.

An announcer starts the ceremony, and we all scramble to find seats in the limited space. There's plenty of standing room, so I opt for standing behind Holly's chair. My mom sits next to her with Charlie in her lap.

Baby Boy comes to stand next to me. Robin is standing on Duke's lap and jumping up and down to reach her uncle. I still don't know what the fuck it is about girls and this prick. Without even looking back, Duke lifts her over his head and

Jeremy takes her. She rests comfortably in his arms and places her head on his shoulder.

My brain is assaulted with images of the bastard with his own kid. My stomach rolls violently. The pot brownies I ate last night aren't sitting right with me all of a sudden.

The ceremony drags on with the only highlight being when Chey takes the stage. She's dressed in her white uniform with black shoes and her chef's hat. She looks like the Pillsbury dough boy—silly as hell. But she wanted this, and she's good at it. I'm proud of her for doing this. She made a hard choice, one I'm not sure I would have made, and it's paying off. Once they get through the list of the graduates, there are a few closing words, and then the kids toss their chef's hats in the air. When everybody stands to cheer on the graduates, I lean down and ease Holly up.

Wrapping my arms around her, I whisper in her ear, "Can't believe she's grown." She nods and tears up as Chey approaches us. I step out into the aisle to give her a hug. She's still a good twenty feet away, but I want to be first. Jeremy steps out beside me and her eyes dart between us. Robin is off with Duke once more. Chey gives Jeremy a wink and picks up her pace until she's running. He's her guy now, I remind myself. Dear Old Dad is second fiddle. My shoulders slump, and I give her a sad smile.

She runs faster, and in a second, her smile gets so wide that I swear it could light up the fucking room. She slams into me with such force that I stumble backward. I'm winded, having not expected the hug, but wrap my arms around her tightly. He may be her man, but for now, in this moment, I still get to be daddy. I let myself pretend she's just graduating kindergarten and we have many more years of these hugs in our future. I'm fooling myself, I know.

She lets go and wraps her arms around Jeremy. It's not a long hug because once Holly waddles out with Charlie on her hip, Chey's attention is diverted. She gives them both a hug, but then snatches her baby sister and gives her kiss after kiss on her cheek.

"I don't care how old I get," Chey says to Charlie who, as always, is absolutely mesmerized by her big sister. "You're always going to have to share Dad and Holly with me. Got it?"

Charlie kicks her feet out and reaches for the collar of Chey's shirt. She's been practicing it for weeks now, and I'll admit, I'm a bit jealous, but Charlie gets to work on saying sis. She's already got mama and dada down, but sissy is her new favorite. I wish Chief could see this. My two girls, each with a piece of him—one with his tribe and one with his first name—for him to spoil.

Chey walks off with Charlie and Jeremy to make the rounds of thanking everyone who came. It's a big deal when one of our own graduates from something, especially higher education.

Mindy walks up and gives Holly a hug. Both of the Mercer women have come a long way from where they once were. You'd never know the horrors they faced just from looking at them. Mindy still struggles, but she's got her sixty-day chip right now, so she's back on track.

Holly worked through her own demons for the most part,

but it was touch and go for a while there. I close the distance between us. Through the sheer sleeve of her top, the butterfly tattoo that rests on her shoulder blade peeks through. She used to fear butterflies once, and they still ick her out, she says. But her tattoo is a testament to her strength. My Old Lady doesn't let her fear control her. She looks it in the eye and gives it the middle finger. She's always been that fearless though, even when she didn't know it.

Chey swings by and drops Charlie in to my arms. Charlie smacks her tiny little lips in my face and giggles uncontrollably. I can't wait to see what kind of big sister she's going to be. I place a gentle kiss to her cheek and savor this time I have with her. Before I know it, she's going to be all grown up and some asshole is going to fall in love with her. I wrap my free arm around Holly and take a deep breath.

"You look a little too happy there, bud. How many brownies did you eat?" Holly asks teasingly. My woman's always been beautiful, but the more time I have with her, the deeper I find that beauty goes. She's the mom Layla couldn't be. She's the rock I need. She's a soft place for me to fall. She's protective and loyal and bossy as all fucking hell. I just hope I can be those things for her in return. Nothing I ever do will be enough to make us even.

"Not enough," I admit. "I'm just happy."

She leans in and nibbles on my ear while whispering, "Get someone to watch Charlie later. I want a little time alone with you."

"You offering to suck my dick?" I ask. My mood perks up

at the idea.

"If you're good, I might let you massage my feet," she says and places a kiss to my neck. I pull her in closer to my side and let myself breathe easy and be content for this moment. After everything we've been through and all the pain we've suffered, we're in a good place now.

Solid.

Safe.

☠ THE END ☠

☠ACKNOWLEDGEMENTS☠

Saying "thank you" is never easy. I'm all too aware that without the incredible on-going support from those around me that these books would be a hot mess and likely unpublishable. The fact that real live people are reading my work and sometimes enjoying it makes my heart swell. It's through your enthusiasm, encouragement, love, support, and criticism that I'm able to do what I do.

To Amy Shearer (Books) for proofing the horrible mess I made of Rachel's awesome edits after I clicked the wrong button in Word (I still don't know what I did!). Thank you for tolerating me, even when I'm at my worst and crying at two a.m. because a character won't cooperate. I think I'm going to keep you, and I promise one day I'll go an entire dinner without talking about work. To Rachel Bateman at Metamorphosis Books for always being so patient and kind with me, and for reading more curse words than MS Word can count. You're irreplaceable. To Brenda Gonet at Gonet Design for once again helping me achieve my vision for the book cover.

To Nazarea Andrews for being my sounding board, advocate, and such a great friend. I don't know what you said to Kelly Simmon (KP) at Inkslinger to get her to take me on, but thank you! I'm so proud to be part of the Inkslinger family. To Danielle Sanchez, you are simply fantastic at what you do. You came into my life as my publicist, but I now regard you as a great friend. Bet ya had no idea what you were getting into, huh? Well, now you're stuck with me! Thank you for helping me share my stories and vision with the world. To the rest of my girls in Indie Ignites. Thank you Chantal Fernando, for staying up late with me every night (or is it early where you are?) and helping me pound out the words. Don't forget our deal—I expect to see you in the States next year!

To my family, thank you for supporting my dream and not shunning me when you realized how many creative ways I can use the word fuck. Mom, you are the absolute best. Period. Always and forever. I am beyond grateful to have you on my "team" of cheerleaders and ass-kickers. You inspire me to be better and to strive for more. To Britt, my Sissy. Thanks for having my back when Mom went off the deep-end because of my deadline. Sorry not sorry that you got in trouble for it. I love you! Grandma, thank you for knowing I write filthy, crude stories and still wanting to read them—but no, you can't—sorry. I'll gift you another book to read!

And finally—Mandie—my best friend, sister, personal assistant, punching bag, beta, hetero life-mate, notebook hider, and buddy—words can't possibly express how thankful I am for you. You are so busy with my nephew (coolest kid ever!) that I never expected you to take me on as well. But you have, and your contribution to keeping this ship afloat is profound. From the bottom of my heart, *thank you.*

   Thank you.

☠ABOUT THE AUTHOR☠

AS A CHILD, JC was fascinated by things that went bump in the night. As they say, some things never change. Now, as an adult, she divides her time between the bad-ass bikers, sexy law men, mythical creatures, and kick-ass heroines that live inside her head. A San Francisco Bay Area native, JC has also called both Texas and Louisiana home. These days she rocks her flip flops year-round in Northern California and can't imagine a climate more beautiful. Her dream is to own her own Harley and she feels compelled to tell you that she is Team Peeta all the way.

JC is the author of the Bayonet Scars series, Men with Badges line, and the Birthright series.

Author's Note

Dear Reader,

Unfortunately, sexual assault isn't just a fancy plot device. It happens frequently and the statistics are horrifying. The only way we can seek to prevent/limit future assaults is through education and awareness. No organization is better equipped to do both than RAINN (Rape, Abuse & Incest National Network). For more information on RAINN, please visit rainn.org. If you are in need of help, or know someone who may be, please contact RAINN's free, anonymous helpline: 1(800) 656-HOPE.

Please take a moment to check them out and thanks for letting me interrupt your regularly scheduled fiction.

Thanks,
JC